a work in PROGRESS

a work in PROGRESS

a novel

K.A. ROSS

Cover image *Handwritten abstract text* by Fandorina Liza, stock.adobe.com, *Couple back view* by Tartila, stock.
adobe.com, *Doodle heart sketch set* by Caelestiss, stock.adobe.com

Cover design by Kevin Jorgensen
Cover design copyright © 2025 by Covenant Communications, Inc.

Published by Covenant Communications, Inc.
American Fork, Utah

Library of Congress Cataloging-in-Publication Data

Name: K.A. Ross
Title: A Work in Progress / K.A. Ross
Description: American Fork, UT : Covenant Communications, Inc. [2025]
Identifiers: Library of Congress Control Number 2024943097 | ISBN: 978-1-52442-782-5
LC record available at https://lccn.loc.gov/2024943097

Printed in the United States of America
First Printing: February 2025

31 30 29 28 27 26 25   10 9 8 7 6 5 4 3 2 1

To anyone who's ever wanted just one more conversation.

Acknowledgments

DID YOU FINISH READING THIS book? I acknowledge and thank you! Did you help me finish writing this book? I acknowledge and thank you too! Let's all do it again sometime.

Chapter 1

UNFORTUNATELY, MY ILL-ADVISED DECISION TO wear sweatpants made me look like a stalker selecting prey from the cliques of well-dressed women hurrying through the waiting area to different offices or meetings.

Whenever one glanced my way, I focused on the coffee cup I was holding. I'd already poured in four creamers to give my hands something to do. The women had to know I'd been invited to the office. Right? I didn't want to be here anymore than I wanted to explain why I'd been standing at the coffee bar for ten minutes. I found myself hoping another man would appear. Then I wouldn't feel like an anomaly or have to individually shoulder the suspicious stares like I was about to steal one of the fake plants off the windowsill as it perpetually bloomed in the cold January sun.

At least I'd shaved . . . yesterday. Fine stubble covered my chin, but you'd have to be close to notice. No one was going to get that close. But, yeah. I should have upgraded my sweats to casual business attire since I was here hoping to hire someone, though I'd much rather have conducted this meeting via text and not in person.

I pinched my fingers around the stir-y, plastic stick thingy to swirl the creamer, making the coffee a weak brown that smelled of half mud and half coconut. My hand shook, vibrating the contents into waves. I dropped the stick and focused on reading the Shakespeare quotes on the side of the cup, afraid of looking up and accidentally making eye contact with someone.

I missed the light tap on my shoulder until a voice spoke in my ear.

"Mr. O'Brian?"

I spun, managing to keep the coffee from flinging onto the bright white blouse of the woman standing behind me.

"Yes? Sorry. Here." Reflexively, I fished around the coffee bar with one hand until I felt a napkin and held it out. "Sorry."

Why had I done that? She stared at the napkin with a polite confusion that reminded me I'd become too comfortable not being around other people.

The woman smiled and bobbed her head uncertainly without displacing a strand of her shellacked, short, black hair. She looked older, but to me that could mean anywhere from forty to seventy.

She put her hand up. "You didn't get me. Don't worry."

I returned the napkin and fiddled with rearranging my beanie. Sweat had gathered under the lip, and I scratched at the curls being flattened underneath.

Before the moment advanced the awkward meter to leave-now-before-you-make-things-worse, the woman spun and walked away, waving her hand for me to follow.

She kept turning her head over her shoulder to talk pleasantries as she led me through a hall to a mass-produced, beige office door. "Can't believe we haven't had more snow," and, "Have you seen the Met's new exhibit on Dwight Gooden? No, you're much too young to have seen him play." Luckily, she didn't pause for a response, because I didn't have any to offer.

Opening the door, she flipped a switch. Overhead lights buzzed, revealing an office as devoid of personality as the hallway. The only decorations on the walls were dark scuffs where they'd been hit with either carts or furniture. I didn't miss this type of office environment.

I sat in the chair with the least number of stains and placed my coffee on the desk next to the blank monitor.

The woman stayed at the door. "Thanks for coming to meet with Nellie."

She wasn't Nellie? Shocked, I opened my mouth to clarify, but she kept talking.

"She'll be here shortly. She's always late." Her tone softened the edges of her words, making Nellie's tardiness sound like an adorable character trait and not a defect. "Come find me if you need anything."

Parting with a smile and an undisclosed name, the woman shut the door. Torn between wanting this meeting to be over and dreading the moment Nellie walked in, I searched for bits of personality around the room to prepare to meet her in person. A single clue lay nestled inside a faux-wood frame on the desk showing another older woman surrounded by puppies. So, Nellie must love her dogs.

We'd only texted a few times after Charlie had forwarded Nellie's number. I'd tried to explain the project, but she'd insisted we meet in person. If I didn't need the project done so badly, I'd have said no.

But the white hair and cable cardigan tied over the shoulders in the photo filled me with grandmother-esque familiarity. Maybe I could do this, negotiate with a woman I'd never met . . . and who didn't know she was the absolute answer to righting my life.

The door smacked the wall behind me. I jerked into a standing position.

"Oops, that was loud!" The new female voice sounded both apologetic and annoyed. "Ugh. Cheap doors . . . I always forget to be gentle." A slender figure strode past me. "I shouldn't complain since Anita's letting me borrow her office, though I think it's because she's hoping I'll fix her printer. She loves to assume that, because of my age, I understand all things IT related."

Several things gripped my attention: an incongruously lemon-colored sweater against the gray walls, a large leather bag almost pancaking my coffee cup, and a dimpled scowl at the computer's dark screen.

Still staring, two new words came to mind: Golden Crown. The bestselling blond hair dye in the Women First collection. Three rows over at Bob's Market, two shelves up and sold right next to Honey Almond. She needed a touchup. An inch of darker hair showed at her part before the hair tucked into a messy low ponytail.

But admitting to her how I knew about the hair dye at Bob's Market wasn't something I was prepared to do. Besides, another fact demanded more attention in the immediate moment.

She was not the grandmother in the picture.

Heat gathered at my neck even as my fingers went cold.

"Who . . ." I swallowed and redirected my blurted question away from the young woman and toward the picture.

She followed my pointing finger and smiled at the frame. "Oh," she cooed, her dimple carving into her cheek. "That's Anita's mother. Love her."

She, Nellie, settled into the desk chair. "I really appreciate you coming in. I'm really curious about your project and would really like to help. Sorry. That was too many 'reallys'."

My Jell-O knees threatened to betray me, so I returned to the stability of my seat.

Breathe.

Nellie glanced my way, hazel eyes narrowing as she said, "He sat uncomfortably, afraid his dark hair and beanie wouldn't camouflage the sweat on his forehead or that it would soak through the underarms of his alma mater's shirt."

My eyebrows shot into the brim of my beanie. "What?" Was she . . . narrating me? And had sweat soaked through? I hadn't worn these during my morning run, had I? No, I'd showered, which meant new clothes.

"I was at work," I said to explain my casual attire, while trying to recall what T-shirt I was wearing, since I suddenly couldn't remember what I'd put on that morning, let alone which college I'd attended. "I telework."

I clamped my mouth over the word soup my brain was pushing out about the work-at-home agreement with my company. None of it was relevant, and all of it was boring and unnecessary.

Nellie raised an eyebrow closer to the color of her roots than her tips. "Well then, Mr. Daniel O'Brian. Let's get you published."

This was it. Desperation and Nellie's genuine smile nailed me in place and kept me from walking out the door.

"I just need a bit more information," Nellie said. "What genre is your book?"

"Genre? You mean type? What did I write? Nothing. I'm an accountant."

Nellie's mouth puckered before her lips turned down.

I readjusted myself on the thin chair cushion and cleared my throat. "My sister. She's the writer."

Understanding lit Nellie's face. "Oh, is she shy? I'm happy to meet with her. I promise I don't bite, unless you're food."

I suppressed the shudder traveling up my spine and forced a casual laugh, a pretense to take several quick breaths to stop anything from welling up behind my eyes.

I meant to say, "She died," but what came out was, "We held her funeral December first at Mary Agnes's Cemetery, and it snowed all day. She was the only immediate family I had left."

Amazing the damage a solid month of solitude could do to social abilities.

Nellie inhaled quietly, but in the silence, it resounded with the impact of a bomb. We stared at each other. My knee bounced, and I put my hand on it, forcing it to be still. Her brows pinched closer together. Understanding? Pity? I kept my hand on my knee to keep from springing out of the chair.

"Sorry," I muttered. "I'm, ah . . . not used to talking about . . ." *my overwhelming grief and guilt.*

Nellie straightened and gave the wall behind me 100 percent of her attention. Her eyes widened slightly as though trying to keep them dry. The inside of my chest tossed with a fever, unable to find a comfortable resting place.

Images of dirty snow piled alongside the hospital parking lot popped into my head, then Elise's empty chair across the dinner table. Out of Nellie's view on the other side of the desk, I clamped one hand around the knuckles of the other to focus all my energy on squeezing the images away. I knew if I didn't, they would root in my mind, blocking out all thought for hours.

"So," Nellie said slowly, "your sister wrote a book?"

"Three."

"What?" Nellie flashed half a smile, maybe waiting for the answer before giving me the other half.

"It was three. She has three stories."

Nellie's voice ticked up. "Three? Impressive."

There was the full smile. Someone, anyone, praising Elise helped calm the turmoil in my chest. Both Nellie's and my shoulders relaxed.

I leaned forward. "How do we get them published? Charlie wasn't much help."

My old college roommate Charlie worked in "books." That was all I knew about his profession. When I'd asked how much he'd charge to get Elise's stories published, Charlie had laughed at me, then given me Nellie's number. I'd never had large amounts of disposable money before, so learning it couldn't solve all my problems had come as a shock.

Nellie spread her hands. "I offer several types of editing for different stages—"

"I'll pay for them all," I interrupted.

"They have different price points—"

"That's fine. You'll do it?" The words burst out before I became acutely aware of how rich-flaunting I sounded. I grimaced and slowed down. "My sister worked on her stories during her last year." I couldn't bring myself to say, "of life," so I skipped ahead to, "I'm her only remaining family. She left me everything. Whatever the cost, I can pay it."

Nellie blinked as I plowed ahead, afraid of losing momentum and falling off the rehearsed-verbiage train into the canyon of unpredictable reactions.

"I just need someone to finish writing them."

Nellie's mouth dropped. "They're not done?"

"Well, no—at least not . . ." *the first one.* It was the only one I'd actually opened and read. It contained a very long, detailed outline, but Elise hadn't actually begun writing out the story. "Don't publishers do that?"

Nellie looked like she'd seen a ghost playing a banjo and didn't recognize the tune. "Noooo. Traditionally a book is completed first. Then the author hires a developmental editor to polish the story. Then the author submits their work to an agent, like the ones who work here. If the agent likes the book, then they send it to a publishing house. If they like it, *then* it gets published."

There were entirely too many *thens* in that process.

Her voice high with apology, Nellie finished with, "So a book has several steps before getting to someone like Charlie, who is an acquisitions editor. None of that happens without a completed manuscript."

My thoughts jammed. "So . . . Charlie recommended you because you're an agent who works here?"

"No. Well, I used to. Now I'm starting work as a freelance developmental editor. That's why Charlie recommended me. He probably thought you had a completed book."

"Why meet here if you don't work here? Why meet in person?"

A streak of red framed Nellie's dimple. "I'm still good friends with everyone here and with Anita, the president of this literary agency. When I told her I was entering the workforce again and," she gestured to me, "had a potential client, Anita offered her office as a place to meet. I wanted to meet you personally. I'm very hands-on."

The back of my chair caught my slouch. "You wanted to meet me in a safe place first?"

I couldn't blame that logic. Yet, she was the one who'd insisted we meet, not me. I would have happily completed this uncomfortable conversation via text or video call. I hadn't left the house since the funeral.

Shaking her head, Nellie put both hands flat on the desk. "Yes, to a safe place, but not in the way you're thinking. Anita is, well, she's kinda my lifeguard. She knows I've been out of the pool, so to speak, and now I want to jump back in because I miss swimming. She's just there to make sure I don't cramp up in the water. And we have a high respect for Charlie. He vouched for you. This is about me." Nellie tapped her chest. "Not you."

Charlie had also vouched for Nellie when he'd forwarded her number. But relief that Nellie didn't think I was a creep didn't solve the fundamental issue.

Charlie couldn't help.

Nellie couldn't help.

Elise always told me she wanted to be an author, and this was the best way to use her money. I just didn't know how to get it done. I couldn't even find the starting line. The learning curve to understand the book world was more than I could surmount alone. But I had to get Elise published. I had to. I didn't know how else to fix—

Pressure built behind my eyes. I pushed the heel of my hand into my forehead, looked at the floor, and struggled to keep a composed face. "You can't help if I only have an outline?"

The soft drumming of Nellie's knuckles on the desk tracked the moments passing with no solution. I needed to strategize how to leave.

"Here's an idea." Nellie's voice sounded closer. I glanced up as Nellie's eyes unfocused for a moment as if working out the final details of a plan. She'd leaned the upper half of her body across the desk, elbows planted on the glossy veneer.

Already in the back of my seat, I couldn't retreat any farther, though I pressed hard against the plastic behind me. She wasn't frightening, but the closeness was something I hadn't dealt with in a month.

"Soooooo, what if we made a contest?"

I didn't follow. "And the winner publishes the books?"

"No, no." Nellie waved her hands and tried again. "I know several people who want to break into the ghostwriting business." Nellie anticipated my next question. "Ghostwriting is where someone writes a book based on whatever material you give them. An outline, in this case."

I attempted putting the pieces together. "We have a contest, and what? Pay the winner to complete the book based on Elise's outline? You edit it, and . . . it gets submitted to an agent to be published?"

"What do you think?" Nellie's chair squeaked as she leaned even farther across the desk.

I stared at the popcorn ceiling, wrapping my mind around the idea. I didn't completely understand all of it, but I didn't need to. This was what I'd been looking for. A path forward. Finally.

One corner of my mouth ticked upward in a smile. "It's perfect."

"His shoulders relaxed and eyelids closed over cocoa-colored eyes as relief flooded his mind."

Was she narrating me again?

"Nellie!" We both jumped as the woman with the white blouse sped into the room. What had Nellie called her? A lifeguard? Anita. "You let your phone die. Again. Sarah called me. She's coming to pick you up now."

Nellie stood, and Anita disappeared back into the hallway. I raised my eyebrow to ask questions that Nellie had already opened her mouth to answer.

"I'll email you the details. We'll get the contest set up. Announce the deadline. Maybe have people submit a first chapter after I post the outline of the book, etcetera. I'll include pricing options for my services and for the winner after they're chosen. Let me know what you decide."

Nellie walked around the desk and grabbed my hand to drag me out of the office. My mind cramped. I'd hardly spoken to a real human in a month; to be touched by one so casually tipped my world off its axis. Dazed, I followed even after she released me to wave at everyone we passed. Outside, I clamped my arms to my sides when the cold flash-froze everything, except my hand—which was on fire.

Nellie had produced enough content for a day's worth of deconstruction. But two thoughts distinguished themselves.

One: Nellie offered the lifeline I needed to get Elise published.

Two: Nellie offered the lifeline I needed to get Elise published.

Yes, the two thoughts had the same conclusion. It was just such an important conclusion, I added it twice.

Still . . . I swallowed, having to ask, "Are you ready for this? Getting back in the water?"

A car stopped next to us. Before Nellie climbed in, she angled herself closer. Usually, whispering into a client's ear after meeting them was a little forward. But at this point, it didn't surprise me.

"I lost my husband over a year ago."

Okay, that surprised me.

Nellie raised her hand and narrated herself. "She wiggled her finger, showing she still wore his ring." Nellie chuckled softly. "I understand how loss yanks us out of life at unexpected and unwelcome times."

Her accuracy stunned me.

"And the answer to your question is yes." She grinned, and the smile seemed to part the car's exhaust exposed by the cold swirling around us. "I'm ready."

Opening the car door, she climbed in and rolled the window down. Warm air from the car's interior hit me like a soft wall. As the tires crunched over frozen snow toward the road, Nellie hauled the top half of her body out of the window to wave goodbye. "I look forward to helping you, Daniel!"

Chapter 2

THE SOUND OF AN UNFAMILIAR ping stumbled me out of my runner's high. I skidded to a stop and automatically checked the straps on my knee brace out of habit and sheer panic that I'd injured it. No pain. I straightened and inhaled in relief. Then tried to remember why I'd stopped in the first place.

Another ping came from behind me. Turning, I squinted through the light rain, then at the ground for any clue about where the sound was coming from. Had I tripped some sort of alarm? Other than a half-buried FedEx package, the snow piles on either side of the cleared sidewalk didn't reveal anything under their dirty gray coloring.

I pulled the package out of the snow, placing it on the walkway leading to the nearest house, and decided to keep running before the rain froze into ice, making my route too slick. One step later the ping sounded a third time, and I realized it was coming from my new phone tucked in the pocket of my sweatpants. I stopped again and dug my phone out of my jogging pants.

I really needed to update the ring tones. Until I customized the settings, I wouldn't be able to tell if I could ignore the call. I glanced at the screen, shielding it from the rain with one hand.

Charlie.

Ever since I'd reached out to him about publishing Elise's books, he'd latched on, and I'd become a fish trying to avoid his hook. I thought this would be another invite for Thursday night basketball, but this text was about Nellie. I had to make this conversation quick, or Charlie would hound me with periodic pings for the rest of my run.

I tapped Charlie's number, held the phone to my ear, and resumed a light jogging pace. I passed several houses with red cut-out hearts in their windows. One especially dedicated neighbor also strung red and white Valentine lights around their front door, something I used to mock, but Elise loved stuff like that.

In my mind's eye, I pictured where I'd placed her box of Valentine decorations in the basement last year. I'd hoped at the time she would still be around to help me put them back up this February.

Suddenly drained, I thought about hanging up the phone, but Charlie answered.

"Dan? I can't believe you called back. Are you coming to basketball tomorrow?" Charlie's voice was normally deep, and I doubted it was the phone connection that made his words high-pitched. He was nervous. I hated that I did that to people. Made them feel uncomfortable or like they had to walk on eggshells around me.

I measured my breath. "How many points would I have to spot you?"

"Twenty. And you can only play with your left hand."

"That's reasonable."

"And you have to wear mini shorts."

"You're a monster." Charlie's chuckle deflated some of my guilt, then I reminded myself the whole point of this call was to have a quick conversation. "I thought you wanted to know about Nellie?"

"That too. Gotta get a plug in for basketball. But how's it going with her?"

I skirted around a large puddle. "Good. Just working the contract and going over details."

"Sounds good. Numbers and facts are your favorite things. How many times have you met up?"

I thought back to the drab office. "It's all been over email and text. Their place is kind of a dump."

Charlie chuckled. "Getting snobby now that you've got money?"

The comment made me double-check myself. I thought the statement was factual, but what if I was being a jerk?

"That's a temp office they're using because of rising New York rent costs. They got kicked out of their usual space and are trying to find a new one. Don't let that put you off. Nellie is one of the best. When I heard she wanted to get back into the book game, I knew your project would be perfect for her."

I trusted Charlie, both with his business acumen and as a friend, even with his doggedness in trying to include me in stuff that I had a ten percent desire to do. Maybe eight percent. If I'd been in the mood, I would have joked to Charlie about how much our situation had reversed since rooming together in college when I'd have to cajole him to leave the dorm room to experience life.

Yeah, not in the mood for any of that right now.

All I had to do was make it through a few more details with Nellie, and the project would be in her hands and out of mine. That, and getting Elise published, were my only goals. Neither should take much time. I could last that long.

A second wind steeled me, and I picked up the pace. Charlie asked, "Are you out running?"

The phone pinged in my ear. I pulled it away to look at the screen. A text from Nellie.

Hey, Daniel! Do you want the bad or good news?

Charlie's tinny voice squeaked up from the phone. I put it back to my ear and said, "Sorry, got a text from Nellie. Can we talk later?"

"As long as you promise to actually do that." The words were lighthearted, but I detected a note of reproach.

"Yeah, sure. Will do."

"Sounds good. Talk soon!" Charlie's voice returned to fun casualness, as though I was a wild animal, and he didn't want to spook me. I stopped myself from sighing into the phone. I really did hate that I did this to people. Better not to talk to anyone at all and avoid all this.

I disconnected the call and texted Nellie a reply. *The bad news.*

The inspector is shutting down the building our temp office is in.

What's the good news?

The inspector is shutting down the building our temp office is in.

I rested against a large tree next to the sidewalk and reread Nellie's texts to make sure I hadn't missed anything. At least our project was still on track.

I responded, *Okay?*

No one is sad about it. But we'll need to find a new place to meet.

Typing, "Why do we need to meet?" seemed rude no matter how much I wanted to ask. She responded before my fingers submitted my question.

Any chance we could meet up today? I know you want to get this started soon.

I winced and leaned down to massage my knee out of habit again before remembering it was fine. Nellie had hit on the one argument that could sway me to meet up in person: I did want this done soon.

I'd invite you to my house, but I've been staying with my mother-in-law, Juanita, and it's crazy over there.

My mind raced through all my nearby options. There were a few coffee shops that might work if they weren't full. Of people. In close quarters. The only other option was the library since Elise's home sat smack in the middle of a residential area.

Eager to get this over with, I texted, *What about the city library?* and included the address.

Perfect! That'd be great. I'll meet you in twenty minutes.

My mental state dived headfirst into what I'd come to coin "brain delay." A condition that consisted of a full-blown panic attack that ballooned inside my head and squeezed out rational thought and outside inputs, allowing knee-jerk reactions and fear to rule. Today's episode of brain delay was especially spectacular.

While my brain short-circuited, I pushed my phone back into my pocket and sprinted down the streets, my usual pace smashed into a frenzy. By the time I turned onto Elise's street, I'd unzipped my jacket and torn my beanie off to allow the February air to cool me down. Rounding past the mailbox, I leaped up the front porch's four steps in one jump to reach the dutch door, my knee twinging in protest. Grunting, I tore into the house.

Inside, my gasps echoed off shadowed walls. Due to the shorter winter days, I'd left one lamp on in the living room to keep the house from being dark when I got back. I followed the straight path its light created into the kitchen and filled a glass with water, downing it in seconds. Forgoing a second round, I snagged my keys off the counter and bolted through the kitchen back door to jump into my car.

So intent on making a self-imposed deadline, my panic at having to meet Nellie again in person didn't register until I saw the full parking lot at the library. I drove slowly, hoping there wouldn't be any stalls open, since not being able to park sounded like a foolproof excuse not to have to go inside.

No luck.

I rolled into the last space in the back of the lot, located right next to a dumpster, whose stench encouraged me to slam my door shut the second I opened it. That would be an acceptable excuse, right? *Sorry we couldn't meet; I barricaded myself inside my car to avoid last night's pizza fermenting with week-old salami saturated with beer.* I liked the excuse but didn't dare send it.

Ping.

A text from Nellie. *My sister just dropped me off. I'm inside at a table in the romance section.*

Why, oh why, was I doing this?

For Elise.

Walking into a library never used to be a chore. Talking to people never used to be a chore. I could do this because I *had* done this before Elise died.

Many times, I reminded myself. If my mind wasn't willing, my body would force it.

I released the steering wheel from my death grip and filled my lungs with the gym-bag essence inside my car, held my breath, and opened the door before dashing for the library's front steps.

My momentum carried me through the clogs of the local high school debate team outside the breakout rooms, showing conformity by all wearing that year's spirit jersey. Then, navigating through the stacks, I also avoided several pitfalls masquerading as elementary-school-age children collaborating with parents and friends on some reading challenge.

After several wrong turns, because romance was hard to find, I rounded a stack to find Nellie sitting at a small table nestled between the window and a fake potted palm tree. My sneakers skidded on the carpet, and I almost fell on top of her.

Glancing up, Nellie stood, a smile on her face, and gave me a full view of her shirt, which had a picture of a bookcase overflowing with books. In neon blue, the caption read, *I Have No Shelf Control.*

"Hi, Daniel. Nice to see you again."

Afraid she'd misunderstand the action of my eyes reading the words across her chest, I snapped my attention to her face to find she was giving me the once-over. But, like me, it was out of open curiosity without judgment.

"Were you out running?"

Unlike me, however, when her eyes reached my chest, they stayed there.

"How many colleges did you attend? You're too young for more than one. And Yale?"

I stared at her, then followed her gaze to look at my sweatshirt. Sure enough, gold-stitched "Yale" blazed across the front. Words failed me. Was there a way to explain that I wore a sweatshirt from a college I didn't attend because it was one of the last things my sister had given me?

"Eh, no. I didn't graduate from Yale."

"Me neither. State college alum," Nellie said proudly, rocking up on her toes to meet my eyes straight across. "Graduated three years ago."

Her attention traveled to the matted man-bun mess my discarded beanie had created on top of my head. I tugged at the elastic band holding it together. Hair wet from the rain flopped over my ears, shedding cold droplets down my neck. I'd needed a haircut for months.

In college, Elise had convinced me to go with her to a new hair salon, under the auspices of wanting to try out a "perm." In reality, she wanted to trick me into going in so I'd have to get a haircut. Joking about my hair was Elise's favorite pastime. When the hairdresser who helped us fit in naturally with our teasing, she'd gained two new customers for life.

Well, Elise's life.

Now that Elise was gone, going somewhere else would be a betrayal of loyalty. But going in meant questions would be asked about how I was holding up, how was I doing, etcetera. Not doing that. So my hair continued to grow unchecked.

I ran fingers through the mess, hitting a snarl immediately. To fill the silence while I attempted to extract my fingers without ripping strands out, Nellie casually said, "Thanks again for meeting me here. If I brought a guy over to Juanita's house, everyone would assume we were dating. Just too many questions."

I freed my hand, unsure of what to say. *It's nice that you're dating again after your husband passed away*, was too familiar. And, *Between graduating from college, getting married, and becoming a widow, your twenties have sure been eventful*, was too callous.

Misunderstanding my silence, Nellie said, "It's a choice to live with my mother-in-law, one we're both happy with. Don't worry; I'm not homeless."

Several seconds passed before I realized I was being rude as well as drawing this out. I mumbled a suggestion that we sit and held the chair for Nellie while she did.

She acknowledged the action with a head tilt and small smile. Angling past her to take the other narrow seat, I quickly inched forward to avoid a pair of giggling children who'd escaped their section of the library and were apparently playing hide-and-seek from whatever parental figure had foolishly brought them here.

Now closer to Nellie, though, I couldn't back away without being obvious about it. It made sense, I told myself. It would make it easier to hear her over the buzz of the other patrons. Uncomfortable, yes, but a necessity and the lesser of two social evils.

Nellie pointed at my knee brace visible past the edge of the table. "ACL?"

"Uh, yes. But I was lucky, just a light tear in college. Didn't end my basketball scholarship."

She nodded knowingly and twisted her blonde hair into a bun, securing it with a pen. The unfastened cap teetered but remained in place.

"I apologize if I smell like a locker room."

Nellie's head snapped back so fast the pen cap dislodged and flew off into the recesses of the nearest stack, forever entombed by the romance authors with last names starting between Te and Tu.

She tilted her head again with another small smile. "You're fine. Trust me."

She held my gaze, her smile not failing for a second. Convinced she was being serious and not hung up on my blurted announcement, I finally nodded. Clearing her throat, Nellie straightened the papers in front of her.

"Okay, so I cleaned up the outline like you asked and posted the contest rules. We're asking for anyone who would like to ghostwrite the book to submit their first ten pages or first chapter by March first." Her eyes slid to mine, asking for a confirmation.

So far, I hadn't heard anything new; this was a recap of things we'd already discussed. Nellie would then go over the submissions and select a winner. I'd pay them, and they would work with Nellie to get the book polished and ready to submit to agents. Quick, easy, over. I nodded politely, still waiting for the bit that necessitated this face-to-face meeting.

"But we don't have to wait until March first to go through all the submissions. We've already had several come in this week. Several overachievers, but there could be some good ones in that bunch. I think it might be best to start going through the submissions as much as we can instead of waiting until the end. That could just . . . bury us in work."

I hadn't stopped nodding; a bobblehead with no off switch. I stared at Nellie. Her head slid to the side as she stared back. "Or you'd rather wait?"

Wait? "Wait to what?"

Nellie spoke slowly. "To go over the submissions together."

I stopped nodding as realization crystallized over my brain.

Nellie reached the conclusion before I admitted it to myself. "You never meant to go over the submissions with me?"

I opened my mouth. How had I missed that? The hardness scale of the wooden chair I was sitting on multiplied by ten. The information must have been in one of the attachments she'd sent. Normally, I read all that stuff. Normally, I go over contracts with a fine-tooth comb.

Normally.

"I'm sorry. I missed—didn't see . . ."

I squirmed. I hadn't read through the contract. I'd only skimmed what Nellie had sent me, so relieved thinking the guilt was almost out of my hands, to pass on the responsibility. And the reason was now obvious.

Elise never told me about her three stories. Certainly not the one I'd found in the trash folder. What she had done was beg me to talk about our fight. I'd said no, we'd do that when she got out of the hospital, all while knowing, but not admitting . . . she wasn't getting out of the hospital.

I needed to get Elise published. That's what this effort was for. But of course it wouldn't be that easy. I'd glossed over the "effort" part of the experience. Maybe that was the missing ingredient. If I wanted Elise to be published, I needed to put in the work, not just pay someone else to do it using Elise's money.

"It's okay," Nellie said, her voice soft. Unaccusatory. Understanding.

I burned with embarrassment that I was reacting this way, causing a feedback reaction that started me sweating. When did I get so good at making other people feel bad or uncomfortable? Why couldn't I get over a done event that couldn't be controlled or reasoned with?

The edges of my vision fuzzed. "No," I countered.

My throat constricted, trying to close. I swallowed several times, grimacing with each attempt. Nellie didn't say anything to push or rush me. The worry she might ask me something I didn't want to answer lessened with each moment. The extra time without pressing expectations gave me the space I needed to get my breathing back under control.

When I was sure I could speak without my voice shaking, I admitted, "I should have caught that. I read stuff like that for work. Usually I'm good at this stuff."

"I have no doubt," she said. I was prepared to argue with someone attempting to defend me, but Nellie wasn't done. "You continue to work for a company even though you don't need the money due to what Elise left you, all because you're loyal to them. And that company is more than willing to let you telework before and after your sister's death because they don't want to lose you as an employee, so you must be very good at what you do."

My shocked confusion over how she knew all that must have shown on my face.

"Charlie told me," she conceded out of one corner of her mouth. She tilted forward, testing the midway boundary of the center of the table. "I'm not offended." She spread her hands in an obvious gesture. "This is about your sister's work. That's difficult. Of course it is. I understand. We can go back to square one with this, and if you decide to have me run the entire thing, I'm happy to do that—"

"No." I swallowed and blinked. Then I repeated more calmly, "No. Thank you. You're right. I need a bigger role in this. I need to do the work. Though," oh, this was hard to ask, "I'm going to need . . . help." My chest ached, either from all the running or the reality of living. I falsely hoped it was the running. That, at least, was temporary.

I chanced a peek at Nellie. The glow from the overhead lamps highlighted her hair, now fully blonde, no hint of her roots. She put her hands in her lap, giving me space. The act was so nonthreatening that I didn't retreat or push back from the color and closeness of her presence.

"Helping is my literal job. Which I do because I love it. And, hey! I think you'll find this can be fun." She lifted her eyebrows at me and activated the dimple on the side of her mouth before swallowing and glancing away for a moment. "You asked me if I was ready to help you. I have to ask, are you ready for *me* to help *you*?"

I waited for a new wave of embarrassment or guilt to overwhelm me. But staring at Nellie's face, set in determination, I only sensed support. "Yes." I pulled my sweaty shirt away from my chest and looked at her with relieved embarrassment. "Though, maybe not here—"

I gripped the table as something slammed into the back of my chair. I spun, expecting to find a kid latched onto it, then almost ended up on the floor when a rolling cart filled with books hit my chair again. The engine was revealed to be a surprisingly strong and small white-haired lady who poked her head around the cart and gasped in horror.

"Oh! Oh my. So sorry sir!"

Nellie slid out of her seat and steadied me out of mine. "Please, no worries. We're just leaving."

She reached out to squeeze the woman's hand in assurance, grabbed her coat off her chair, and led me through the stacks to the stairwell. Our voices would echo here, but luckily, we were the only ones there for the moment.

Nellie patted my shoulder and walked around me to lean one hip against the railing, using her coat as a cushion. She rubbed her forehead and laughed. "Agreed, this may not be the best place to meet."

"Definitely not." Suddenly overcome with fear of Nellie suggesting another place to meet that would still include the proximity of strangers, I blurted out, "What about my house?"

Instantly I regretted the words. That was way too forward. Plus, inviting someone I'd only met twice to Elise's home seemed 100 percent creepy on my part.

Bouncing on her toes, Nellie proved me wrong. "Perfect. I've got your address. Does Thursdays at this time work for you?"

How did she know my address? *The contract, idiot.* Did I just invite someone to Elise's home? No one but me had been inside since she'd died. Why did my chest hurt? *Breathe, you idiot.*

Nellie was typing on her phone. "I'm texting my sister to come pick me up. Let's call tonight a wash and start again next week."

If she wanted to start next week and really was this enthusiastic, then maybe I hadn't made a mistake in inviting her. Nellie clearly didn't think so.

Breathe, breathe . . . breathe. One exhale later and the tightness in my chest retreated to a distance far enough not to suffocate me but continued to hover on standby to dive right back in at the slightest invitation.

Nellie tucked her phone away, and for the first time, a new expression crossed her face. A sly, teasing grin. "The stench that wafted between them was greater than any body spray could cover. Truly, soap intervention was required."

Nellie's tone left no doubt that she was teasing, I was so surprised I didn't have time to suppress the laugh huffing from my throat. "You said I didn't smell!" Then, not wanting her to respond to that, I asked, "Do you always narrate people?"

"You don't smell, sorry! Not too much, promise. I played ball. I get the locker-room stench. Just couldn't help myself." Nellie broke into giggles that elicited more unexpected laughter from me. The pulsing from my chest felt like an out-of-body experience that I couldn't stop and didn't want to. Her rolling giggles mixed with my deep chuckles, the echoes surrounding us before traveling up the staircase. "And yes, I love narrating. Don't be surprised if you pick it up."

"I'll . . . look forward to it." Oddly enough, I didn't think that was a lie.

Nellie's phone pinged. "My sister's here." She inclined her head toward the exit. "Shall we?"

As we walked, I tried to smell myself without being obvious and concluded, maybe with unfounded hope, that it really wasn't that bad. To distract both of us from thinking too hard on the topic, I asked, "And I need to, in the meantime, before we meet next week . . . ?"

"Nothing. I'll bring everything with me, and we'll go over it together until you feel comfortable."

I held the door open for Nellie, and we walked into freshly falling snowflakes, highlighting every orange cone of light streaming down from the streetlights surrounding the parking lot. A car sidled next to us, different from the one I'd seen pick Nellie up from the office when we met.

Nellie offered her hand softly encased inside a woven mitten. I shook it, and she climbed inside the car with a farewell wave. Then she was gone. I stood still in the falling snow, feeling as though the world had slowed into silence after taking me on a bright and cheerful carnival ride. When I heard a group of teenagers leave the library behind me, I made my way to my car and drove home.

The single lamp I'd left on at Elise's house offered a sorry and solitary welcome home. I left it on and climbed the stairs to shower, hoping the bit of colorful wonderment that I hadn't realized I'd been experiencing until it left would come back, at least until I went to sleep.

When it didn't, I lay awake in the dark, staring at nothing and wondering, *What did I agree to?*

Chapter 3

I FINISHED MY RUN EARLY, giving myself more than enough time to shower and wander in agitation around an already clean living room before Nellie arrived. But my chest wouldn't settle. I didn't know whether I could actually help get Elise published, even under the guidance of an industry professional. Maybe I would be so incompetent that Nellie would cancel the project. Or nuclear Armageddon could start. Really either option would work.

The doorbell trilled, and I jogged into the vestibule with forced enthusiasm to open the front door. Nellie and I had discussed the details of our new scheduled meeting and unanimously agreed to keep it casual. Given her proclivity for bright colors, I was curious what "casual" would mean for her. I didn't expect it to be a Thai House orange jacket. Looking up from the jacket, I found Nellie wasn't the one wearing it.

"Daniel O'Brian? Your weekly order. Sorry we were late tonight."

Shocked into temporary confusion over how I'd forgotten, I reached into my back pocket.

"No, sir, you've already paid. Remember?"

That's right, I had. I still dug for my wallet, remembered it was on the side table next to the door, and fished out a tip. The delivery man smiled a thank-you and waved farewell with a twenty in his hand. He walked back to his car over Elise's lawn, now showing more brown grass than snow.

Nellie would be here any minute. If she saw the amount of food for two people, she might misunderstand and ask questions. Since I wasn't in an answering mood, I ran the bag of curry and pad thai into the kitchen, shoved the cartons inside the fridge and slammed it shut just before I heard a "Hello?" from the direction of the front door.

I wiped my hands against my jeans to rid them of any evidence that may have leaked from the cartons. "Come in!" I returned to the vestibule to find

Nellie peeking past the open door, the front of her coat unzipped. "So," I said, ushering her inside, "'Casual' is a shirt that says, 'The Book Was Better?'"

"Or 'casual' is yet another gray, alma mater, long-sleeve T-shirt."

While maintaining her hold on a large box, Nellie shrugged out of her puffy coat. No yellow sweater today or neon-blue flourishes. Instead, Nellie's shirt shouted bright pink. Complete with her jeans and loafers, her outfit didn't define casual as much as it declared cheerfulness. But her hunched and rounded shoulders betrayed a slight nervousness. I must be contagious.

I reached forward, but instead of giving me the box, she relinquished her coat. Waving her past me into the living room, I hung her coat on one of the decorative hooks in the vestibule that Elise had found at a flea market in Vermont last summer. When I returned to the living room, Nellie was slowly spinning with her mouth open.

She'd switched on another lamp, flooding the space with dancing light as the tassels hanging on the lampshade swayed back and forth. The box lay deposited on the couch like an afterthought.

"Wow." Nellie whistled and continued turning. She squinted teasingly when her gaze passed me. "This must be your sister's work."

Elise had a gaggle of friends who all loved her home. But Nellie was an unknown quantity. I had no idea how Elise's home might look to a female stranger. To Elise it was a sanctuary. I didn't want to see it any other way.

Half apologizing, half pleading, I tried to explain. "Elise loved gardens. I know it seems . . . a lot, but she could tell you the name of every flower . . . It's a bit chaotic."

"It's perfect." Nellie completed another turn. Her fingers outstretched, she brushed the grass-cloth textured walls while staring at splintered and weathered picture frames with their country settings, the stylish but lumpy throw pillows, and the handblown vases the colors of the rainbow on the fireplace mantel. "No, it's not too much. This has a method to its madness. Planned and thoughtful. No wonder you didn't want to meet at the office or library. They're caves compared to this. This," Nellie said, taking a final turn by twisting her heel into the carpet, "this is a home."

Just like when we'd first met and Nellie complimented the number of stories Elise had come up with, a bit of the pressure on my chest lessened.

"Yes," I agreed, finding myself explaining more than was necessary for someone who wanted a quick meeting. "It took her years to put all this together. Finding each piece. Her house was a treasure hunt for her."

"It's a beautiful garden." With her shirt, Nellie looked like a prize freesia in this space. She took a deep breath, no doubt inhaling the hint of fresh pine the living room always smelled of.

"Okay." Nellie shook her head as though trying to reorient to reality. "We should get started."

Before she sat though, she laser focused on a single frame. And why not? It was the only one with a towel draped on it. Nellie raised one eyebrow at me. I shrugged, not having a verbal explanation ready. She reached out hesitantly and raised her eyebrow again in a silent question. Instinct told me to shake my head, to leave the towel right where it was, but the desire to help make Nellie comfortable in Elise's home and ease the nervousness in her shoulders triumphed over my hesitancy.

I nodded.

Nellie grasped one end of the towel and pulled, revealing Elise's last purchase. A hand-stitched embroidery sampler from the eighteenth century that read, *Be kind and compassionate to one another, forgiving each other, just as in Christ God forgave you.*

Nellie stepped forward and squinted at the faded thread at the bottom.

"Ephesians 4:32," I offered in case she couldn't read the notation.

Nellie's shoulders relaxed, and she smiled at the frame, then at me. I smiled back, mostly not to lose any goodwill but also a plea for her not to ask why I had it covered.

Nellie obliged by clapping her hands together. "So, back to work." She sank onto the couch. "Oh, good heavens above, this cushion feels like a cloud."

She cleared her throat. Then again. Probably trying to work around the question that must be running through her mind. A cottage house in the suburbs but still close to the city and where everyone had a backyard and cleared streets and sidewalks after every snow.

"Divorce," I blurted out.

Nellie's eyes shot to mine at the unexpected word.

"Elise came into money from her divorce. My ex-brother-in-law is a pretty wealthy guy."

Nellie blanched. "Yeesh, divorce. Sorry to hear that. That can be so messy. He's not coming after you trying to get the money back or anything, is he?"

"I—" The thought of Edward coming after me shocked me. "Is that a real thing that people do?"

Nellie crossed her legs and drummed her fingers against one cheek, the action almost hidden by the hair curling around her face. "You know, probably not. Someone sent me a book to edit where that was the plot. But I don't think that was researched. The rest of the manuscript was pretty bad. So, sorry, no. Probably not a thing."

Only now I was worried it was. As Nellie took the lid off the box to rummage through it, I searched through any memory of Edward from the past year. I'd last seen—but had not spoken to—him at the funeral in December, and nothing since.

"Here we go." Nellie hefted a stack of papers out of the box and dropped half on the coffee table, a reclaimed nineteenth-century steamer trunk Elise had salvaged, and handed me the other half. I frowned. The stack reached from my hands to halfway up my forearm.

"Um, how many submissions is this? And why print them out?" I asked, angling my body as far as I could from the stack weighing my arms down.

"Forty-three. And because I like working with paper as much as possible. Don't get overwhelmed yet. There's still one week left before March first when all submissions need to be in." I must have looked lost. "Yeah, we had way more interest than I was expecting. But we have until May to go through all the submissions and announce the winner. We'll just take the submissions one at a time, as much as we can each week."

"Glad we only asked for one chapter per submission." Wow, was I complaining already?

I dropped into the armchair next to the fireplace and squirmed as Elise's favorite chunky robin-egg-colored quilt, inconveniently draped over the chair, dug accusing knots into my back.

"Don't worry. That's not all I brought." Nellie started pulling something out of the box.

I caught a whiff of salsa as Nellie put a container on the coffee table and peeled the lid off. The aroma spread around the room, squashing the lingering scent of pine. A hungry hurricane swirled in my stomach, reminding me of all the times chips and salsa had sustained Charlie and me through at least a hundred study sessions in college.

Leaning closer, I said, "It'd be rude to decline."

"Indeed, yes." Nellie threw me a cheeky grin as she also grabbed a bag of chips from the box and yanked on the corners to open the top with a loud pop.

A horn honked outside. Nellie slapped her forehead. "Shoot!"

She ran to the door. I dumped my pile of papers on the coffee table and followed. Copying Nellie's lead, we both waved to the woman behind the wheel, who must have been waiting for Nellie to signal she was free to leave. Unable to smile realistically on cue, I could only hope I didn't look like a psychotic waving clown. Nope, just a friendly client.

The driver must have approved, or at least didn't object. She gave a final wave to Nellie and drove off without any suspicious glances indicating worry over leaving Nellie with me. Wearing non-sweat-stained clothes and sporting combed hair that didn't resemble a squirrel's nest must have helped. I winced, imagining how I must have appeared last week at the library. A sweaty mess who looked like an unmade bed.

We stayed on the porch as the car puffed plumes of exhaust out into the fading evening sky. Though it was none of my business, I had to ask, "That's the third person I've seen drive you somewhere. Are they all your sisters?"

Nellie ushered us back inside the house and closed the door, impatient for either the work or the food. "In a way. I have one biological sister and several foster sisters and sisters-in-law. I collect families. Is it okay if we eat in here?" Nellie waved at the living room.

"Definitely. One sec."

I ran to the kitchen and returned with china plates and cloth napkins. Overkill for salsa maybe, but Elise hadn't liked disposable kitchenware, and I hadn't found it in me yet to buy any and bring them into her home. Nellie held out her hands eagerly for the plates, like she was as excited to eat the salsa as she was to bring it to me.

Someone shrieked outside. High, long, and whiny.

I grimaced. "Sorry, neighbor's kids. They fight for a minute or two and go inside, but they'll be back out playing with each other within thirty minutes."

Nellie sat on the couch and dumped a pile of chips on my plate next to a mound of sweet-smelling salsa. She handed it over, then licked the remains off her thumb before putting food on her own plate.

I groaned after my first bite, the flavors proving far superior to any store-bought brand. "How are we supposed to work when we could be eating?"

Nellie chomped a chip, swallowed, and said, "Pacing."

She gestured to the pile of papers on the coffee table. I eyed them, impressed. It must have taken a lot of time to print them out. Nellie handed me the top bundle from my pile and grabbed her own. Nellie deflated into the couch cushions with a sigh and began to say something when another scream rang from outside, followed by a slammed door.

"You say we have at least thirty minutes?" she asked.

"Hopefully."

"Well, sometimes siblings fight. Anyway, we'll go over the first submission together—you okay?"

Sometimes siblings fight. I rounded my shoulders to reset myself. "Yeah, sorry. Go on."

Nellie hesitated for a moment, then wrapped her hair in another pen-secured bun. "So, these are the first chapters people submitted based on your sister's outline. Honestly, I'm seriously excited to read how they wrote the scene where the main character keyed her ex's Mercedes-Benz. Oh, you're waving your hand to speak. That's cute."

I stared at my hand, frozen in the air.

Nellie stretched across the coffee table and pulled it down for me. "Learning how to talk to people again is the worst." She sounded sympathetic, not annoyed. I could only assume she was speaking from experience.

I wiggled my fingers to send a message that they shouldn't move again without telling me. "Are my cheeks red? They feel red."

"Yes." Nellie chomped another chip. "For the record, please feel free to interrupt me at any time. This is going to be interactive, lots of back and forth."

I sat on my hand. "I wanted to say, that's one of the things I didn't understand from Elise's outline. She made it sound like keying an ex's car was romantic. How is keying your ex's car romantic?"

Nellie positioned her legs underneath her and almost bounced on her knees in excitement. "That's one of the things I love about what your sister did. She showed the couple at their low point at the beginning so the story had someplace to go. Most people don't get that. They love writing about instant love. I haaaaate that. This way, the reader can take that journey with them. That's my favorite part in stories, when people show their true feelings. Right?"

"I just don't think Edward would like that part of the story."

My response wasn't enthusiastic enough for Nellie. She threw her hands up and laughed. "If he's the rich ex-husband your sister based the story on, then no, he probably wouldn't. Unless he still loved her, in which case he'd love the ending where they get back together. But he's not the target audience, and that's who we want to buy the book when it's done."

I couldn't argue with that.

"So," Nellie continued, "we're going to start reading through the submissions to weed out ones we don't like because they either don't align to your sister's vision for the story or they contain too many writing flaws and errors. Some are okay, but not too many. I'll work with whomever we ultimately decide on with my editing passes."

"What are some of the writing errors that I should watch for?"

Nellie's mouth silently moved as she considered her answer. "The most obvious will probably be cliché writing. Where they use phrases you've heard a million times."

"Like 'a million times'?"

"Clever, that. Very astute."

"I do have a sweatshirt from Yale."

"Sooooo." Nellie's mouth resisted a smile that her voice did not. "Clichés tend to pop up in physical descriptions. I've read books before where all the main characters had blue eyes. Describing those can be so repetitive. Watch for descriptions like, baby-blue eyes, deep-blue eyes, ocean blue, etcetera. It's all been done. You're laughing, but it's true."

I was sure my slight chuckle didn't qualify as a laugh; I hadn't worked up to that in months—but wait. I *had* laughed, and recently, back with Nellie when we'd met at the library.

Huh.

I liked that. And I liked that this laugh caused Nellie to giggle.

"It's harder than you think. Here, describe my blue eyes." Nellie raised up on her knees on the couch cushion. She tilted toward me, eyes wide.

I stiffened. "If one of your sisters drove by right now and saw you, they might break down the door to find out what was going on in here."

Nellie shook her head, amused but not deterred. "Describe my blue eyes without using a cliché."

I scooted to the edge of my seat, trying not to snort at Nellie staring straight at me with unblinking, demonic doll eyes. "Yeah, so those are green."

Nellie flopped back onto the couch and let her legs dangle toward the floor. "You passed." I leaned back too, enjoying my win, only to stop when Nellie asked, "How would you describe green eyes?"

I threw my head back. "Oh, come on!" I pleaded in mock protest.

"I'll bring more salsa next week . . ."

I exhaled and looked at Nellie again. Her features weren't exaggerated this time. She just sat with a Mona Lisa smile on her face. She thought this would be hard for me. In a way, it was, though probably not in the way she assumed. All this, talking with someone, joking, sharing food, sharing thoughts, all things I used to do but thought I'd forgotten how. But here I was, falling into the pattern using dusted-off familiarity as a guide, a familiarity that brought comfort. It felt good. And warm. And shocking.

I met Nellie's gaze. "Like Depression-era green glass."

Nellie's eyebrows went up in astonishment and together in confusion. "Like what?"

I pointed to the fireplace mantel. A sea-green, bubbled glass bowl filled with white seashells sat in the place of honor, the focus of the room. "Nine antique stores over two months. That's how long it took us to find that exact one. It was our 'Centerpiece Adventure.'"

Nellie's nose scrunched in curious amusement. "Centerpiece Adventure?"

"Ah, yeah . . ." My initial hesitation to talk to anyone about all Elise's and my adventures was based on the belief that sharing something that precious was heretical. I'd been so absorbed in this little describe-the-eyes game that I'd let the bit about the Centerpiece Adventure slip. It took a heartbeat to remember that sharing a memory didn't mean losing it or that Nellie would automatically deride or mock it. In fact, her smile indicated understanding. Something I needed the person leading the charge to get Elise published to have.

"Yeah," I repeated, hoping my quick grin would smooth over my hesitation. "We had a lot of adventures. So, in answer to your question, your eyes look like Depression-era green glass."

Her eyes narrowed, and tiny lines formed between her thick, dark eyebrows as she scrutinized the bowl. "Yeah," she conceded. "That's accurate."

"Like 'cocoa brown' eyes?"

Nellie groaned and rolled her face to the side at the reminder of our first meeting. "That was a bad example. Nine times out of ten, brown eyes are described as food. I shouldn't have chosen cocoa; it's overused. Plus, your eyes aren't that dark. More like the color you get when you mix melted dark-chocolate chips into milk-chocolate pudding."

My stomach rumbled, and Nellie unapologetically giggled and flashed her trademark dimple before pointing to our stack of papers.

"I printed off two of every submission. Let's go through the first together."

It took longer than I wanted. Nellie continued teaching me what to look for in a good copy, only to have to repeat the instructions on the next page. She continued patiently, never showing any irritation and occasionally mocking me with gentle ribbing. The frequent salsa refueling helped. When I objected that I was making the process too long, she shook her head. She explained once I understood the basics this would go faster, so it was worth the time expenditure. But we would never get Elise published at this rate.

Midway through reviewing the second submission, I stood to stretch. "I'm ready," I announced.

"To read through the next page?"

I clarified, "To move on."

Nellie shrugged, but sensing my determination, handed me the next stack while she finished the one we'd started together.

Two lines into the manuscript, my eyebrows rose.

After the first paragraph, I snorted.

From the corner of my eye, I noticed Nellie straighten and glance in my direction. When I pursed my lips together in an unsuccessful attempt to not chuckle, Nellie gave me her full attention.

"What?" she asked. I started to tell her when she stopped me. "Read it aloud."

Scanning the rest of the first page, I said, "Uh, you don't want that."

"Anyone can narrate. I could narrate an instruction manual and make it sound good. Try it, I dare you."

It might have been the challenge, or the relaxed way Nellie now held herself, but something in this situation sparked a competitiveness so dormant I almost didn't recognize the feeling. It created an idea that shot straight for my mouth, bypassing rational thought or risk analysis. Nellie couldn't have known, but growing up as Elise's younger brother meant I had a Master's in playacting.

I sucked in a breath. In a few seconds, Nellie wouldn't care about how I was reading and would be more concerned about what I was reading.

"'The knife tickled his earlobe as she continued to press the tip into his skin as she pricked the blade closer and closer to his throat. The man's voice rose in fear,'" I did the same, wobbling each of my next words, "'Didn't your mother tell you not to play with your food?'"

I glanced up to see Nellie's eyebrows draw together, then hit the roof when I read the next line, "'She snarled, raising the knife—'"

I pantomimed the action, bringing my arm up and clenching my fist. What was possessing me to act this way? It had to be the ghost of the person I used to be.

Nellie lunged forward as I read the next line, "'—she stabbed it into—'"

As Nellie snatched the papers from my hand, I couldn't help but casually comment, "I don't remember a murder scene in Elise's outline."

"Oh no, no, no, no, noooo . . ." Nellie's hand covered her mouth as she read the page. "How did a slasher submission slip in? Oh!" She slapped her forehead. "I printed off the last three chapters right before I came over. I didn't check them to see if any went off genre. Or, you know," she smacked the pages, "didn't follow the basic and obvious RomCom instructions. Argh, I'm sorry!"

I was only half-listening since my chest had decided to start somersaulting end over end. I didn't know yet if it would land on embarrassment over pretending this moment was like any other moment where I used to joke and kid around, or on encouragement to keep the act going.

For a moment, a very brief one, perhaps inspired by the hilarity of watching Nellie's reaction over asking me to narrate what turned out to be a slasher submission, encouragement won out. Long enough for me to quip, "You should be. I'm strictly a cozy mystery type of guy."

Luckily, Nellie's focus was inward, so she didn't notice the way my face might also be reddening when my stomach flipped a final time and flooded me with embarrassment. I took several quick deep breaths while Nellie wasn't looking at me. I hadn't dated anyone since Elise had called to tell me about her diagnosis, so the inappropriateness of joking (let alone playacting) about a murder, even a fictional one, to a recent acquaintance didn't occur to me until it was too late.

Yet I couldn't deny that the rush of the challenge and resulting mischievousness had produced a definite thrill. A familiar one attached to enough good memories of joking around with Elise or Charlie that my head drifted on a sense of euphoria for a few seconds.

Nellie snapped the pages down and sucked her lips inside her mouth before releasing an exaggerated exhale. "I'm guessing my face is red now?"

I wanted to say her cheeks were scarlet, but that seemed too cliché. Even though I now shared Nellie's embarrassment over the situation, I still said, "You look like a boiled lobster."

Nellie snuck a snort of approval my way, a gold star to reward my quick thinking. "That was some pretty good word play. Unlike, 'Didn't your mother tell you not to play with your food?'" She shuddered and dropped the slasher submission back in the box. "Well, okay. Let's move on."

My fading euphoria had enough power to push out one more tease. "Without tickling anyone."

And that was enough of that. Even though Nellie snorted again and grinned in appreciation at my comment, my embarrassment briskly swept away the last of the euphoria.

The next twenty minutes were filled with Nellie's promised back-and-forth interaction and my prediction of being interrupted occasionally by the neighbor's kids fighting. Taking several notes that I constantly referred to, I admitted to myself that this was like any formula on an Excel spreadsheet; there were rules. I could get the hang of this.

Nellie wasn't so sure. She kept insisting that it was hard to quantify something in a story that made you identify with it, that rejecting bits solely because of grammar flaws might mean missing the heart of a story. According to her, sometimes patience and sympathy were required. I nodded along until she set me loose to start marking my own submission again.

I actually enjoyed seeing my progress. I marked up the next manuscript, grinning at each red circle and hoping one of the characters would speak some cheesy dialogue. Drawing red ink through those lines gave me purpose, a gentle revenge for all the rom-coms I'd been forced to watch. Though, Nellie again warned not all cheesy dialogue was bad in a romance. Sometimes it was expected. Even looked forward to. I disagreed.

At some point, Nellie asked, "Do you think your sister would have liked this part with the MC? Sorry, MC stands for main character." She pointed to a line on the paper so she wouldn't lose her place as she looked at me.

"You can say her name. Elise," I offered, trying to hurry past the correction so Nellie wouldn't see it as a criticism. "And yes. Since they get back together at the end, it makes sense that the writer put in that bit about finding her ex's journal."

Nellie nodded and put her attention back on the page. "As much as I'm helping you, it's great to have you here to help me zero in on the author's original intent, what your sis—what Elise had been going through in her divorce and what she meant by some of the things she wrote."

Outside, the sister wailed for her younger brother to let her swing. My grip on the manuscript tightened. Nellie had returned to reading and didn't see me put the papers and pen in my lap. I curled my fingers into fists several times until the fuzz on the edge of my vision went away. I quietly took several breaths, sneaking peeks at Nellie all the while to make sure she hadn't noticed. But she remained stretched out on her back, neck propped up by the couch's armrest.

Sometimes I knew when this would happen. These crazy physical attacks on my senses. I could understand them happening when I could see them coming. Like happening across one of Elise's blankets and unexpectedly having the scent of her perfume escape when I unfolded it. Or hearing a crosswalk signal, the beep-beep-beep reminding me of sitting in Elise's hospital room. Even if I didn't want them, I could at least understand having a reaction in those cases.

But sometimes they hit with no warning or care that I could detect. As much as Nellie was helping me, I didn't want her to see this. Because then I would have to explain why they happened and the reason for the weight of guilt around my core. I blinked several times as my vision sharpened, and I could discreetly pick the manuscript back up.

Elise had always wanted to be a fiction writer. To write fake stuff about things she made up and put together. Now, reading her outline, I saw Elise and her real life all over it. True, her MC didn't have her name, and the circumstances in the story were different from Elise's life. But Elise was telling her own story. Her MC's heartache was hers. The challenges she faced reflected ones Elise had lived through.

All on her own.

The worst part was that it was all news to me. I didn't know Elise had felt this way . . . because she'd never told me. Because I hadn't been there when Elise's divorce to Edward was going down. Whatever had happened during that time remained a mystery.

And then it hit me, what the problem was. It wasn't that I didn't know how to critique books. I was learning that. I just didn't want this insight into Elise's mind, afraid that it would reveal something I should already have known. Or something I could never make up for. But I had to. I had to give her this gift, to get her published. Something she'd always wanted but couldn't do for herself.

So the problem wasn't that I couldn't do the work. The problem was that I *could*.

With a final silent inhale, I accepted the problem.

I snagged the last chip off my plate. The loud crunching caught Nellie's attention, giving me the distraction my thoughts needed. Unfortunately, at the same time, Nellie's phone buzzed in her pocket, the vibration loud enough to be heard through her jeans.

"It's my sister," she predicted before digging the phone out to look at the screen. Just like that, our time was up. Nellie stretched and took our plates into the kitchen. I piled everything into Nellie's box, including the unread manuscripts.

"Don't want to go through them alone without me?" Nellie teased, coming up behind me. I shook my head and followed her into the vestibule. "I'll store these at my office and bring them back next week. What's on the agenda for the rest of your night?"

"Work," I said. There was always work to catch up on.

Nellie sucked in her cheeks, creating two dimples. She might not have approved of my answer but didn't say anything as she tried to arrange putting her coat on while holding the box and looping her bag over her head.

A little too much going on.

I stood and reached over to grab the strap of her purse so she could focus on not dropping the box. A few inches taller than Nellie, I saw where the strap had twisted due to her half-hearted efforts to put it on. Moving to untangle it, the back of my knuckles brushed against her neck, the loose hairs from her pen bun tickling my skin. For someone who had been actively avoiding people, this sudden intimacy racked my brain like I'd snorted water.

I jerked my hand back, causing it to get caught in the strap. The force of my pull nearly knocked Nellie off her feet. Worse, the strap tugged on her neck, strangling her. The container of salsa tipped out of the box, its lid sliding off, splattering us both as I struggled to disentangle myself.

"I'm sorry, so sorry." I winced at her now salsa-covered shirt. Removing tomato stains was a chore. My embarrassment worsened as Nellie coughed several times to regain her breath.

"S'okay . . ." she wheezed. She took in a lungful of air and expelled a final cough. "You were trying to help. And look at you!"

Bits of tomato, cilantro, and onion covered me from shirt collar to belt, but I wasn't worried. "Men's gray T-shirts were built for this sort of thing," I assured her.

Nellie dropped the box with a thud onto the hardwood floor, her coat folding on top of it. By the time I glanced up, she'd stripped off her shirt in a flurry of pink fabric. The instinct to cover my eyes delayed long enough for me to catch the black tank top Nellie wore underneath. She caught my expression and misunderstood the reason for it.

"This is my sister's shirt. If she sees it before I can soak it—" I wondered what punishment a sister would inflict when Nellie finished with, "—she may not let me borrow her pleated olive midi skirt on Friday."

I swallowed to get some moisture back in my mouth.

Stuffing the stained shirt into her bag, Nellie attempted again to juggle everything she had to carry and put on. Sensing disaster, I stepped in. Holding my arms wider, I exaggerated my movements and slowed them down, carefully looping straps and coat sleeves.

When we were done, Nellie stood successfully ensconced in her coat, holding the box with her bag draped securely across her shoulder. Everything was in place. Including her goofy grin. I'd probably resembled a clown on stilts while helping her.

"Were you narrating that in your head?" I asked.

"Still am."

I looked down as if that would hide my embarrassed smile.

"Charlie said you were a funny guy."

Ah, yes. That funny guy, my old self. The one who was laughing in all the family pictures Elise kept in her room on the second floor. 'Course, all of them had been taken back before the diagnosis. Before the fight.

"What all has Charlie said about me?"

"What all has Charlie said about *me*?" Nellie countered.

Not wanting to appear like I'd been caught talking about Nellie behind her back, I quickly admitted the truth. "That you're the best."

Nellie nodded and gave me a significant wink. "Same."

It took a second, but I realized what Nellie was implying. I groaned. Now I had friend guilt.

"Not a fan of compliments?"

"Not that. I'm just . . ." I sighed. "I'm a bad friend."

"What are you going to do about it?"

The implication wasn't lost on me, fresh off my decision to stick this project through for Elise; if I could do hard things for her, I could do hard things for others.

A car horn blasted from outside, surprising me with a feeling of annoyance. We said our goodbyes, but I didn't linger in the hallway after Nellie left. I found my phone and sent Charlie a text.

Too late to come to b-ball tonight?

By the time Charlie replied, I'd already changed and was grabbing my keys.

Seriously? No, dude, come! We start in fifteen minutes.

I typed one-handed as I locked Elise's kitchen door and sprinted through the invigorating night air toward the detached garage. *I'll be late.* I raised the garage door and climbed into the front seat before my phone pinged.

Better that than never.

As the car engine thrummed, a thrill in my chest pushed out air so quickly, I had to breathe faster. My knees bounced like I was already bringing the ball down the court or rolling around a defender's pick to hit a floater over their outstretched arms. More and more bits of familiarity were filling my brain, connecting emotional comfort to memories and making the feeling closer . . . and attainable.

I sent a silent thank-you to Nellie in whichever sister's car had picked her up tonight.

Then a shriek sliced through the air and hit my chest, puncturing the building anticipation. The neighborhood kids were fighting again. I remembered Nellie's words: *Sometimes siblings fight.*

More shrieks broke the connections I'd made between memory and comfort. Paralysis hit before I could back my car out. Breathing slowed. Anticipation vanished. I sat perfectly still, except for my chest, which rose and fell with each new breath.

My phone pinged. Charlie. My car read the text, *I'm excited man. See you soon.*

The words snapped the part inside holding me in place. Finger by finger, I loosened my grip on the gear shift and turned off the ignition. Moments later, I stepped out of the car and closed the garage. I hurriedly typed an apology to Charlie before turning my phone off. The sounds of the screaming sibling fight stalked me as I retraced my steps to the kitchen door, struggling to both unlock it to let myself through and relock it behind me.

The frame around the uncovered embroidery sampler stared pointedly at me once I reached the living room. Well, it could stare all it wanted at the backside of a towel. I re-covered it and left the room, turning off all the lights behind me.

Chapter 4

NOT AGAIN, I THOUGHT.

The evening had been all planned out until . . .

I stared at Nellie's text asking if we could meet thirty minutes earlier. It would be another race against the clock since it was too late to change my standing dinner order with Thai House.

The doorbell trilled, and I raced to answer it. Over the last few weeks, Nellie had taken to knocking on the door when arriving for our review sessions, so this had to be the delivery man. The same orange Thai House jacket, the same twenty-dollar send-off tip, the same rush to the kitchen to stash the cartons of curry and pad thai in the fridge. The only difference being, this time, I had a few minutes to ignore my growling stomach before answering Nellie's rap on the door.

As I went to invite her in, it occurred to me that this overcaution might be teetering on paranoia. Nellie probably wouldn't ask anything if she saw the cartons, and even if she did, I could deflect by telling her how Elise and I had found the kitchen chandelier at an estate sale in Boston.

Nellie greeted me with the same beaming face I'd come to expect and look forward to. "You're smiling," she said. "You must be having a good day."

I stopped my hand from reaching up to touch my face to confirm what shape my lips were making. Thinking back on my day, I couldn't recall what had made it good. Any other hour of it, I'd have argued against the assertion.

"You're smiling too," I countered.

"I'm always smiling."

In what had become tradition, Nellie and I waved at whichever of her sisters sat behind the wheel of the car that had dropped her off. As it pulled away from the curb, I said, "That's the fifth different sister I haven't met." I eyed Nellie to see if I could catch any hint of why she had never introduced me. Nothing. "Why don't you drive?"

Nellie shrugged without answering and carried the box of manuscripts inside. "Did you watch the game with Charlie? He told me he has a big watch party every year." She'd stopped in the living room in front of the TV, riveted as the two announcers sat recapping the NCAA Men's National Championship game.

"No," I admitted, taking my normal seat in the armchair next to the fireplace. I'd thought about going, which was more than I would have done a month ago. I called that a win.

Nellie put the box down, and I noticed she wasn't wearing a coat. Just a Hawaiian-inspired long-sleeve shirt, unbuttoned enough at the top to allow a black tank top to peek through. A mini early-spring heat wave had gifted us with near seventy-degree temperatures, and she was taking advantage.

"Did you and Elise ever play basketball together?" Nellie asked.

"Ha!"

Nellie raised an eyebrow. "There's a story behind that reaction."

"Well . . . yeah. I mean, Elise didn't really like basketball. She liked watching me play, but never wanted to herself. But whenever we were going on a weekend adventure, we played HORSE to see who got to pick the music for the first two hours of driving."

Nellie pursed her lips, considering. She shot me a sly glance. "Doesn't seem fair if you're the one who knew how to shoot."

"I always started with already having the H-O-R-S."

"Ahhhh." Nellie smiled in understanding. "That's a little more fair."

She picked up the first stack of papers. However, before she handed one to me, she dropped them back in the box.

"How's your knee?"

I glanced down, trying to find the cause for her question. "Um, it's fine?"

"Good. Let's play." Nellie tugged me to my feet, which, in my confusion, I allowed. "Don't worry. This is off the clock, and you won't have to spot me any points. Come on. We both played in college, and I know you have a ball somewhere around here. We passed by your neighborhood basketball court coming in, and it's empty. We have to go."

I pointed to the papers lying rejected in the box. Somewhere in there could be the perfect author to write Elise's story, the entire purpose for Nellie's and my association.

But Nellie continued to coax me into the hallway. "We'll get to those. Promise. After we play. This won't be like the library."

Nellie had few boundaries—a fact proven with every meeting we'd had. I also knew she liked to push mine. I'd be blind not to notice, expect, or even be glad for it. But those pushes and pulls had always been inside Elise's home. Playing basketball wasn't an unknown situation, but playing it with her was. I'd started looking forward to these meetings. I didn't want to mess with that dynamic.

"You're in jeans," I protested. "My joggers might give me too much of an advantage."

"That's never once stopped me from playing."

"You're serious?"

"*Yes*. Get your knee brace. Where's the ball?"

I needed an excuse, fast. "You played in college?" It wasn't a change in topic, more of a bounce to a parallel conversation.

"Yes. And I played yesterday. And hopefully today. The next game is always the most important one." She stepped closer. "Come on. It's too perfect a day not to get out and play."

I stared, locked in by Nellie's anxious pleading. I tightened my lips, wondering how best to say this. I finally said, "Her sea-green eyes laughed in anticipation of his answer."

Nellie's eyes narrowed until she realized I was joking, using narration. "Wow. That was really bad. Spectacularly so."

I shrugged in agreement.

"And eyes can't laugh," she corrected. "But see? My mouth can! Hahahaaaaa . . . So? Are we playing?"

I sighed. "Okay."

Nellie squealed at my capitulation.

"Give me a sec to put my brace on."

Nellie texted her sister to postpone her pickup while I jogged upstairs. When I came back down, I called, "The ball's in the basket next to the front door," but Nellie wasn't in the vestibule. Craning my neck, I spied her standing in front of the towel-covered embroidery sampler in the front room.

"You can take it off."

Nellie spun at the sound of my voice. Huh, look at that. I'd surprised us both.

"It's okay."

She narrowed her eyes as we both studied what I'd said. "You're smiling, so I think you're telling the truth."

"I . . . agree."

Nellie gently tugged on the towel, revealing the message again. *Be kind and compassionate to one another, forgiving each other—*

"Why do you keep covering this up? If I can ask."

"Umm." I fumbled a gesture in her direction. "Why do you ask? If I can ask."

Nellie's dimple reflected off the glass covering the sampler. "It reminds me of what Juanita, my mother-in-law, put on my husband's grave marker; *I will not leave you comfortless: I will come to you.*"

I took a step closer, my face reflecting next to hers. "Why does this remind you of that?"

"They both bring me comfort." She glanced up at me, giggled, and glanced away.

"I'm smiling again, aren't I?"

"Come on." Nellie tucked her phone into her jeans, and I followed her into the vestibule.

I grabbed the ball and tossed it her way as we left the house. I couldn't determine if I was excited or not. Bees buzzed in my chest, so I was definitely feeling something. But Nellie had promised this wouldn't stop us from looking over the manuscripts later, so . . . I was gonna do this.

Once outside, I found myself in a battle with either the bright sun or the new green plants pushing up through the dirt. One of them was on a mission to make me sneeze. Nellie outstretched her arms to catch the greatest number of rays and disturbed a group of chattering birds, who told us off for walking too close to the waist-high fence they were sunning on.

Nellie couldn't resist bouncing the basketball as we walked down the sidewalk, and I couldn't resist breaking down her form and technique as her shirtsleeves whipped and snapped in the breeze with every pivot. She caught me staring and bent her knees to dribble closer to the ground.

"Don't get any ideas before we start playing," she warned with a competitive wink.

At such an obvious invitation, I swiped at the ball, catching it with my fingertips. Nellie pulled it in at the last second to keep it from spinning away from her control. Then she firmly tucked the ball in her arms. "Have you ever heard that you can learn more about someone in one hour of play than one week of talking? I don't necessarily believe it, but I do think you can discover things about someone by playing that you wouldn't any other way."

I swiped unsuccessfully again. "What are you hoping to learn about me?"

"Hopefully that you're not very good at basketball," Nellie said bluntly.

I smiled again, but this time, I knew I was doing it.

"I mean," Nellie continued after bumping into me with a teasing elbow, "you don't even have a hoop at your house, so maybe you don't practice and are all talk, no show."

"I did have one," I confessed. "But Elise's room overlooks the driveway. She never complained, but I found out the sound of me playing was keeping her up. I took it down."

I'd revealed too much. My chin jutted back, trying to camouflage into my neck. Most people would question why I hadn't just stopped playing. Taking down the net was, admittedly, overkill. But Elise recognized the gesture, the primary reason for my action, seeing it for what I hoped she would.

She'd teased me at the time that my efforts to ensure she had a good night's sleep were a far departure from the "Late-Night Adventures" we used to have. They were basically competitions to see who could keep the other one up for as long as possible. Weapons of choice in those battles included hidden alarm clocks, low-battery replacements in fire alarms, and remote-controlled kids' toys. When Elise sent me a text every five minutes from ten p.m. to five a.m. before a big date, I repaid the favor by hiring a bagpiper to serenade Elise outside her window at two in the morning. After that, Elise and I shook on a truce, officially ending the Late-Night Adventures.

I didn't have a succinct way to tell Nellie all that, but thankfully, she didn't ask me to. She just smiled as we rounded the corner and the park came into view. I huffed a quick sigh of relief.

In front of us, the court sat empty. I'd hoped it would be. I came all the time and knew it should be free this time of day, but the warm weather might have enticed a few others to come out and play. Thankfully, Nellie and I had the entire place to ourselves.

"Guess I do have some evidence that you might be good," Nellie said as we crossed the street.

I raised my eyebrow.

"Basketball has a grand tradition of smack talk, which is all basically bad prose. And you? You're really good at bad prose, which means you get to practice a lot."

I swiped at the ball again, this time getting enough of my fingers around the curve to steal it, catching Nellie off guard. She ran after me as I sprinted ahead. I dribbled to half court, reassured by the familiar scent of sun-warmed cement, and stopped at the mid-court line. This "home" always felt comfortable. I inhaled and relaxed. Turning, I slowly bounced the ball from one hand to the other, taunting Nellie on the sidelines.

She reached into her jeans pocket and tugged out an extra hair band. Her hair was already piled into a messy bun by a scrunchy, so I didn't understand what the second was for until she shot it, rubber-band style, my way.

While I yanked my own hair back to secure it, Nellie rid herself of her long sleeves. "Back to taking your shirt off?" I teased. It was a little bit of a shocking thing to say. Correction: a LOT shocking. Not sure why I said it or how I found the capacity to behave like I would have before Elise died. Nellie had to be rubbing off on me.

Nellie tossed the Hawaiian shirt onto the park bench, aiming for the end that didn't have obvious splinters in the faded wood. "That's my sister Jenna's shirt. I can't get it dirty."

"But you can get the tank top dirty?" I picked the ball back up and started to dribble.

Nellie stepped onto the court, her posture transforming. Bent knees and elbows, arms extending as she neared me. The only thing unchanged was her devious grin. "The tank top is mine. I can do whatever I want to it."

She lunged for the ball. I put my shoulder between it and her. "I thought that was a myth."

Nellie pivoted, swiping around my other side, but came up empty when I matched her movements. "What's a myth?"

"That sisters always share their clothes."

Nellie feinted left, and I fell for it. She snatched the ball from me, stepped back, and sprung into the air, arms outstretched. The ball swooshed through the hoop. We both glanced at her feet—several inches behind the three-point line.

0–3.

Nellie kept her shooting arm extended in triumph. "He realized with dread that he was going to lose."

I retrieved the ball and teased, "Had we officially started yet?"

And so we did. I squeezed every leverage I could out of my several inches of height advantage, and Nellie used her low center of gravity to pivot around me to steal the ball again and again. At some point, I stopped to take off my sweatshirt, enduring another joke at my propensity to wear gray shirts with a university's name on them. When the score became 16–13 in my favor, I held up my hands in the *T* gesture for timeout.

"We should have brought water with us," I huffed.

"Yeah, but we'd just have sweat it all out." To confirm, Nellie swiped at her forehead with the bottom of her tank top.

Still needing a breath, I thought of a way to keep her talking to extend this pause in the game. "How would I say, 'Someone smells' in Nellie language?"

Nellie threw back her head and barked a laugh. "*Nellie language?*"

"Yeah. Perfect descriptive prose?"

I loved how Nellie's dimple carved a satisfied smile into her cheek. "I assume that you're taking a dig at yourself and not making a commentary on me."

"You assume correctly."

Nellie wrinkled her nose at some memory. "Old socks. But I always thought that was way too cliché. I think 'overcooked burrito' is more accurate."

"That sounds like overly pink purple prose."

"Overly pink purple prose?" Nellie eyed me.

Too late, I realized I'd given myself away. That was one of her signature phrases, though not one she'd ever said to me in person.

"You've been watching my YouTube channel!"

Caught.

Nellie's channel gave editorial advice for aspiring authors. I'd found it weeks ago and was secretly watching all the videos about editing to get better at reviewing the submissions for Elise's story.

I covered my eyes with one arm and groaned at my self-sabotage. I held out the ball to Nellie. "Just take it."

The weight lifted off my fingers, but Nellie didn't accept it as an offering to drop the topic. "No wonder you picked up how to catch filtering words so quickly."

Watching someone's YouTube channel could be easily misconstrued as stalkerish. Lucky for me, Nellie believed I'd done it for the content. Which I had been. But . . . I'd also been watching because they were . . . relaxing. A good way to detox from work's virtual meetings while eating dinner. And a good way not to feel alone in Elise's kitchen.

Nellie clapped her hands. "Okay, let's go. Hey, stop stalling! Daniel! Daniel? What is it?"

The ball rolled across the court from where Nellie had dropped it. From the corner of my eye, I watched her assess my frozen form, then she followed my gaze until she saw the car I was staring at as it glided down the street. I recognized the manufacturer but would be surprised if either Nellie or I could name the model. Even in an affluent neighborhood like this, that car was a giant Snickers bar in a Halloween bucket filled with candy corn.

Nellie whistled. When I didn't respond, she asked, "Do you know who that is?"

I swallowed, again wishing I had some water. "That's Edward's car."

"Your rich ex-brother-in-law? Elise's husband?" Nellie whipped her head back to look between me and the car's taillights as it turned a corner. "He's headed to Elise's home."

I sighed. "Yep."

"Should we—" Nellie used her head to indicate the direction of the car.

I sighed again. "Yep."

Nellie gathered the ball, her shirt, and my sweatshirt (something my brain delay hadn't thought of), and we walked off the court. Every memory I searched through couldn't provide an explanation for this visit.

I'd last seen Edward at the funeral, but he'd disappeared without saying a word to me after the service. Elise always spoke highly of him. I couldn't remember a single time she'd complained about him, even when things had to have been going downhill for them in their marriage. We'd still been talking at the time, and she'd never said a word. But because I hadn't been around for the divorce, I couldn't say with any certainty what Edward had been like, or how he'd acted toward Elise during that process.

Him suddenly showing up? Something was wrong.

Nellie didn't dribble the ball on the way back. When she spoke, she kept her voice low. Either because she sensed the seriousness of the situation or because she saw this as a game where we would whisper secrets to each other and conduct a sneak attack.

"Why is he here?"

I lowered my voice to match hers. I wish it was because I wanted to play the spy game too. Instead, I went along with it because my mind was too busy trying to come up with an explanation to her question.

"No idea."

I'd researched to see if Edward could take back the money awarded to Elise in the divorce settlement. Nothing indicated he could, at least not that I could find.

Nellie scanned the neighborhood by turning her head left to right and back again and seemed disappointed when she didn't find a nervous accomplice lurking around. "Is Edward a good guy?"

An even more difficult question to answer. I'd tried to figure that out during the five years they were married and had nothing. Edward had called Elise a number of times after her diagnosis, even though the divorce had been finalized. She never seemed drained or upset after those calls. Packages wishing her well arrived on her doorstep at regular intervals. He'd even come to see her at the hospital right before the end. When she called and asked him to see her, I didn't think he'd do it. But he had. He'd come when she asked. That meant something, I just didn't know what.

On the other hand, Elise's sickness had crippled her for months before the end. In all that time, she'd only reached out once. Why not more?

A piercing roar split the air. Nellie, wide-eyed, lifted her foot to reveal a plastic dinosaur toy that had adventured off its lawn onto the sidewalk. Nellie and I stared, not breathing. The dinosaur roared again with flashing red eyes.

Nellie grabbed for my arm, almost tripping over her own feet as she pulled me along. I couldn't help but suspect she was having more fun with the situation than I was. Though I didn't think I was having any, I found myself following her as we ran across the street to shelter behind a plumber van parked on the curb, panting from the sudden exertion and spiked heart rates.

Nellie clutched her chest and searched the ground for new threats that could expose our position. I rested my back against the van as she hissed threats at my neighbor's lawn gnomes to behave. Then she repeated her threat to the easter eggs so well hidden to not have been found by the neighbor's children in the nearby flower bed.

She was definitely having too much fun with this.

Closing my eyes and trying to reset my breathing, I reviewed the timeline for Edward's involvement in my life.

He'd married Elise five years ago. Everything had been fine until three years ago when Elise and I stopped talking. Then two years ago, Elise and Edward divorced. Elise and I didn't start talking again until eighteen months ago, when she called me about her diagnosis, and I moved in to help her. Her divorce and our fight were never discussed after that. Like they never happened.

I didn't see Edward again until five months ago, when he came to see Elise in the hospital. She'd sent me down to the cafeteria so they could speak in private. I had no idea what was discussed.

The next Edward sighting was four months ago at Elise's funeral. He came but left quickly, not speaking to anyone. That brought me to today, with Edward just waltzing into Elise's home, uninvited and unannounced.

"I think we're safe," Nellie whispered in my ear. Though hushed, her excitement crept through. She had clearly cast herself as a master spy for this chapter of my life. "So, what where you going to tell me about Edward?"

Also whispering, though with considerably less excitement than Nellie, I told her, "I can safely say that Edward—never call him 'Ed,' by the way—is a pretty self-centered guy. But the man took care of Elise. And she returned the favor. She could have gotten so much more money out of the divorce. I met with her lawyer to go over her will once, and he was still smarting over the money she left on the table. As far as I know, Elise kept everything with Edward on good terms, both before and after they separated."

I eyed Edward's car. He'd parked it in Elise's driveway but left the bumper jutting out over the sidewalk. Any walking neighbor or kid on a bike would have to swerve around it. Given how much it would cost to cover a scratch and perfectly match the paint color, I cringed, hoping everyone would give it a wide berth.

A perfect metaphor for Edward. Opulence to inconvenience you.

Edward wasn't in the car. Nellie and I both looked at the house where the outline of someone closed Elise's lace white curtains in the living room.

I grabbed Nellie's arm at the same time she pulled me back. In an uncoordinated jumble, we jockeyed for the best vantage point behind the van, me facing one way, Nellie the other. Squished beside me, she squinted through the van's windows toward Elise's home.

"Did he see us?" she breathed.

I checked the windows of the neighbors' houses to make sure no one who could misunderstand our actions was watching us. "You should call your sister to pick you up."

Nellie abandoned her post to stare at me incredulously. "I'm not leaving."

"But you don't—have to—why stay?"

Her usual grin returned. "This is exciting."

"Yeah, now it is. But I don't know why he's here. That could become considerably less exciting. And maybe awkward, especially if money is concerned."

"Then you'll need backup. Someone for moral support or a logic check," Nellie added, probably trying to convince me. Then she added action by slapping me lightly on the back. "Besides, we have an entire stack of chapters to go through. If we're going to keep this project on track, we need to work on them tonight. Can't do that if I leave."

Checkmate. The need to get Elise published. Nellie would win with that argument every time. I turned to face the same direction as Nellie, our shoulders still pressed together. Neither of us saw Edward approach the living-room window again.

"Okay, but if things get weird, I'm taking you home myself." I wondered if the threat of finally having to introduce me to her family would sway her.

Nellie swiped at her nose as a breeze blew a loose strand of blonde hair across her face. She considered for a second. "Deal." Inching closer to the van's window, she asked, "He has a key?"

"Elise must have given him one." I'd always suspected but figured she hadn't because he'd never visited her once that I knew about, even after she got sick and I moved in.

I rubbed the van window to clear the glass from my breath's condensation.

"What else can you tell me about him?"

I shrugged, the action moving Nellie's arm as well. Wow, she really was close. "For someone I saw a lot, I can't say I know him. Other than the fact he loved Elise and is infatuated with himself. Since Elise and I spent all holidays together, he took us on a lot of destination Christmases and trips to the Hamptons for the 4th of July, stuff like that. Elise and I spent most of the time together since Edward always had something going on. I honestly can't remember ever spending any one-on-one time with him."

"And you won't start today." Nellie put a hand on my shoulder. "Let's go."

We pushed off the van and walked as naturally as we could around it. I pulled my hair free of Nellie's hair band and handed it back. Nearing Elise's home, I couldn't deny that some of Nellie's enthusiasm was rubbing off on me. It diluted my sense of dread in a refreshing way.

Before we reached the driveway, I grabbed my sweatshirt out of Nellie's hand. "What?" she hissed. I balled up the fabric and stuffed it behind one of the budding rose bushes Elise had planted to line the driveway.

"It used to be Edward's. Elise wore it all the time, then gave it to me last fall when I couldn't find my sweatshirt and was going out to play one night." I couldn't think of a reason Edward would be offended by it, but instinct warned me not to bring it into the house.

Nellie whacked me on the shoulder.

"Ow," I protested.

"You said you thought sharing clothes with your sister was a myth."

Leading us up the driveway, I took Nellie around to the kitchen door. Surprisingly, it was open. Only the screen door separated us from whoever was making sounds inside the kitchen.

I tentatively called out, "Hello?"

"You're here!" Edward appeared at the screen door and opened it.

I thought I heard a low "Whoa" escape Nellie's lips. Understandable. At Edward's height, he could have been a center for the NBA. The trimmed hair at his temples should be beginning to show gray and probably would when he decided the time was right. And his wavy-set hair was just as shiny as Elise's polished mahogany kitchen cabinets. Ordinarily I would have described his eyes as "deep blue" but guessed in Nellie language that would translate to something less cliché and closer to "arresting azure."

Edward's face, a tanned skin tone punctuated by dimples on each side of a broad smile, welcomed us into Elise's home like we were his guests and not the other way around.

"Come in. Come in." Several bags bearing the signature of an upscale restaurant sat on the table. Edward returned to pulling containers out of them. "This house is adorable. Or quaint? That's what she called it." I wouldn't be surprised if Elise's home cost less than the business-casual tan suit and leather shoes Edward was modeling. "I could never live this far from the city."

Nellie came to stand next to me. We exchanged raised eyebrows. Elise's neighborhood wasn't that far from the city.

"Who won?" Edward pointed to the basketball. "You, Daniel?"

Even with such a simple question, I was at a loss for words. I pointed to my brace.

"Ah, right. Bum knee. I'd forgotten. So, *you* won." He pointed at Nellie, then looked closer at her face. "I don't know you."

Nellie extended her hand. "Nellie Vasquez."

On her YouTube channel, Nellie went by her maiden name, Nellie Sudder. Despite her professed excitement at the situation, using what I presumed was her married name indicated Edward was rattling her too.

Edward shook Nellie's hand with his left, then placed his right over their intertwined wrists. "Absolute pleasure." Releasing Nellie, he returned to unpacking the food. "No offense, you two, but you smell like old socks." Nellie and I shared another raised eyebrow, only this time, Nellie's cheeks puffed out as she held in a laugh. "Ms. Vasquez, would you mind getting us plates? Daniel, napkins?"

Nellie raised her shoulders a pinch, unsure where to go. I gestured across the kitchen at the corner cupboard. Not wanting Edward to order Nellie to also get forks and serving spoons, I opened the utensils drawer and held them up for Edward to see.

"Um, Daniel?"

I turned to see Nellie throwing a confused look over her shoulder. She'd opened the wrong cabinet. I crossed to her and closed it, catching a glimpse of the hair-dying equipment and towels inside. It'd been several months since I'd even thought about that cupboard or made plans to clean it out.

"Go sit," I offered to Nellie. I skirted around her to get the plates and joined everyone at the table. Edward served himself first, of course, then passed the containers to Nellie. From what I could see, they were filled with nothing but vegetables.

"Is this all raw food?" Nellie asked.

Edward confirmed with a knowing smirk and popped the first bite into his mouth.

"It looks good," she said, trying to convince herself. Nellie took a few portions and passed everything on to me.

Edward wiped his mouth. "You're still an accountant with Milford Company." He hadn't phrased it as a question, but I nodded anyway. "Are you determined to keep working even with the money Elise left you?"

Nellie raised her eyebrows at me again, Edward was getting right to it, but I couldn't respond to her without Edward noticing. I played it safe. "Milford's a good place. Good charter. Good people."

"That's right!" Edward slapped the table, causing the silverware to jump and clink against the plates. "I remember Elise told me about them." In fact, I was the one who'd told him when Milford hired me out of college. "Anyway, Daniel, I want to talk to you about some investment opportunities."

Small vibrations originated under the table when Nellie started to bounce her legs. To keep Edward from detecting it, I lightly placed a hand on her knee. It wasn't hard to do; Nellie was sitting very close. The bouncing stopped.

Deciding between the julienned carrot slaw and a collard wrap, I asked as casually as I could, "Is that why you're here? Business talk?"

"And to share a meal, get a report on how everything's going." Edward waved a hand and continued with his sales pitch. "I know most people shy away from high-risk investments, scared away from the minority of horror-story cases. But there's real opportunity there. Don't let the few naysayers frighten you away."

Discreetly, Nellie's hand brushed mine, and she double tapped my wrist. We must have transitioned from shared eyebrow raises to silently communicating through touch. I took the action to mean, *Don't give him any money*. I needed to redouble my efforts to find out if people could recoup divorce funds.

Edward shot me a winning grin. "I know someone who would be happy to manage your investments if you move forward on this."

I had no doubt Edward knew someone. They probably worked under him and were instructed to volunteer. "I have to follow Elise's advice on this," I hedged. "Only risk what you can afford to lose."

Edward's face stilled, then his features contracted. A wrinkled nose, pursed lips, creased brow. Then it all disappeared. It happened so quickly, I couldn't deduce what it meant. I'd said what I'd said to deter Edward. Now I wondered if he thought I said it as a subtle dig toward his and Elise's divorce.

Edward smoothly went on. "I'll send you some information. Look it over and get back to me. It will change your mind. So, Nellie, tell me about yourself." Swiveling to face Nellie, he cut me out of the conversation.

Bits of spiraled spaghetti squash hung out the sides of Nellie's mouth. Caught unaware, she slurped them up and swallowed. "Yeah, me. I'm a freelance editor and work with authors. Daniel hired me to help get Elise's stories published."

All must have been forgiven, if he'd even been offended in the first place, because Edward swiveled back in his chair to gape at me in astonishment. "She would *love* that." His surprise that I could do something Elise would *love* rubbed me in an already raw place. Edward turned back to Nellie. "What's the strangest request you've helped an author with?"

"Hmm, strange? Yeah, uh . . ." Nellie wrinkled her brow as her eyes drifted toward the ceiling in thought. "There was this nice gentleman I was helping write a space fantasy. He wanted to come up with his own swear words for his characters to use. We went back and forth with different options for *weeks*." She chuckled so quickly her hand went to her nose, anticipating a snort. "He was sweet but also intense."

I forgot the weight of Edward sitting across the table from me. I leaned forward, ignoring the fact that it pressed my knee further into Nellie's. "What did he finally decide on?"

Nellie's dimple speared into her cheeks as she smiled. "*Cotstoee.*" When Edward and I both opened our mouths to attempt sounding out the word, she clarified, "Cots-two-ee. Cotstoee."

I chuckled, my chest prepared to launch into full laughter when Edward sneered. "What a cracked mind."

Nellie's dimple smoothed out as her smile dropped. She focused on swirling her fork around her plate.

Edward either didn't notice his offense to her former client or didn't care. After another bite of his cucumber salad, he said, "But it must take all kinds of people to write. Elise always wanted to be an author." He winked at me.

Talking with Edward about what Elise would have wanted caused the carrots I'd just swallowed to land awkwardly in my stomach. To change the subject, I said, "Nellie doesn't like to drive." *What was that?* I coughed weakly and turned toward Nellie, wondering how to justify saying something so random about her. "I could teach you?"

Nellie's lips parted and her mouth dropped. The fork she'd been raising clattered back onto her plate.

I hurriedly added, "She also has a ton of sisters. More than anyone I've ever met."

Blinking rapidly, Nellie thankfully took the reins of the conversation, closing her mouth and planting a polite smile over it. "Yes. And I have several mothers thanks to the foster program."

"The foster program?" Edward asked. He puckered his nose. "I've heard horror stories that come out of there."

Nellie's fork dropped to her plate again with a clang. "Don't be scared because of the minority of horror-story cases. It can be a lifesaver for a kid. Don't let the few naysayers frighten you away."

Edward stared at Nellie like he hadn't just met her. Then his head flew back, and he laughed at her use of his own words against him. Propping his elbows on the table, he wiped at his eyes. "I like you."

Nellie laughed back, her voice pitched higher than normal. "Oh, good."

Still chuckling, Edward stood and pointed at his cucumbers. "These could use some dipping oil. I sent a bottle to Elise when I traveled to Abruzzo last September. Don't worry. I'll get it," he graciously offered at his own request.

With his back turned, Nellie and I exchanged all the eyebrow raises we'd been saving up. It wasn't until I heard the fridge open that my heart rate spiked. I turned, halfway out of my chair to see Edward standing still, looking at the Thai food in the fridge. Particularly the top carton marked *pad thai*.

Though cooled, the smell of cooked spices wafted around the room. Nellie sniffed. "Is that Thai food?"

Slowly, Edward closed the fridge and stared at me. He made his way back to the table, never taking his eyes off my face.

Everything was fine. Why wouldn't everything be fine? Thai food wasn't unusual, nor was storing cartons of it in your fridge. Edward must know that. Besides, even if Edward knew what it really meant—and how could he—it still wasn't a big deal. It couldn't be to anyone but me.

But if it wasn't a big deal, why was I hiding it? Like so many other things, it was something I didn't want to explain. There was no logic to it, which made it pretty indefensible.

As Edward retook his seat, I broke eye contact first. I didn't know what part of me had just been exposed, or which part Edward might be judging me for, but it all hurt. I shifted, unsure what was happening. Too many emotions and not enough explanations for them.

My face had to be giving away some of what I was feeling since I didn't have the energy to both control my expression and hold back the tide of emotion drowning me inside.

"This was lovely. Apologies for not staying longer." I knew Edward would say the next words, his catchphrase, before he said them. "I gotta go."

Edward abruptly stood, catching Nellie in the middle of another bite of food. Startled, she reached out but couldn't swallow in time to say goodbye before Edward shook her hand and disappeared out the door. Moments later, his car roared to life, and he backed it out of the driveway.

I walked to the sink before Nellie could look at me, trying to determine what had just happened. I needed to gain some breathing room and get my face under control since I could feel my cheeks twitching. I opened a cupboard and filled two glasses with water. Better composed, but no less confused, I sat back at the table and offered one cup to Nellie.

She scooted her chair next to me, the action pressing her leg into mine. "Wow. That was fascinating, fun, unexpected, and not at all useful. Except to deepen the mystery, of course. I love mysteries; they're my favorite part in a story. I certainly couldn't find any concrete reason for why he came tonight. Or why he left so quickly."

I shrugged in a what-are-you-going-to-do sort of way. I couldn't talk about what I couldn't understand. I'd given up something to Edward; I just didn't know what. "Agreed. But hey, we should get started on the submissions."

"But—"

I smiled as naturally as I could, like the awkward dinner hadn't happened, and picked up a container, literally dangling a carrot under Nellie's nose to entice her. "We can eat in the living room."

Nellie gave in and grabbed the slaw from me. Scooping several portions onto her plate, she muttered, "This stuff *is* pretty good."

By the time the horn honked for her to leave, we'd finished off the food Edward had brought and gone through most of the submitted chapters. Those that had passed our first round of evaluations were separated by red-markered stars at the top. By that standard, it had been a successful evening. We were that much closer to getting Elise published, so I should feel good . . . happy even.

Nope. My current state didn't reflect either of those emotions.

I opened the door to allow Nellie, carrying the box of manuscripts, to walk through, but found twisting the handle and pushing against the weight to be harder than before. I dropped my eyes, curiously afraid to let her know I didn't want her to leave or me to be left alone in an empty house.

"It's Sarah." Nellie half-waved with the hand holding the box.

I leaned heavily against the porch railing and hoped it didn't snap. I needed to pull myself together. I told myself I'd see Nellie in seven days. "Ah, Sarah. The super protective sister."

"She's been worried ever since I told her that you tried to strangle me. Look." Nellie cocked her head to the side, giving me a glance at her neck. "Totally healed."

Fresh sweat broke out at the memory. "Please tell me you didn't tell her that."

She gently bumped me with one arm and offered a mischievous wink. "Nooooo . . ."

Sarah blared the horn again. Suddenly, against all understanding and planning, I wanted to stretch this moment out. "We'll meet again next week?"

Nellie's head flinched back, obviously confused by my question. "Of course. Wouldn't miss it."

I smiled at Nellie, and she turned to go down the stairs, thankfully missing when I dropped the expression that took too much energy to maintain.

I waved at Sarah, who rewarded me with an appraising and curt nod. Nellie turned and walked backward toward the car. "What an unexpected turn of events." Nellie paused, letting her foot hang in midair for a moment. "But not necessarily bad." Then she spun and walked the rest of the way to the car.

"See you next week!" I called after her.

Back inside, I considered covering the embroidery sampler but didn't. I even folded the towel and firmly tucked it into a kitchen drawer. But Nellie's air of optimism dissipated soon after. The release of the day had been fleeting, like the warmth of a paper fresh off the printer. Charlie, bless his heart, still texted about playing b-ball. I actually considered it. All the way through showering and falling onto my bed to plead for sleep.

Chapter 5

Four times in two minutes.

I pretended to read while slowly rolling my wrist to check my watch. From her reclined position on the couch, Nellie put the manuscript she was reviewing down on her chest and sighed at the ceiling.

Five times in two minutes.

This reviewing session was quieter than our others. The usual back-and-forth comments, the narrating, and the sharing bits we liked had all settled into a comfortable silence.

Nellie sighed again.

An almost comfortable silence.

I wanted to point out how close we were to the finish line of going through all the submissions. Only a handful of chapters still needed the initial review. Next, we should be ready to go through the finalists and select a winner. But voicing my thoughts would interfere with the bet I made with myself two minutes ago when Nellie had first sighed. As restless as she was, there was no way she would make it to five minutes before cajoling me into some type of activity.

The clock Elise had purchased on her honeymoon at the queen's hamlet in Versailles chimed. One, two, three, four, five . . . nothing.

Nellie rolled over on her side to stare at me from the couch. This time when she sighed it was elongated and an obvious play for my attention.

I put an elbow on the arm rest of my chair and placed my chin in my hand. "Bad submission?" I said conversationally.

Nellie rubbed her eyes. "Yeah." She started to read out loud, using a valley-girl voice with a smoking habit. "'My heart was so full of love I thought it would explode like a water balloon filled with chocolate milk.'"

"I thought you liked it when people say cheesy things?"

"It's not about the cheese." Nellie's fingers curled in the air like she was trying to grab something, and said earnestly, "It's the emotion. What do the words make you feel?"

I nodded along until Nellie's pointed gaze told me she expected a response.

"Honestly? Well, hearing the words 'filled with chocolate milk' makes me, well . . ."

"Want to make a run to the bathroom, right?"

I nodded, grateful Nellie had found a more delicate way to say "need to pee."

"Or, how about this." Nellie flipped back a few pages and continued reading. "'I could never trust anyone who donated my Christmas gift to the Animal Gift-Giving Event at the zoo!' Or even worse, 'How could I ever give my heart to another when it was bruised and smashed like a rotten crab apple hit with a cricket bat?'"

"Gotta love that pink purple prose, huh?"

Nellie waved her hands in frustration, causing some of the pages she was holding to drift to the rug. "The author is evoking the wrong sentiment. The cheesy dialogue isn't making me feel the right way. I mean, the answer's so obvious. If you don't know if you could give your heart to another, then you're not ready. And, well—"

Nellie inhaled so hard she coughed. When she finished, I thought she'd go back to reading, but her eyes fixed on the green sea-glass bowl on the mantle. "I, just . . . think, well when you love someone, you love all of them. You know? Not only the good. All of them."

That sounded suspiciously like Nellie's thoughts had strayed from the chapter she was reviewing and to personal experience, provoking questions to start crawling around inside my mind. Those questions might have leaked out of the mouth of someone not raised by a mother and older sister who practiced and modeled common courtesy. Which I had been.

Well, cotstoee.

I sat on my questions like a seat cushion, glad when Nellie demanded, "Tell me more about Elise."

I decided talking about Elise constituted a new activity, and I'd won my own bet. "Well, she always wanted to be a writer—"

"No, I already know and love that about her. Tell me something unexpected. Something I haven't heard."

"Oh." I looked around the room at Elise's carefully curated living room with all its flowers, colors, and textures. "Okay, for someone who loved gardens, she didn't like being in actual nature. Hated camping."

Nellie smiled. "Bet you love it."

I liked that she'd accurately guessed that about me. "Yeah. But," I held up a hand, "I never got lost in the woods when I was seven."

It'd been a while since I'd thought of this story. Everyone in my family knew it, and all the different renditions of it, so I liked the appeal of a fresh audience.

"When we were younger, our parents took us upstate for a camping trip one holiday, and Elise got lost. I don't remember much, except feeling sad we couldn't make s'mores that night. Don't judge. I was four!"

Nellie's grin made no promises.

"Anyway, she was on her own for a full night before they found her. She loved the Peter Rabbit books growing up. Might have saved her life. She didn't go wandering around and get more lost than she already was. Instead, she stayed by a big tree and made a small burrow under one of the roots. She pretended she was a bunny and used pinecones as her imaginary bunny family. One for Mom, Dad, and me. Weeks later, she still struggled to sleep after what had happened, so my parents bought her two stuffed bunny toys. She named one E. Bunbun, after herself, and Daniel Nibble Hop for me."

I paused, lost in a pleasant memory and wondering again what had happened to those stuffed animals. I knew Elise would never have thrown them out. I helped pack them in a box for her when she went to college, and again when I helped her move into Edward's penthouse. But I hadn't found them when I'd gone through her things after she died.

I blinked. Focusing on Nellie, who had a sleepy, contented look on her face, I said, "Sorry. That was a long story."

"It was sweet. I love stories."

"Tell that to the submission on the floor." Nellie groaned so I had to point out, "If you'd review like me and let the student become the master, this might go easier for you. Critiquing is about clear-cut rules. Right or wrong. No, no." I held up a hand to her objection, knowing what she was planning to say. "It's not about connecting, identifying, or sympathizing. Either the story is good, or it is not."

"Oh, you are so wrong," Nellie said. "A story doesn't have to be perfect to be loved."

I smirked at her stubborn jaw and slowly returned to reading, forcing her to do the same to keep us on track. Nellie sighed, but my smirk widened, and I didn't look up. She groaned again in capitulation and picked the manuscript back up. After reading one line, she threw it back on the floor.

"Tell me how Elise met Edward." Nellie raised herself up on one elbow, prepared to wait me out if I didn't concede.

The combined weight of my manuscript's pages thwacked onto the side table as I tossed them. "Okay. But you'll be disappointed. There's not much to tell. He was her 90s-movie summer romance. They met at a party at the Shore one night. That's it. Elise could make quite the impression and be the life of any party. Even more so when people realized that was really her. No pretenses."

Nellie narrowed her gaze, probably not believing there wasn't more to the story. I shrugged and picked my manuscript back up to read, keeping track of Nellie out of the corner of my eye. While also trying not to give in to a smile.

Nellie picked up a framed picture from the side table next to the couch that showed Elise and me flanked by our parents the day she left for college. Nellie brought it closer to her face, one eyebrow raising. I almost stopped everything to ask what could be so interesting about the picture, but Nellie put it back and retrieved the papers off the floor to start reading again. A minute later, she chuckled like she was enjoying it.

"You're lying," I accused, sure she was pretending to get a reaction from me.

"No, really! This is one of my favorite parts, the forced confession."

"I thought your favorite part was when the characters acted on their true feelings, or mysteries."

"I have several favorite parts. This story can only go up from . . . here . . ." Nellie's voice grew soft as she read the next few lines. "Nope!" She slammed the pages, an impressive feat for paper, into the box.

I held out my arm, knowing what was coming. Seconds later, Nellie pulled me to my feet. "Elise has a beautiful home. Crafted to be inviting and pleasant, but we gotta get outta here. Let's go get some food, take a break. We need to get you—er, us out of the house. Somewhere with not a lot of people. We'll work better once we've recharged. I hear there's a good Thai food place nearby."

"That, no. That's . . . not . . ." I struggled to speak. We couldn't go to Thai House. I'd be recognized. They'd ask about my order. My standing order. The one Elise had created during our first "Hot-Food Adventure." Even as poor college students, we'd never missed a week.

I struggled through my brain delay to offer an alternative. "What about Indian?"

Grabbing her jacket, and apparently up for any type of food, Nellie proclaimed, "Indian it is."

Clutching my arm, Nellie walked by my side as we exited the house and headed to my car. Was she afraid I was going to bolt? She didn't let me go until she veered off to climb into the passenger seat. It could be my imagination, but the more I thought on it, Nellie seemed to be initiating a lot of physical contact recently, and it made me want to go stand in the fridge.

I was sitting behind the wheel when my mind broke free of its brain delay and caught back up to the situation in real time. Was this a date? Had Nellie asked me on a date? This wasn't playing basketball or comfortably talking about submissions while munching on salsa. This was actually going *out.*

Another warm April day had preheated the inside of the car, so luckily Nellie didn't question when I blasted the AC, oblivious to my counter goal of using it to dissipate my nervous sweat.

Pulling out of the driveway, I reviewed every part of our conversation. Had I missed something? I should have pushed back harder on the idea of going to get food. Instead, I'd regressed into making a questionable decision because of being overwhelmed. I wasn't sure I wanted to go on a date with all its extra protocols and expectations.

"I noticed you kept the embroidery sampler uncovered in the living room," Nellie said.

"The one that reminds you of your husband's grave marker?"

Sure, ask her about her deceased husband on a maybe-date. A completely natural way to start a conversation.

Nellie's mouth opened, but her gaze went vacant.

I meant to say sorry, but "Uhhhh" came out.

Nellie blinked, focusing again, though her voice still sounded distant. "You know, I used to visit Luis's grave every Sunday. At the beginning, I needed to. Then, after that first year, I got to the point where I felt like I *had* to. Does that make sense? Like, what kind of wife would I be if I didn't?"

Trying to guess where this was going, I asked, "Did you go last Sunday?"

Nellie smiled, something I hadn't anticipated her doing in this conversation about cemetery visits.

"I did," she said. "But it was because I wanted to. Not had to or needed to, but *wanted* to. I felt closer to him there than I have in a long time."

You'd think having a potential date discuss feeling close to a former spouse would be a mood killer. It wasn't. Nellie had entrusted me with a special revelation, and I felt honored. Maybe that's why it was easier than I would have thought to answer her next question.

"Do you visit Elise's grave often?"

"No. Not yet. I mean to; it's on the list. But not yet."

Nellie patted my arm. "Nothing wrong with that. Grief hits everyone differently. The trick is to give everyone, and yourself, the grace and space to move on."

I was in the middle of nodding in agreement when Nellie said, "Tell me about your parents."

I choked and was sure Nellie caught the small cough and lump in my throat.

"I mean," Nellie hurriedly said, "from all the pictures in Elise's home, it seems like you had a good family life with many adventures." Without having to look at the road, Nellie focused on watching my face for a reaction. Softer, she said, "Sorry if I'm wrong . . ."

I blew out a breath, caught between the worry of discussing my parents and the worry about whether or not Nellie and I were on a date. If we were, I was severely underdressed again. And my car was too dirty. And might smell like a gym. And was my hair even combed?

I needed to stop delaying and giving Nellie the wrong impression that she'd hit on a sore subject. She had, of course, but I didn't want her to feel guilty about it. There was a difference between casual inquiry and genuine curiosity and concern. I had no doubt Nellie was asking with the latter.

"You're not wrong. We were close. They died right before my first year of college." I didn't explain how. Only that it was "unexpected," knowing Nellie would respect my not wanting to elaborate. She did, nodding as I continued. "I switched colleges my freshman year to be closer to Elise, who was in her final year before graduating. We were already close before that, and then we were . . . all. All our family, all of what was left."

Nellie shivered, and I switched the AC off. To compensate, I blasted the heat under the guise of warming her up while I intended to use it as an excuse for why I was sweating if she asked. Why would she ask?

Stop overreacting, I told myself.

If I could take the dating question out of the equation, this could be fun. Just getting food with a friend. Something I hadn't done in ages and missed.

Leaning forward, Nellie spread out her hands in front of the air vents to catch the warm air on her fingers. "Please tell me if I push you too far. Or too often. It's hard for me to tell."

"I'm fine," I assured her. It wasn't a full lie. Part of me was fine, somewhere. Surely.

"Your shoulders are up to your ears, and you're strangling the steering wheel."

I unclenched my fingers and forced a deep breath while I worked out a way to describe my "brain delay" to Nellie. "It's fine. Really. I know I need to be pushed. In the moment, I don't always think to . . . I don't always think. Better thoughts come after, so I can't always tell you in the moment if I'm being pushed too far. But afterwards, when my head is clearer, I know it's the right way to go." *Unless you're not sure if you're on a date or not. Maybe then, don't go.*

Nellie chuckled in agreement. "In times of stress it can be easy to forget there are other options."

"There's a Mexican restaurant that's closer. Want to try that?"

Nellie did a double-take of my face, probably searching for the reason for the change in subject. "No. I rarely find any restaurant that can hold up to my mother-in-law's cooking. You should try it."

Was that another date invite? My ears were on fire.

"I wish I could show you, but she's super busy. Lately, we barely get any fresh homemade meals. In fact, we're preparing dinners for her. I mean, I'm decent, but nowhere near as good a cook."

Okay, so Nellie didn't want me to meet her mother-in-law; she was just being polite. My mind still milled in confusion. At the stop light I chanced a glance at Nellie.

She met my eye and said, "You can ask me."

There it was. A direct invitation to ask, "Are we on a date?" Just say it. Clearly, she was thinking it as well.

I chickened out. "Hmm?"

"You can ask about my parents."

I hadn't expected that. The light remained red, so I turned to Nellie. "You sure?"

"Yeah." If her mannerism was any indication, the topic wasn't painful. At the green light, I drove through the intersection as she explained, "I don't know who my dad is. Never met him. I've become okay with that. My foster mother was good friends with my mom's family growing up. Mom had my sister and me in high school before she dropped out. My foster mother took us in when she bailed."

Figuring no question was off the table, I almost asked about how her husband, Luis, had died, but the question unexpectedly squeezed my stomach. Quickly pivoting, I asked instead, "Are you close with your biological mother?"

"Uhhhh, no. But we left things on a good note. She's in Florida. I last saw her about two years ago." Nellie counted on her fingers, "Helen, biological mom; Clarisa, foster mother; and Juanita, my mother-in-law. Three mothers. That's pretty good." Then her voice lost its song quality. "You lost your entire immediate family in like, what? Seven years?"

"Eight." I'd responded too quickly to brush off the question as nothing important. I hurried to cover. "I have a few cousins, some extended family. But they all live out of state. If I see them at all, it's usually during the summer." I meant to convey I still had some family, but as I said the words out loud, I didn't feel comfort. Just an immense sense of loneliness.

"Wow." Nellie stared out the windshield. "I'm so sorry."

"I don't want to make this about me. And it sounds like a good part of your childhood was difficult."

"Let's not compare pain," Nellie said. A wise offer I was more than happy to take her up on. "It's just something we have. And we can all agree it sucks."

"But you feel like you're moving beyond it? Going to Luis's grave because you want to? Or being able to start working again?" I frowned. "Are you still hoping to be a literary agent when all this is done?"

Nellie studied the question, either that or the crack in my windshield, for several moments. "It was always my dream. Ever since my first year in college. All I *ever* wanted was to work in books." The corners of her mouth trembled before losing a battle. She brought a hand to her cheek as she stopped fighting the smile spreading across her lips. She turned toward the window as if to hide her expression. "And working with you . . ."

Then she turned and stared at me so pointedly that my eyes broke contact with the next stop sign to reconnect with Nellie's. She'd been wrong earlier. Eyes could totally laugh. ". . . working with you has brought something back."

"Your love of stories?"

"Definitely my love of stories."

Nellie released my gaze as I pulled through the four-way stop. "What is *your* dream? Top HR accountant in New York?"

I couldn't tell her what I didn't know, but not responding would end this conversation, and in the moment, I didn't want that. I made something up. "My dream is to dominate on the basketball court."

"Oh." Nellie patted my arm again, her fingers lingering longer than before. "I'm so sorry you've had to give up on that dream."

I rewarded her teasing with a side glare. I wasn't sure I could accurately explain to someone how much this banter was carrying me away from the lump of guilt rotting in my soul. These simple words, laughs, shared confidences; they filled up the space in my chest that had been dormant and dark.

Nellie started tapping her leg in time to a song on the radio I hadn't realized was playing. I turned it up and skillfully deflected all of Nellie's playful attempts to get me to sing the words before we reached the restaurant.

Parking the car, I ran around to Nellie's door, surprised she'd waited for me to open it for her. So, this was a date. Maybe?

The is-this-a-date debate continued when Nellie linked her arm through mine as we walked to the front door. "I find clichés are most accurate when they refer to food," she said. "Have you ever tried super-hot phaal? The phrase 'tongue on fire' was invented so it would have a description on menus."

"Closer to 'mouth on fire' since everything in the vicinity of your taste buds goes up in flames." I held open the door. "But the second before the heat knocks out your tongue, it's delicious."

"Sounds like we'll need some chocolate milk."

"Only if we have a heart full of love that would explode it like a water balloon."

A waiter with a ready smile and silver bowtie sat us down at the only empty booth and saved my evening by asking, "Will this be one ticket or two?"

"Two," Nellie said.

Not. A. Date.

I rested against the vinyl back of the booth and smiled behind the menu before giving my order. But as Nellie gave hers to the waiter, my sense of relief dissipated. Replaced by . . . what? Gradually, I realized what my relief was inadequate to hide.

I *did* want to go on a date with Nellie.

More accurately, I wanted her to want to go on one with *me*.

Nellie shot me a wink, oblivious to my internal, earth-shattering revelation. The waiter jotted down our order, and I watched him leave with our menus. I was going to need that menu back to cover my face in case my color was changing along with my rapidly climbing temperature. Nellie smiled at me, talking about the bad submission she had been reviewing. I tried to force myself back into the conversation she'd started without me. Too late.

Nellie noticed my grimace and stopped mid-story. "What?"

I gestured toward the back of the retreating waiter. "I can't decide what I want."

I sucked on my lower lip and looked down, worried she would pick up on the double meaning of what I'd just said. Or, more specifically, that she would tell me I didn't have to worry about deciding on a relationship with her because she wasn't interested.

Great. Now I also had to worry about how to eat on a stomach that had just dropped out on me.

"I'll share with you if you're willing to take a chance."

"Sure, yes. Thank you!" I downed half a glass of water, stopping only when the ice froze the roof of my mouth.

Believing she'd solved the issue, Nellie started typing on her phone. No doubt to text whichever sister was responsible for picking her up to let her know about the new time. All this driving Nellie around, and with all the short-notice time changes, it had to be annoying.

"You must have a good relationship with your sisters," I commented.

Nellie spared a smile my way as she continued typing. My own phone pinged. Since Nellie wasn't finished, I pulled my phone out and read the new text.

Whoa.

"What is it?" Nellie asked, and I realized I'd spoken out loud.

"Edward." I scrolled down the message again to make sure I hadn't missed anything. "His company is hosting a party this weekend. He wants to know if I want to come and bring someone."

Nellie looked as confused as I felt. But we disagreed on one thing. "You have to go," she insisted. "Find out what is going on with that guy."

"How will going to a party help with that? I'll just stand around awkwardly by myself surrounded by people I don't want to talk to."

"I'll go with you!"

The waiter stopped by to refill my water glass and walked away without Nellie and I saying anything to each other. Out of the corner of her mouth, Nellie finally whispered, "He struggled to find something to say to stop the awkward staring."

I opened my mouth, but only an exhale came out.

"Please," Nellie pleaded. "There's bound to be someone there who can give us some kind of information. We can investigate Edward together, especially since it's a work party. And we'll have each other to lean on in the crowd."

But is it a date? I thought, back to my original conundrum.

"It'll be our first date," Nellie said.

Relief slammed into excitement and mixed explosively with worried anticipation, causing a laugh to erupt from my throat. So maybe Nellie did have an interest in dating me. As though I'd just stumbled off a roller coaster, I held my stomach to quell the queasiness.

Nellie squinted and tilted her head.

I turned my relief into a joke to help hide it. "You mean our 'second' date."

Nellie bit the inside of her cheek. "Second?"

"You invited me out for Indian food tonight."

"Ah, I see." Nellie transferred to biting her lip in an unsuccessful attempt to hide a smile. "Does that mean I'm paying?

"Her green eyes narrowed, realizing she'd been played."

Nellie snorted, then tried to cut off the sound midway through as the waiter appeared with our corn pakoras. She sounded adorable, which was apparently a word I used now. Once he'd retreated, Nellie said, "I never should have taught you how to narrate."

She nibbled to test the spice level. Her eyes bugged out, and she opened her mouth to suck in air against her tongue. She gulped several swallows of water.

Then she eyed the pakoras and took a larger bite.

I chuckled as Nellie's eyes watered. Hot as the food was, neither of us could resist.

"Well," Nellie said in between mouthfuls and sips of water, "according to romance lore, if I'm paying I'm owed at least a handshake tonight."

This time I was the one who snorted, coming dangerously close to inhaling water up my nose. After clearing my throat several times, I double-checked the text and choked out, "The party is on Saturday. Two days away." I raised my eyebrows at Nellie. "Is that too short of notice?"

"No, I can make that work."

Maybe I could too. So long as Nellie was with me.

"Oh." I snapped my fingers. "I should let you know when I was at Bob's Market on Monday, I saw he was having a sale on the Women's First hair care products if you need more Golden Crown."

Nellie's hair had grown out again. An inch of dark brown separated her scalp from the blond in her hair.

I sampled the pakora but had trouble swallowing when I noticed how Nellie was staring at me. Forcing the food down my throat I choked out, "But I don't care either way. It's fine—no worries." How bad did I sound telling Nellie how to look? And so soon after finally getting confirmation regarding a date. "I shouldn't have said anything, sorry."

"Well, that clears everything up." Nellie's confused tone did not agree with her words.

Our dinner's smell preceded the food. The waiter's arrival couldn't have been more perfect. I smiled in deep appreciation as platters arrived to distract Nellie from how awkwardly I'd steered the conversation. Wanting to make sure we'd changed the subject, I said, "Remember, after this, we have to finish that stack of chapters tonight."

Nellie's regular smile returned, tinged with a bit of attitude. "Fine. But since I'm paying, I'm getting a dessert to go."

Chapter 6

THE CLOCK'S TICKING HURRIED ME out of one room and into another. And then back again.

Popping out of the bathroom, I ran to the closet to pick the blue shirt— no, the gray with white pinstripes. Returning to the bathroom, I grabbed my phone when it buzzed across the tiled counter.

"Come on, Charlie," I muttered as I hung the new shirt on the doorknob. It was rude of me to expect Charlie to help after standing him up to play b-ball with the guys week after week and month after month. But I was desperate, and Charlie must have sensed it. Probably because other than asking for his help getting Elise's books published, this had been the only other time I'd reached out for help.

The fact was I only had one suit, so Charlie couldn't help me there, but I owned two dress shirts and needed a second opinion to pick one. I needed this night to go well. So again, I was desperate.

Charlie's text read, *Go with the gray and white stripes. It's classic without being formal. The blue shirt is fine with jeans but looks stupid with the suit. Don't shame me by wearing that. My sympathies that the dress code isn't sweatpants and T-shirts.*

Whistling at the near miss, I typed back a thank-you before applying another round of deodorant. I didn't want to ruin the shirt before the date, or quasi-date—what was this thing?—even started. Two days ago, I thought it was a date. But every single one of the past forty-eight hours had convinced me, until I was ninety-percent certain, that the main reason Nellie had asked to come was because she was curious about Edward.

Was I excited?

Yes.

Was I worried?

Also yes.

I had to keep moving or the fear of not knowing how I would react in a crowd might trigger a negative reaction. Going out tonight with Nellie was enough of a motivation to get out of the house. But also, I was sick of me. More specifically, sick of how everything exhausted me. Or how I avoided things I knew I enjoyed. While a party among some rich and influential people, including my suspiciously behaving ex-brother-in-law, wasn't ideal, hopefully the social norms of being a stoic man who had his emotions always in check would keep my unwanted reactions at bay.

Now if only I could pin down if Nellie really did see this as a date or not. Date sweats I was used to. Date sweats I could handle. Date ambiguity was an entirely different beast.

Maybe her reaction to my suit would be a clue. I buttoned my shirt and eyed it. If all the movies I watched with Elise were any guide, meeting up with a potential partner for a big event that required fancy clothes usually resulted in a slowed-down moment. With staring. Lots of staring. If Nellie did that, chances were good she thought this was a real date.

The tile counter buzzed with my phone's vibrations again.

Charlie'd written, *This the first date you've gone on since Janet, right?*

I'd broken up with Janet when Elise called to tell me about her diagnosis. It took a dedicated moment of concentration to remember, but yeah, I hadn't dated anyone since.

Regardless, Charlie texted, *make sure you play it casual. CASUAL.*

I typed, *Always*, with my thumb over the send button when a car door slammed out front.

I acted on impulse, suddenly wanting to meet a member of Nellie's family. Whipping my suit jacket over my shoulders, I sprinted down the stairs and out the door, hoping to catch the car before whichever one of Nellie's sisters was behind the wheel drove away. I might have made it if Nellie hadn't stopped me in my tracks as she walked toward the front door.

Her eyes widened, and her mouth dropped. More extreme than the slowed-down moment I'd hoped for. I thudded to a halt on the top step.

"What did you do to your hair?" Nellie asked in a voice loud enough to draw Elise's neighbors to their living-room curtains.

"My . . . hair?"

Nellie retracted her expression. In one second, she'd transformed from confused shock to mischievous smiling. "Never mind."

She continued up the walkway, playfully skipping the first few steps up the path. "I've decided to help you out by giving you a full-length description of how I look, since I know Charlie and any other basketball buddies will ask. This is a French knot." She pointed at her hair, twisted up and tucked inside a roll, sans pen, and turned in a full circle while still moving forward.

Still hung up on her hair comment, I couldn't do much more than nod.

"And," Nellie continued as she pulled open her long black coat, "This is a periwinkle tea-length dress with a pencil skirt. Make sure you mention all those words. Guys eat up those details." She winked. I attempted a smile and nodded again. "My sister helped me pick it out. She loves keeping current on all the fashion trends."

Finally ready to join the conversation, though still rabidly curious about her reaction to my hair, I asked, "Which sister? Biological, foster, or sister-in-law?"

"All the same to me."

I offered a hand to help her walk up the steps. "So, is this her dress?"

"No, Jenna picked out the outfit, but the dress is Sarah's. Oh, but the shoes are Jenna's." Nellie reached the top stair and extended an ankle attached by a silver buckle to a pencil-length heel. Nellie lowered her voice. "Heads up—I can only stand in these things for fifteen minutes before I'll need to sit down."

Nellie followed me into the house and through to the kitchen, where I snagged my keys off the counter. There wasn't enough time to take a photo of my hair and send it to Charlie to ask what he thought. Not something I would do, even under normal circumstances, but his fashion acumen could pinpoint the problem if one existed. And man, I really wanted to know. Instead, I tried to sneak peeks of my reflections in any window or mirrored surface I passed.

I led Nellie out the backdoor, and she said, "Now narrate yourself. Tell me what you look like."

"Maybe you should instead," I suggested slowly. "You're better at it."

Heels clattered against concrete, and Nellie reached the car first, placing herself between me and the door. With both hands, she reached up toward my hair but pulled back. "Okay, you win. What happened?"

Our faces were inches apart, but she didn't meet my eyes. Instead, she angled her face to study my hair from every side. Unable to stop herself this time, she lightly touched the ends while looking like she'd seen a team shoot a game-winning three pointer.

I jerked my head back with an uncertain laugh, the best alternative given how close we were, and the fact that, well . . . "Are you petting me?"

Her eyes widened. She retreated into the car with a frozen smile, opening her door before I could—we were on a more formal date after all—and closing it. I stood alone, gaping into the trailing wake of her floral-perfume cloud. I instantly regretted having said anything. I ran around the car and climbed into the driver's seat.

Nellie started, "Sorry—"

"No, it's fine." I insisted.

"Oh good." Nellie sighed in relief and angled in her seat to get a better view of me as I started the car. "Please tell me how all . . . this happened."

The return of her playful voice left me hopeful that whatever had shocked her about my hair wasn't bad, maybe even something she liked. I started the car, using the navigation to lead us to the hotel where Edward's company was hosting the party while I explained.

"Elise and I have been going to the same lady to get our hair cut since college. It's a bit of a drive, but we can't imagine supporting anyone else. I haven't seen her in months and wasn't sure she could get me in on such short notice. But she made an exception when I told her about the—" *date* "—event tonight."

I didn't mention it, but the visit had gone better than I'd feared. After a brief but seemingly sincere offer of condolence, Ava hadn't mentioned Elise. The time spent in her chair felt less like a hair appointment and more of a visit to a favorite aunt's home.

"I wanted to get a haircut, but she persuaded me to let her style it instead." When Nellie didn't react, I repeated, "Styled! She shampooed it, put some stuff in, and stuck me under a dryer."

Still no reaction. Nellie's eyes were back on my hair again as she failed to hide an open-mouthed smile.

"I didn't know guys did that," I said, unable to hide my shock. "Maybe it's more common than I thought; there were two men in the waiting area behind me." Like Nellie, I couldn't resist and reached up to feel the straightened strands brushing an inch past my shoulders. Used to an interlocking wavy mess, having straight hair felt different. I could tell when each individual strand moved. "Does it look too 80s? Or 70s? Is it bad? It feels weird."

"No!" Nellie insisted. "No. It doesn't look bad." Then her voice dropped. ". . . Not at all . . ."

It hit me that she didn't dislike my hair. She liked it. She really liked it. That must be why so many guys were lined up for Ava to style their hair too. I needed to make another appointment ASAP.

Nellie waved her hand, maybe afraid she'd overplayed it and wanted to do some damage control. "I mean, overall the effect is not . . . unpleasant." She turned to look out the window at the next stop light, but I caught her sneaking glances my way.

Huh. "Good." *Thank you? Are we on an actual date?* I couldn't believe I was back in this situation. How had that happened?

Nellie nestled back in her seat, though still peeking at me in a way that was obvious from my peripheral vision. Keeping her voice neutral, Nellie said, "I think we should talk about moving on."

I leaned forward, then had to act like I was readjusting myself in my seat. "Moving on?" I asked as casually as possible. Charlie would have been proud.

"To Elise's next book to see if you want to find a ghostwriter for that one too."

Aaaaand another readjustment to hide my disappointment in Nellie's response. Normally, I'd be all for talking about getting Elise published, but not right now. If this kept up, I would have to find the courage to just ask Nellie, which really meant finding the courage to potentially hear her say no, this wasn't a real date.

A ping sounded from Nellie's small purse, a silver clutch that matched the silver lines embroidered in her dress. Great. Now that she had me noticing those details, I might actually make the mistake of telling Charlie. I made a mental note NOT to do that.

"Ugh." Nellie shook her head. "I forgot to charge my phone."

I debated teasing her that she'd done that before but didn't. We didn't have much time before we made it to the hotel where the party was held. Before I offered the use of my charging pad, Nellie tucked the phone away and said, "Not a problem. I am going to focus on tonight."

She asked several questions about Ava, calling her my "stylist," that I happily answered. But unfortunately, it was a safe topic, and I couldn't get any insight into Nellie's mind. By the time I recounted one of Elise's failed perm attempts in college, we'd reached the hotel's valet lot.

Well-dressed people got out of the cars in front of us with coordinated outfits, including outerwear, shawls, hats, and wraps. The obvious quality acted as price tags. Our winter-black coats would stick out like beetles on a gilded platter.

Though we had a second before we had to leave the safety of the car, I felt the need to whisper as though my voice could carry through the closed doors. "Maybe we should leave our coats in here."

"Definitely," Nellie agreed out of one side of her mouth. "I hope they have heat lamps on the roof." The early-spring wind fighting our efforts to get out of the car agreed it was too soon for a bare-shoulder party. I handed my keys to the valet, and Nellie and I dashed into the shelter of the lobby.

Inside, we slowed our gait, trying to look like we belonged. I held out my phone for the bellman at the elevator to scan the invite Edward had forwarded. He waved us through, and I unclenched my fist in relief, even though we'd been invited and had every permission to be here. We placed our backs to the wall of the elevator, giving Nellie a full view of everyone else piling in after us. As more high-heeled and dress-shoe-wearing people joined us, I could tell she was concocting a narration in her head.

Catching my eye, Nellie subtly nodded toward an already inebriated older gentleman. She probably had pegged him as a Winston Churchill impersonator. When he unapologetically belched loudly, like his namesake, I had to convert my laugh into a cough. While I pushed my lips together to keep more laughter from coming out, Nellie snaked her arm through mine, trying to tease the laughter out of me. A battle of wills, Nellie almost won when look-and-act-alike Winston stumbled into the chest of the unimpressed woman standing next to him.

The elevator dinged to a stop. Being the last to get out, Nellie and I gaped at our new surroundings before we had to start acting casual. As Nellie predicted, heat lamps surrounded dedicated spaces, creating cocoons of heat over the small, round food tables, the intimate seating areas, and the large talk-and-mingle square in the center of the rooftop. Lamps cast enough light that no one would have to squint to see their date while also setting a seductive amber ambience.

"I wore too much color," Nellie whispered. Either an errant wind or a straightened strand of hair tickled my ear as she spoke.

She wasn't wrong. Even though her dress's periwinkle was a soft, light blue, among all the cool gray, white, and tailored silver clothes, Nellie'd fit in better with the rooftop garden just outside the cultivated atmosphere created by the lamps than the other guests.

"So Jenna was wrong about what's fashionable this spring?" I asked.

Nellie considered it, then raised her chin. "No. Jenna is a savant. All these rich doodads don't know what's up."

Without having to consult each other, Nellie and I selected a table on the edge of the activities. The small top allowed us to rest our elbows on it while we stood. No chairs.

Nellie sighed. "This was a mistake."

My mouth went dry. "I, uh . . . what was?"

"These shoes!" Nellie shifted her weight to roll each ankle in turn. I closed my eyes for a second, laughing at myself. I pitied Nellie's ankles but was glad the shoes, and not our date, were the reason for the mistake.

Nellie rolled back her cap-sleeve-covered shoulders and surveyed the tittering crowd. Giving me an encouraging grin, she pointed out the only other woman wearing a stand-out color. Everything matched: red lipstick, red dress, and red heels. She dominated an argument with a blond man holding two glasses of champagne. He backed up with each point of her finger.

"Our first couple of the night," Nellie said. She pitched her voice higher to imitate the woman. "I drink red wine only, you fool! Everything must match, else what is the point of an ensemble?"

I chuckled too loudly and glanced away in case the couple being narrated looked our way. I responded, "His grip tightened as he suspected the laughter around the room was directed at them. A moment later, one glass shattered."

Nellie and I paused, but no explosion of glass followed. Nellie slumped her shoulders when my prediction didn't come true. Then she straightened them, laser-focused on something behind me.

What? I mouthed as I fought the impulse to turn.

Pulling in toward me around the table, Nellie whispered, "Edward!" She grabbed a drink from a passing waiter and used the action as an excuse to point over my right shoulder. "Oh my word, that suit! Black on black on black. That'll make his baby-blue eyes pop . . . Yes, that's a cliché description. Ignore it. Moving on . . . He's got some confidence. I bet he's wearing designer socks too."

Nellie inched the starched cloth napkin that came with her drink toward the edge of the table until it fell off. She dived after it, lost from view, until she triumphantly popped back up.

"I knew it."

"How can you tell?" I asked.

"They're monogrammed at the ankle."

"Daniel!"

Nellie and I locked eyes. I hoped I didn't look as delighted as she did; who knew what Edward would think of that. I turned. Edward extended a hand while the man next to him gave my suit and shirt a thorough once-over. At least he had the decency not to smirk.

Everything about Edward's companion was silver. Trimmed hair, wire-rimmed glasses, expensive watch, clipped goatee, cut suit, and narrowed eyes. Somehow, even his calculating expression said *silver*.

After he'd released my hand, Edward introduced us. "Daniel, this is Antoine. He's the head of our accounting department." We shook hands, and I held my grip a moment longer than Antione. "He needs talent like yours."

"Yes," Antoine said with a smile tight around the edges. "If you send in your resume, I'd be happy to personally review it."

Was this why I'd been invited to the party? Was Edward trying to find me a job? Why? I didn't need the money. Unless Edward found a way to take back what was in the divorce settlement. But if he was intent on taking money away from me, why try to find me a job to make up for it? Antoine clearly considered me to be the boss's charity case.

I matched Antonie's smile. "I've heard fabulous things about your department. If I'm ever in the market, I'll keep you in mind."

Antione's lips curled before he bowed slightly in acknowledgment, no doubt wondering if he'd just been rejected by the favor he was giving to Edward.

"Think about it," Edward said, clapping a hand on my shoulder. "Give him your card," he ordered Antoine, who obediently fished inside his jacket pocket for a business card lined, of course, in silver.

I nodded my head and accepted it with a polite, "Thank you."

Several people called Edward's name, and he flashed a smile. "You two enjoy yourselves. I gotta go; I'm needed elsewhere. I don't know how people function without me." With that, Edward and Antoine walked away. Antoine couldn't resist a final look in my direction. Maybe still trying to puzzle how a cheap suit had rejected him.

I turned around to find Nellie had pushed her untouched drink to my side of the table. "What was that? He brought you here for a job interview? Had you asked him if you could get hired?"

I shook my head and downed a few mouthfuls of Nellie's drink. I winced as the alcohol hit my throat. I had to stay calm or risk becoming emotionally paralyzed in front of strangers. "Was that guy—"

"A jerk," Nellie agreed. "Even more arrogant than Edward."

I wasn't sure that was possible. "More than Edward?"

"Yeah. No, wait. Edward isn't arrogant. He's . . ." Nellie pursed her lips and stared down Edward's retreating back. "There's something else going on with him. Not sure what, though." When I snorted, Nellie put her hands up in capitulation. "Let's shake him off. I think there are more characters worthy of a narration around here."

A perfect distraction. Also, I liked that Nellie didn't want to dwell on Edward, instead wanting to spend time with me. A point for Team This-is-a-Real-Date.

"I'm in."

"We just have to make sure at some point in the evening we include my favorite part of a romantic novel."

I snorted again. I'd lost track of the list of Nellie's "favorite" parts. "Which one again?"

"The misunderstanding. If done correctly," Nellie brought her fingers to her lips and kissed them away, "so good."

Trying to shake off the lingering worry Edward had placed in my mind, I hunted for our next couple to narrate. A few candidates vied for the honor, since several of the rooftop corners were claimed by people pretending they weren't at a party and in full view of everyone around them.

Nellie gestured with her head at the blond guy monopolizing the end of the open bar with the woman in the red dress. He was the only one in the room not wearing a jacket over his white silk—satin maybe—shirt. Far enough away from the nearest heat lamp, the guy was clearly leaning into his drink for warmth. Or he was getting his warmth from the red dress leaning against him and sipping from his glass when he put it down and happened to look away.

"They must have made up," I muttered. "Wonder what that relationship is like."

"She probably loves to tickle his earlobe with a knife."

When the woman tapped the side of the drink at the bartender for a refill, I said, "Wait until the bartender tells her they don't serve chocolate milk."

Nellie shivered.

I scoffed. "In an attempt for attention, she trembled, hoping to lure him out of his jacket."

"No, I really am cold!"

I stopped the game and eyed Nellie. Her arms hugged her waist, and her lips quivered from chattering teeth. I couldn't get out of my jacket fast enough. "Sorry! Thought we were still playing."

Nellie chuckled. Though as the laugh traveled up her throat and hit her chattering teeth, it caused her shoulders to shake. In my attempt to take my jacket off as quickly as possible, the sleeves whipped over the table, hitting the drink Nellie'd given me. The stemmed glass wavered and sloshed its contents over the side. Nellie ignored it as she put on my jacket, as if not wanting any of my residual body heat to escape before she could bask in it.

I dived to grab the napkin and mop up the drink, unaware Nellie'd moved beside me until she bumped against my arm. "The slasher enthusiast had a good idea. Huddling for warmth is a classic trope in romance."

Another point for Team This-is-a-Real-Date.

Wearing my jacket, she couldn't feel the heat rushing through my skin, but I still joked to distract her in case she could. "If you're just here for my drink, I'm not sharing."

Nellie smiled and snuggled closer. Glancing down at her, it hit me that this joking around felt 100 percent familiar. In moments when I let go, our senses of humor aligned, and I was myself again. It was freeing and invigorating. The effect warmed my core, and I didn't miss my jacket. And I didn't think the warmth in my chest came from my drink. I pushed the glass away, wanting to feel the full effects of this, naturally and fully.

Using the hand not holding my jacket closed around her chest, Nellie pointed at the blond guy again. "I bet he secretly stalks her on YouTube."

"Only because she eats all his salsa and then doesn't order him a dessert."

Inching away, Nellie looked up at me, the corners of her mouth twisting into a smile. In that break in our conversation, a couple passed us, their laughing voices within earshot. Nellie started to respond to me but froze and placed a hand on my chest at something they said. In solidarity, we raised our eyebrows at each other.

"Did he . . ." Nellie craned her neck around me to look at the retreating couple. ". . . just say *cotstoee?*"

Heedless of how ridiculous it might look to have both of us leaning to the side, I followed Nellie's action, refusing to believe what I'd just heard. "No. It—no."

Nellie slid her hand from my chest to my arm and gently righted both of us. "*He did!* Edward must have stolen 'cotstoee' and used it at work, and people are picking up on it!"

I couldn't stop shaking my head. "I—no. Your client got published, right? That must be how they got it."

"Edward is using *cotstoee* at work!"

"Not possible."

Nellie narrowed her eyes, the effect more pointed with the black eyeliner and mascara. My heart skipped a stone until she added a sly smile to the glare. "I'll be right back," she said, taking my jacket and her warmth away.

No sooner had she gone than the blond guy took her place. I hadn't seen him move and didn't know how he could have overheard us. My first instinct warned he'd come to confront me, at least by how he held himself. He'd gelled every bit of his inch-long hair into spikes, giving him the appearance of a 90s movie jock villain. Someone with too much confidence who'd had too much to drink and was about to do something I'd regret.

His hair gleamed with the charm of a spiked helmet as he leaned in. "Hey, you the reason he didn't bring Shayla?"

The jerk didn't come across as so drunk as to have mistaken me for someone else. But still drunk enough to do something stupid. I didn't want to be around when that happened.

I sidestepped around him with an, "Excuse me."

The jerk moved with me, quicker on his feet than I'd anticipated. "Your sister was his wife, right? Elise? You're her brother?"

Just like that, my confusion turned into annoyance.

"Then you have to be the reason ol' Ed didn't bring Shayla, right?"

Ol' Ed? From his tone of voice, the jerk was making either me or Edward the butt of a joke.

"What?" he teased when I clenched my jaw. "Did your sister tell him never to date again? What did she do that Ed would be so afraid to have Shayla meet you?"

Just like that, my annoyance burned to anger.

Taking shots at me was one thing, but taking shots at Elise turned me into an extrovert looking for a fight. I had to shut this down; this clenching of muscles, my tightening chest, the anger in my veins trying to curl my fingers into fists. Jerks like this either stayed until they got the reaction or praise they wanted. I had to get away from him before I allowed myself to become an active participant.

I tried to move around him again, but he continued to match my attempts. Physically pushing past or away from him would escalate the situation, and if he touched me, I wasn't sure my coiled muscles wouldn't retaliate. I didn't want that. Yet. But if he was going to force an interaction, he wouldn't get anything from me. I kept my face stone neutral.

Pleased he'd cornered me, the jerk tipped forward again, the contents of his drink lapping dangerously close to the lip of the glass. "I think they're serious. Course, that all depends on if Shayla calls Ed tomorrow after he told her not to come tonight."

The jerk had to be Edward's assistant or something close to that and had overheard him talking in his corner office. If, indeed, Edward had a corner office.

I tried backing up. After one step, the jerk moved to follow me but lost his balance. He fell against me, sloshing my shirt with a red liquid. I stumbled another step back, staring at the stain as we both attempted to right ourselves.

Edward appeared beside me; his presence was the only thing that kept me from lurching forward to grip the jerk by his collar. Edward grabbed my elbow to steady and steer me toward him as he looked at my shirt. Slowly, he turned to stare at the jerk. The power dynamic between the two of them was immediately evident. At the bar, the woman who'd shared the jerk's drink tried to cover her face with one hand.

Oh yeah, Edward definitely had a corner office.

"Having a good night, William?"

The jerk, William, started fidgeting. First rubbing his hands together, then down the sides of his pants. "Yes, sure! Definitely, Mr. Degirmenci . . . just hessing around."

I could only guess that "hessing" was a drunken mixture of "messing" and "horsing."

Edward regarded William, a cold smile hovering out of reach over his lips. After four seconds, the stare elicited a confession.

"We were just curious why Shayla—I mean, Miss Harris, why she's not here. Sir, I apologize. And to you, um . . . Elise's brother. I thought Miss Harris was supposed to come. I sent her the invite and everything like you asked."

Edward stepped forward, positioning himself with his back to me as he stood in front of William. With a warning growl befitting an awakening grizzly bear, he said, "Why don't you go home, hmm? Sleep this off?"

"Why don't you approve my promotion next time?" William snapped. Then he swayed, the realization of what he'd just said bringing more clarity to his gaze.

I was shocked. All this happened because William was upset he didn't get a promotion and was too drunk to realize that bringing this up at a work function with his superiors was a bad idea? At least, he hadn't realized it before blurting out his grievance in front of his boss. Now, in the silence bouncing off the surrounding judging stares, William's words and actions seemed to be catching up to him.

What brain function remained behind Willam's glassy eyes led him to attempt a half-smile and chuckle that did nothing to ease the atmosphere. "W-why don't I just go sleep this off?"

"Excellent idea."

William backed up with less stumbling than I would have expected and, honestly, hoped for. He looked toward the bar, but Miss Red Dress had deserted him. William didn't waste time searching for her. In the next few seconds, he disappeared behind the elevator's closing doors.

Edward hadn't moved. He and I remained in a small bubble of inaction. Those around us who'd noticed the incident stood several feet away. For that reason, even though he faced away from me, I knew Edward was addressing me when he said, "Shayla and I started dating seven months ago."

I did the math automatically in my head. Edward might be lying, but if not, he'd started seeing Shayla well after he and Elise's divorce had been finalized. Edward turned, probably guessing by my middle-distance gaze what my thoughts were. Under his scrutiny, I struggled to pick which emotion to react with. Anger? But why? Because Edward was dating again? Embarrassment? For being judged by Edward's coworkers and underlings? Anger at my sister's name being used as a tool by some idiot wanting to dig up gossip on his boss?

Something warm wrapped around my arm. I didn't have to look. I knew it was Nellie securing her arm around mine. My head cleared enough for me to admit I wanted a reason to be mad at Edward because I wanted a reason to defend Elise, to prove I could be a good brother. I wanted this pent-up emotion to go somewhere. Anywhere. I could walk away feeling like Elise's hero.

But I wouldn't be.

I could pretend the feeling. At least until I saw Elise's disappointed face in my mind if I did something like that to Edward who, as far as I knew, hadn't done anything wrong. She never would have insisted Edward not date again. The fact stabbed my building anger, deflating it.

"It's fine," I said.

Edward gave me a hard stare, trying to force a confession from me like he'd done with William. But I didn't have anything else to say on the subject and could only shrug.

Edward suddenly smiled at both of us. I could have imagined it, but it seemed like the entire room took a collective breath. Or maybe my ability to focus on the sounds around the room had returned, as opposed to what was only in front of me. Edward swiveled from side to side, sharing his smile with everyone nearby who must not feel as though their social standing, or relationship with Edward, would be threatened by openly listening in on our conversation.

Stepping forward, Edward took Nellie's free hand. "Ms. Vasquez, you look resplendent tonight. A wild blossom in a winter garden. And thank you for making him smile, even more than my promise of riches. Speaking of which, see if you can talk him into listening to my investing advice."

Then Edward redirected his attention to me. "It reminds me of when you and Elise were always clearly plotting some sort of joke. Never thought I'd miss those moments."

With that, Edward dropped Nellie's hand and waved at someone near the elevator. "Sorry to dash off again, but . . ."

I'd heard Edward say, "I gotta go," so many times, I automatically finished the thought in my head.

Edward continued, "But let me know if you ever need anything. Investment advice," he waved at my suit, "tailor recommendation, a place to stay, etc." Two gulps later, he'd drained his drink, the bottom of the stemmed flute pointing straight up at the ambient light blocking the stars.

When Edward exited via the elevators, the rest of the room faded back to low conversations with only the occasional glance in our direction.

Elise would have been pleased and proud of me. I hadn't taken any frustrations out on Edward. I hadn't projected any perceived slights on her behalf. For a moment, I crested on a wave of euphoria, but two heartbeats later, the extracting cost of tonight's events caused my mind to crash down without anything to break my fall. Since Elise's death, I'd failed at handling extreme emotions like this.

I muttered thickly to Nellie, "This is why I don't miss talking to people."

"You're not wrong."

We returned to our table to find it didn't offer any shelter. No matter what part of the roof I had my back to, the hairs on my neck stood up. I struggled not to rub my hands together to restore circulation. If I appeared cold, Nellie would try to return my jacket.

Nellie slid a delicate white plate to me with a candied citrus rind atop a cheesecake drizzled in raspberry sauce. Before William had ruined the night, I remembered she'd slipped away, apparently to get me a dessert. "Do I get credit for not eating it?"

I drew air to laugh. I tried twice, each time only managing a weak smile. "Sorry," I offered. "That really was funny."

"No, you're right. We should go."

We started for the elevators. The weight of the eyes following us decreased with each step. Unfortunately, anxiety filled the void. It stalked up my spine, attacking all other senses. One by one, they shut down, starting with hearing. Bits of individual laughter melded with the tinkle of glasses raising together. I tried to differentiate the sounds, but everything swirled like I was at the bottom of a fishbowl.

I focused on the ground to spot if it was getting closer. I didn't want to collapse. Please, not here.

Vaguely, I became aware of Nellie's hand in mine with her other on my arm, gripping it tightly. In solidarity, of course, but more for support. She kept me upright until we reached the elevator, where I had to put out a hand to steady myself on the cool, glossy gray metal.

Nellie repositioned herself as a barrier between me and the party. "Breathe," she whispered behind me.

I would not collapse. I would *not* collapse. I drew air in through my nose and pushed it out through my mouth. It took several attempts, but finally, the anxiety slunk back down, pulling me straighter as it retreated.

I'd done it.

Nellie felt my strength return and came back to my side to link arms as the elevator dinged open. Luckily, we had the lift to ourselves, so I took a deep breath when the doors closed.

"You okay?" Nellie asked.

I nodded and inhaled another deep breath, resting the back of my head against the elevator wall.

"You sure?"

"Yeah." I smiled to convince her. "Sometimes it happens so fast."

"I always hated when that happened," she said, referring to what had to be her own experience.

I looked at Nellie and didn't see her sister's dress or shoes. Or her styled hair. I'm not sure I even saw her face. I more felt her. Steadying, supportive, and best yet, understanding.

"Sooooo." Nellie chewed on the word to draw it out. "What sort of pranks did you and Elise used to pull on Edward?"

The question was a perfect segue to feeling better. "Several," I admitted. "My favorite was when we reset his ring tone for Elise's number to 'Baby Shark.' Then Elise called him during a board meeting with a new client."

Nellie's mouth dropped. "Was he mad?"

"No. Edward told us the call made everyone laugh and broke up the tension in the room. Helped him negotiate the contract."

Nellie snorted a laugh as the elevator buttons counted down to the lobby level.

"Sorry we didn't get a chance to narrate any misunderstanding," I said. "I would have enjoyed that."

As the elevator dinged before opening its doors, Nellie asked me again in an urgent tone, "You sure you're okay?"

"Yes. Why—"

The doors opened to reveal several well-dressed people waiting to get on. Before they could enter, Nellie took off my jacket and threw it at my chest. In front of everyone, she cried, "You donated my Christmas gift to the Animal Gift-Giving Event at the zoo? I've never had a worse misunderstanding!"

Oh, she was good.

She fled the scene in tears. So many tears. Leaving me with glares from those still waiting to swap places with me in the elevator. I gave several polite nods as I shuffled past them. Once I made it out to the valet station, I located Nellie behind a pillar looking every bit the impudent student who'd successfully swiped the teacher's apple.

I ran my fingers through my hair, amazed when they didn't get caught on the straightened strands, and asked, "Why is that your favorite part again?"

Nellie grabbed my jacket back to dig the parking ticket out of the pocket. Handing it to the valet, she said, "I told you, if done correctly, the misunderstanding is the best part. Now I feel fulfilled. This evening needed to end on a high note so it wasn't a waste." She peered at my face. "It wasn't, was it?"

I rubbed my neck, trying to massage the guilt of having a good time away. "No."

Nellie walked me to the curb. "And it's the longest period of time I've seen you go without that haunted expression on your face."

I groaned and turned away. "You have to stop looking at my face."

"It's hard not to." Nellie's voice was devoid of her usual tease. She'd layered it with a serious tone. I glanced back at her to see if her face would match her words. We stared. Waiting to . . . what? Neither of us said.

"Your car, miss? Sir?"

Nellie jumped, grabbing my forearm.

"Yes," I told the valet as he handed me my key. "Thank you."

Reluctantly, Nellie and I parted. I walked around the car and climbed into the driver's seat while Nellie went to the passenger's. I tossed my jacket in the back seat, too warm to need it. I'd barely turned the car on when it asked if I would like to hear an incoming message from Charlie.

"Yes!" Nellie replied.

How's the date going? Any sparks yet?

I knew Nellie was going to respond before her mouth opened and she tapped the reply function. "It's going great," she said. "Wanna double date next week with us? Nellie will plan everything."

The car jumped as I ran over the curb. I waved to a few startled hotel workers and started down the road again. My heat level ratcheted up to boiling while we waited for Charlie to respond.

Nellie tapped her fingers on her knee. "He hoped she couldn't see his red cheeks in the dimness of the car's interior."

"My face isn't red!" It probably was. "It's the reflective taillight of the car in front of us."

There was no car in front of us.

"Well, my face is red. Whew." Nellie rolled down the window and propped her elbow on the frame. "And my neck."

I finally admitted, "Mine too."

Nellie reached over and placed a cool hand on the groove of my neck. "Oh, and your heart rate just went up."

I regretted what I was about to say. I swallowed—shoot, she could feel that too—and said, "This is a fun game, but I don't want to wreck my car."

Nellie chuckled and removed her hand but placed it on the rest between our seats. "Better?"

The car pinged a response from Charlie. *I like it! Let us know when and where to meet so we can arrange for a babysitter.*

I slid a glance toward Nellie. True to what she'd said earlier, she was looking at my face. Still trying to play it casual, I asked, "When should we plan it? Probably not something too short notice. In two weeks?

"No. That's too long notice."

My eyes bulged. "Next weekend?"

"Perfect." Nellie leaned forward and tapped the console screen to reply to Charlie's message. "Next Saturday at the Blue Parrot, 8 o'clock."

Marking the calendar now.

"Yes." Nellie made a fist in triumph. "Our third date. And the first one you get to pay for."

So this had been a date. A full date. And Nellie wanted to go again, even though Edward wouldn't be there. She'd even invited Charlie and his wife.

I was ready to discuss this more when Nellie asked, "Do you mind if I use your car?"

The question made no sense. I knew she didn't drive. Not until she started typing numbers into the console screen did I remember her phone had died. Nellie dictated the text, "Hey, sis. This is Nellie. The evening ended early. Can you pick me up at Daniel's in twenty minutes?"

Still wanting to discuss the dating situation, I wasn't prepared for Sarah to text back immediately. *Oh no! It ended early? What happened? Don't worry. Just like we discussed, having the first date since Luis died end up sucking is normal. Still can't believe you were able to go through with it. Respect, sister!*

A different type of silence filled the car. At least until Sarah texted again. *Shoot! I'm so sorry. Forgot you weren't texting on your phone. Did Daniel see my last text? Delete it before he does!*

Nellie sat so far back in her seat the leather creaked.

I tapped the NO button when the screen asked if we wanted to reply. Nether of us spoke for six blocks. I didn't know if I should be more concerned about the texts or the fact that Nellie remained silent beside me.

I cleared my throat. "You don't have to answer this, of course, but—"

"I don't want you to misunderstand. Please don't misunderstand." Nellie rushed the words like they'd been tumbling inside her mind and just now found an outlet. "Remember when I told you Anita, my old boss, was my lifeguard? And how grief hits you when you don't expect it, but it's not related to anything you're doing? And remember what I told you then about it not being you? It's me?"

I nodded, but Nellie continued talking without looking at me.

"It's been almost two years since Luis died. And I'm still going through stuff. I will probably always be going through stuff for the rest of my life." She gave me a genuine half smile when I glanced over. That one expression did most of the heavy lifting for removing my worry. "Sorry."

I shook my head. Of all people, I understood. "You don't have to apologize to me."

Nellie reached up and gave my hand a brief squeeze. "Thank you." Her half smile became whole. "It doesn't mean I don't want to date. Or date you specifically. But because you're the first guy since Luis . . . there's some annoying new emotional ground I have to break, and then deal with, to make sure this can happen. All these things were only supposed to be shared under the sisters' cone of silence." Nellie waved her hands to indicate the shape said cone would look like if it actually existed in the physical world.

"Oh well." She sighed and placed her hand back on the rest between our seats. "Just know I'm here because I want to be. And I want *you* to be. Didn't know if I was coming on too strong before. All the standing and sitting so close, initiating physical contact with you . . ."

My mind blanked a white screen, then flipped back at lightning speed to review the past several weeks. Nellie was right. Especially the night Edward had shown up at Elise's house. Playing ball, always bumping into me, crouching behind the van, our legs touching under the table . . .

Nellie reached over and gently lifted my chin to close my mouth.

"How—how was I so oblivious?"

"I prefer oblivious to disinterested."

"I thought you only came tonight to find out what was going on with Edward," I said, relief making my voice louder than normal.

"Oh, that too! Mostly to hang out with you. But yes, that too. What is up with that guy hovering between arrogance and mystery?"

I welcomed the cleansing relief washing the hot doubt from my mind. For the first time that night, I took a full breath and let it all out.

"What?" Nellie asked with a playfulness in her voice that brought the heat back to my neck.

"Just glad."

"That?"

I put my hand over hers, guessing it was what she'd hoped for when she left it on the console between us, and was rewarded when she wrapped her fingers around mine. "That it's my turn to pay for the next date. I'm finally going to order some dessert."

Chapter 7

MY KNEES BOUNCED TO THE rhythm of the rain hitting the windshield. The extra energy, though welcome, was surprising. I'd run for an extra thirty minutes that afternoon to get rid of all my nerves. Or to try to get rid of them.

This date would be different, I reminded myself. Gone was the ambiguity regarding Nellie's intentions. She wanted to date me, not just get information on Edward. But dating nerves born in the teenage years didn't die until you did. And they were heightened by anticipation or the thrill of being close to someone. I had a healthy combination of both.

My current destination increased those nerves. Nellie had finally given in, forwarding me the address to her mother-in-law's house where she was staying. I'd get to meet part of her family. Maybe even some of the chauffeur sisters who apparently all liked to hang out together.

Nellie already liked me, a thought that both puffed me up like a kite and thrilled me like I'd been chosen by the most popular girl on campus. Now the chore was to get her multiple families to like me too. A particularly daunting task, given that part of that family belonged to Luis, her late husband.

My knees continued to bounce. I made the final turn onto her street, rapidly scanning the house numbers for Nellie's address. The houses weren't as spaced out as the ones in Elise's neighborhood, but the properties appeared to be well-kept and cared for.

I almost missed it. My GPS told me I'd arrived, but darkness covered both the inside and outside of the two-story house. Parking against the curb, I got out of my car, covering my eyes to squint at the house number half hidden by the rain and overhang scroll work of the front porch. The front door opened to reveal a single lamp in the entry hall next to—

The door shut as Nellie's silhouette slipped out. She held the hood of her long black coat up around her face, leaving only her wide smile visible. She grinned as she ran down the porch steps and past me. I rushed to open her door and sprinted back to the driver's side. By the time I entered the car, Nellie had already flicked her hood off. The coat's shell had protected her face from the tiny droplets sliding off it. But as I started us off down the street, Nellie found a mirror in her bag to correct minute details around her lips and eyes.

"Your house wasn't what I expected," I said. "Guess I thought it'd be full of light, and people, and cooking. All that stuff."

Nellie flipped the mirror shut and returned it to her purse. "Usually it is. Juanita is working late, and Margarita went to a show with Sarah. Jenna is . . ."

Nellie's voice filtered away. My shoulders sagged, probably trying to reach the pit in my stomach. Though meeting your date's family could be nerve-racking, I'd been looking forward to it. And this didn't sit right. I didn't think Nellie wanted to hide her family from me, else why would she have set up this date? One I wanted to go well.

Focus on that, I told myself. Not on the far-fetched possibility Nellie didn't want me to meet her family. I knew I had a good thing going and didn't want to upset that.

This week had been a welcome surprise. Waking up to the world suddenly didn't carry the automatic impulse to go back to bed. Everything shined with an excitement. Sometimes during work, I'd had to stop and remember why I was feeling so happy. The feeling slipped outside my memory and infiltrated other thoughts with the sneaky ability of a joyful virus.

After work on Monday, I'd gone shopping for the date. On Tuesday, I'd participated in a spur-of-the-moment pickup basketball game at the park. On Wednesday, I'd even clocked out of work early to plant Elise's small backyard garden, literally digging up some guilt over the desiccated tomatoes I'd never gotten around to harvesting last fall.

Even though something wasn't matching up with Nellie and her family, I did know I was excited for this date. I didn't want to *not* be excited for this date. So I turned off my questions and tuned back into Nellie's words as she finished with ". . . so as long as she doesn't mind cooking tomorrow, we should be fine."

Guessing at the part of the conversation I missed, I said, "Your family will probably be sad they didn't get to eat Mexican at the Blue Parrot."

Nellie rewarded me with my first dimple flash of the night. "No doubt. It's the only restaurant we've ever found that comes close to Juanita's cooking. And it's actually Venezuelan food, not Mexican."

Nellie started describing the best types of dishes available at the Blue Parrot, giving my hunger a chance to override my nerves. I hadn't determined yet which of the dishes to try when we arrived.

After parking, I ran around the car to open Nellie's door. The rain hadn't slacked off from her house and a trickle of water attempted to become a stream down my back. But Nellie stayed in the front seat, transfixed by her phone.

"I let it die again?" she muttered. It wasn't a question, more of an annoyance. She looked up to share it with me, noticed the torrent, and hopped out with an apologetic, "Agh! Sorry!"

We ran to the front door. I held it open for Nellie, then for an elderly couple shuffling up the walk. Once we'd all escaped the rain, I skirted around the older couple as we exchanged quick smiles of appreciation and greeting.

I caught sight of my well-dressed group near the hostess station. As I neared them, Charlie's wife, Willow, saw me. She reached out for an enthusiastic hug. I'd only seen Willow a handful of times over the past year, but I had been there for the glorious beginning of her and Charlie's courtship. Charlie had first introduced me as "one of those guys who only needs to read the instructions once before he can play a game," and then Willow had proceeded to teach me Hearts and beat me three times in a row.

Charlie joined in to introduce Nellie to Willow, but as the hostess took us to our table, he eyed me. "Did you buy a new suit?"

"And a new shirt." Both were pale blue in different shades. I figured it had to be the style since ninety percent of everything on display in the store was colored in the same palette.

"Maybe next time also buy a raincoat? The rain makes it look like polka dots." Then, he beat me to the punch by pointing out I'd copied his style, though his suit was darker, and his shirt upped his game with a diamond pattern.

I stopped myself from commenting on how he'd cut his hair. Gone was his signature flopped-over Superman style. At some point, he'd buzzed it an inch from his scalp. Saying anything would only serve as a reminder I hadn't seen him in months, an act entirely my fault. At least the light-brown hair and eye color were the same. Enough about him was familiar to keep me from feeling uncomfortable. This was Charlie; I could relax.

"Yes," I said, falling back into the ribbing relationship we'd had back in college. "But I'm not gutsy enough to leave three buttons undone at the top in a casual display of male vanity."

Charlie smirked and reached up to fluff his collar in a guilty-as-charged way. The hostess sat us at a table on the edge of a wood-sealed dance floor. Lanterns both lit the area and strategically ensconced private corners in shadow. Under them, each table gleamed a different color, the same with the chairs surrounding them. Though nothing matched, it coordinated in a celebration of color. Nellie must have been in her element.

Charlie continued to eye me. He was about to zing me. I knew it. Something you learned after rooming with someone for three years.

"Your hair got long. And fuzzy."

"No, it's not!" Willow protested. She pointed at me. "It's not fuzzy. That is curly."

I held up my hands, staying out of their disagreement. I'd much rather Charlie and Willow match wits over the definition of my hair than admit I'd tried to replicate the straightened look Nellie liked so much. I'd attempted to use a few of Elise's gadgets, but the end result was so muddled, I didn't know how to fix it and ducked back in the shower to get my hair wet and let it dry on its own. It was a wavy mess, but one I was used to.

Charlie and Willow's debate went on hiatus when Nellie suggested we look at the menu. Though I suspected she was having a great time narrating the argument in her head. Reaching across the table, Nellie pointed out her recommendations to Willow. I heard snippets about braised tomatoes in cumin seeds sautéed with minced garlic and onions and had to change my mind on what to order twice before the waitress arrived.

At an apparent truce with her husband, Willow pointed across the table at Nellie and me. "Charlie told me Daniel hired you and you're going through what Elise wrote to get her published. How's that going?"

Nellie and I shared a glance, and she giggled.

"What?" Willow insisted.

"Every part of a book is Nellie's favorite part and I—well, I find some of the romantic prose hard to get through," I said.

Nellie hit my arm.

"You do too!" I insisted.

Willow wrinkled her nose. "What's so bad about it?"

"Daniel thinks stories are cut-and-dry. Right or wrong, same as a formula in an Excel file. Either something works according to preset rules, or it doesn't."

"And Nellie thinks stories with flaws have a soul."

Willow shared a glance with Charlie and rested her chin in her hand. "Fascinating. What's something else you disagree on?"

I thought back to the most repeated offender. "How characters are described. What they're wearing, etc."

Charlie lifted his chin. "I bet I'd be good at that."

Willow scoffed, but I issued the challenge. "I dare you."

Grinning in acceptance, Charlie turned to look at his wife.

I tried picking out what Charlie would comment on. Willow had selected black wide-legged pants with a silver-threaded and sequined sleeveless top to showcase her russet-brown skin tone. Her hair twisted back in an effortless bun, but I knew from Elise it easily could have taken an hour to perfect. Any one of those items would be a minefield for Charlie. Suave as he was now, back in college it'd taken him two weeks to get the courage to ask Willow out; she tongue-tied him better than anyone I knew.

Charlie picked up Willow's hand and caressed the back of it with his thumb. "Everything from the sexy hips her mother gave her to her soft shoulders that hold more than I could ever hope to." Willow leaned in as Charlie traced her jawline. "She is, in a word, perfect."

They kissed in a we're-the-only-people-in-the-room sort of way. Nellie and I shared conspiratorial glances since watching them felt like an invasion of a private moment. When they finally broke apart, Willow nestled against Charlie as he put an arm around her shoulder.

Nellie nodded with a grin, and I wondered how Charlie'd pulled that off. He rested back in his chair and said, "Now you."

I knew where Charlie was going with this but tried to get out of it with a joke. "I think you already described Willow quite well."

Charlie raised an eyebrow and gave me a teasing look. I laughed but stopped when I heard how nervous it sounded.

Nellie put up her hand like she was sharing a secret with Charlie and Willow and whispered loudly, "He looks like a boiled lobster."

A challenge.

I accepted.

To play the game, I'd have to use Nellie's language. I couldn't take Charlie's lead and describe Nellie's physical features. We weren't at that level of intimacy. I'd have to use clues in what Nellie was wearing.

I took in a breath and looked Nellie over while trying to keep my gaze from becoming too ogley.

She wore her hair down, but not in its normally straightened form, so tight curls bounced over and around her shoulders. The first time I'd had a date who'd worn her hair like that, Elise had explained women liked curls for movement while dancing. At the time, I'd felt bad for any guy without a sister to explain girls.

So, I could maybe say something about Nellie's hair. And if Nellie wanted to dance . . .

I glanced over the side of the table. Nellie obligingly extended her foot for me to see her shoes. Dark leather with flower stencils. More comfortable than the heels she'd worn last week. More evidence for dancing. Now for the main event.

A lemon-colored, sleeveless, tea-length dress with a square neck. From what I remembered before she sat down, it had reached below her knees and gathered at the waist under a braided belt, where enough fabric bunched up that it could flair out when she twirled. I would have simply called it a yellow dress before learning to "speak Nellie."

Nellie definitely planned on dancing tonight. With me. Anticipation tried to get me to squirm in my seat and demand we hit the dance floor immediately.

Lastly, Nellie wore a gold necklace with a pendant the color of sea-green glass. It matched the eyes watching mine with their usual teasing glow. Though they opened a smidge wider than usual. And I could tell Nellie was also holding her breath.

If there were any good descriptions in the submissions I'd read through that could help me out here, I couldn't remember even one of them. Charlie loudly cleared his throat, and I spoke the first words that came to my mind. "It's my favorite thing she's ever worn."

I didn't know if it would land but thought it might have when Willow put her hands on her cheeks to try and contain her grin. Charlie slow-clapped while I kept my eyes on Nellie, the one whose reaction I most wanted to see. She smiled, setting off a chain reaction I felt all the way down in my new dress shoes. We might have kept staring at each other if the first course of our dinner hadn't arrived.

Everything we ate, from the appetizers to the main and side courses were as good as Nellie described. I could have paid more attention, maybe even remembered the names of the dishes for later, but the constant furtive glances Nellie and I kept passing back and forth kept most of my mind occupied and abuzz.

There may have been a better, more descriptive word to explain what was going on in my head, but jolts of electric emotion blocked me from finding it. Every hair tuck and every shift in her seat riveted me. If Nellie's flashing dimple was any indication, she was having the same problem.

Nellie's words came back to me about loving all of someone. At that moment, I loved how her dark eyebrows pinched as she laughed, how she spoke Spanish with the waiter, how her foot tapped the floor in time with the music. All of it.

It shocked me that, with all the amazing flavors I was consuming, all the music pounding in my ears, the colors blending all around me, I remained entirely focused on what lay between Nellie's necklace and her matching eyes.

"Hey!" Charlie called.

I tore my attention away to see Willow pluck a shrimp off Charlie's plate and pop it into her mouth.

"Yes?" she challenged with a sly wink.

Charlie held out his plate to her. "I meant to say, darling wife, would you accept another one?"

As Willow selected another shrimp, Nellie said, "That's a strong marriage right there."

"What can I say?" Charlie shrugged. "I give, and she takes."

Nellie snorted, and she mocked her fellow industry professional. "Wow, Charlie. That was really cliché."

Before thinking better of it, I asked, "How do you forgive each other when you disagree on something?"

Nellie laughed into her drink and had to put the glass down. "It's too early in our relationship to be asking for advice on *that*, don't you think? So far, we've only fundamentally disagreed on what constitutes a shooting foul. Of course, this is our second date in a week. Therefore, we must agree on at least a few things."

I joined the table laughing, relieved I didn't have to admit the comment was about my relationship with Elise, not Nellie. I closed my eyes and was pinching the bridge of my nose as if in embarrassment when I felt the familiar tug on my hand. I opened my eyes to be drawn in again by Nellie's face as she pulled me to my feet.

Not until we stepped onto the dance floor did I register the beat of the music. I resisted for a moment, suddenly unsure. The song swirled faster than I'd danced to in . . . a while. With a gentle nudge, Nellie kept us moving forward. In the middle of churning couples, Nellie directed my hands and placed one on her hip and the other in hers. Then we were dancing. Multiple songs passed, slow and fast, loud and soft.

The experience simultaneously sharpened all my senses and dulled my anxiety. Little things like heat generating from my palm contrasted against the thrill of holding Nellie's hand so I could twirl her around me. Or the feel of her back through the fabric of her dress as her hips swirled us around the music. Or the panic of having Nellie close enough to whisper lyrics in my ear, but willing to fight anyone, including myself, from pulling me away from her. I was on one terrifying thrill ride I would pay to experience over and over again.

Only when the band announced a short break did we follow suit. Collapsing in my chair back at the table, I felt sweat press into my shirt when I leaned back. Willow held out her hand to invite Nellie to get some drinks.

Charlie played it cool until the girls were at the bar across the room, then he stretched across the table. "Dude! When did you learn to dance like that?"

"Tonight," I gasped out.

Charlie leaned back and stared at me. "Liar," he declared.

I wasn't sure if Charlie could tell from the table how much Nellie had been leading, or how easy it was to follow when I exclusively focused on her.

"I can't let that stand. I gotta show that up." Charlie stood but sat again when Willow caught his movement and waved him back down. "Guess I'm not invited."

He draped one arm over the back of Willow's empty chair, allowing the button over his stomach to threaten to pop when he deeply inhaled. "That was a great dinner." Charlie's good-natured grin took on a familiar tease. "You were a bit preoccupied though."

No doubt the payback smirk was years in the making for all the teasing I'd done when he and Willow were dating. I nodded at the girls, who had gotten their drinks—well, at least Willow had—and seemed in no hurry to return. "Think they're talking about us?"

Charlie snorted. "Oh, for sure. Or not. Hard to tell with Willow. Oh yeah, by the way . . ." I could tell from the switch of his tone that our conversation was about to take a hard left. "Earlier, when you were asking about when Willow and I disagree with each other, you were talking about you and Elise, weren't you?"

Ah, the perils of making an odd comment with someone who really knew you around to hear it. I rubbed my neck. "You caught that?"

"Yeah. I have a suggestion for you."

"A suggestion?"

"Ask for help. If you're struggling with anything, reach out. I may not have the answers, probably won't, but you won't be alone. I'm glad to see you getting out of that house. We've all missed you."

The conversation had definitely transitioned from guy ribbing to a late-night let's-fix-the-world roommate chat. I drained the last bit of water from my glass to have something to do. "Wise words."

"So tell me how you've been." Charlie chuckled when I winced. "It's a simple, easy question."

He wasn't wrong. And he deserved an answer. "I'm fine."

An *honest* answer.

I took a breath. "I'm getting better, I think. The guilt is still there, but I don't feel it as much. The bubble haze of crap around my head clears out sometimes." I looked at Nellie, laughing at something Willow said while the other woman swirled her drink. "Maybe I just needed time. Isn't that what people always say? It must be true."

Charlie nodded at the table. "I get it, man. You're hurting. Elise was your best friend, a permanent fixture in your world. Readjusting when that's gone doesn't happen overnight."

This was the conversation I'd been afraid to have. With anyone. Even a hint of it would drive me away. From Thai Food Palace, from Ava the hairdresser, even from Charlie.

"Yeah," I said, dipping my chin.

Charlie grinned at me. A second later, we both chuckled and smirked.

I decided to change the subject. "How are you doing?"

"Well, Sam's still not sleeping through the night."

Charlie took a long swallow of his drink while I covered my eyes. "You have a kid." What was worse was Charlie had mentioned a babysitter, and I'd obviously glossed over all of that.

"Yep." Charlie took another long swig in an attempt to empty his glass. "Sorry," he said, coughing without putting the drink down. "We don't get many adult nights out anymore."

I couldn't believe he was apologizing to me. "I knew you had a kid. I swear I did."

Charlie waved me off. "Sam was born last June, about the same time you told me Elise had to stop taking her daily walks since she was so tired all the time. I knew you were focused on other things. You didn't go into it, but I knew that meant things had taken a turn for the worse."

June had been a bad month. I hadn't thought Elise could hold on another six months, but she did. I still apologized again. "I'm sorry. I've been a bad friend."

"Don't worry about it. However, we do accept diapers as 'I'm sorry' gifts. Seriously, don't say sorry. It's fine."

"Can I say thank you?"

Charlie nodded his head once. "I can accept it for me. But I can't speak for all the guys. Maybe actually come to one of our games and talk to them. Just remember, we've all been a bit worried, concerned is all. Especially after—" Charlie's face tensed.

"What?" I asked.

"That thing with Edward."

"Which one?" I asked slowly.

Charlie's eyes widened, and he whipped his phone out of his jacket pocket. He scrolled for a moment and then smacked his forehead. Holding out the phone, he showed me a text thread marked *Draft*.

"I didn't send it. I'm such an idiot. Least now I know why you didn't text back. I just thought you were being non-communicative again."

My spine straightened as I leaned forward. "Charlie, what happened with Edward?"

"Is Edward's last name Degirmenci?"

The steak sitting in my stomach started to cook again. "What'd he do?"

Charlie leaned forward too, our foreheads inches apart. He hissed, "After the game this week, a couple of the guys stayed around talking, and this random pair of sunglasses, at nine o'clock at night no less, shows up and starts asking us questions about you."

"How did you know he was connected to Edward?" I hissed back.

"Marco."

Marco was another friend from college. Smartest guy I knew. "How'd he figure it out?"

"Marco got the information off the guy's phone. Got us to distract the sunglasses, snuck up behind him, 'cause the phone was in the guy's pocket, and then he . . . just . . ." Charlie gestured but didn't make any sense with his hands.

"You don't know what Marco did."

"No one knows! Marco does . . . cyber . . . IT stuff. I don't know how to explain it. Anyway, he got the information off this guy's phone."

"Is that legal?"

Charlie paused long enough to give me a withering stare.

"You're right," I agreed. I was focusing on the wrong part of the story. "So, who was the guy?"

"He's a background investigator. Edward hired him."

Energy flowed out of me, replaced by confusion. I slumped in my chair and stared at the ceiling while Charlie kept talking. If anything else, he became more animated with his retelling of the story.

"We had to pull Marco back, he was so riled up. Wanted to full-on stalk the guy back to his car so Marco could follow him to where he lived and then try to break through his firewall and steal all the info off his computer." Charlie stopped for a breath. "Now, that would have been going too far and probably illegal." Raising his eyebrows, Charlie asked, "Do you know what's going on?"

"No." I rubbed my neck. "I have no idea what's going on with Edward. He stopped by Elise's house out of nowhere, invited me to a high-class work shindig, tried to get me to apply to work for his company or allow him to invest my money, and we found out he's been dating someone for several months but didn't want me to know."

"Why would he care?"

"Can I get you any dessert tonight?"

Charlie and I both jumped into straight sitting positions at the interruption. Our waitress smiled. If she'd heard any part of our conversation and found it strange, she didn't show it.

"Um . . ." My brain short-circuited. I pointed across the room at Nellie and Willow. "Them."

Charlie smoothly took over. "We just need a few minutes to discuss with our party."

With a parting smile, the waitress moved on. Charlie waved for the girls to return to the table and added a final low-voiced comment to our conversation. "If this guy shows up at your house, call me."

I hated unfamiliar territory or information. I tried waving it off. "Don't worry. I will, but let's stop theorizing about this. I don't want Edward to ruin another date. Let's enjoy the rest of the night without worrying about some odd ex-brother-in-law."

"Or a screaming kid," agreed Charlie with another sip of his drink. As Nellie slid into the seat next to me, Charlie asked, "Time for dessert?"

"Absolutely, yes." Willow dropped into her chair, the umbrella in her drink barely staying up in the sip of liquid left in the glass.

The waitress returned, and Nellie ordered dessert for the table. Everyone agreed the torta de piña was delicious. At least the first few bites. After such a dinner, it was all anyone could manage.

"The spirit is willing," said Charlie. "But the stomach is finite and flabby."

Nellie and I returned to the dance floor while Charlie and Willow stayed at the table, determined to force more bites down. Over Nellie's shoulder, I watched them order another round of drinks. Again, all the awkwardness of keeping track of my arms and legs went away while dancing with Nellie. Even more so when the next song had a slower beat. The perfect segue from Charlie's news about Edward.

The only other distraction I had was watching Charlie and Willow order a third round of drinks. Turns out, Nellie had her eye on them too.

After the fourth song, Willow looked at her phone, then rose to struggle into her coat. Nellie stopped dancing and followed me when I led us back to the table.

"Was that the babysitter?" Nellie asked.

Charlie shook his head, turning around in a circle to search for his coat, which was hanging on the back of his chair a few feet away. "No babysitter. Willow's mother is watching Sam tonight."

I picked up on Nellie's concern. "Did you guys drive?"

"Yeeep." Willow smiled at us, having only successfully put on one coat sleeve. Unfortunately, it was Nellie's.

Nellie's eyes met mine. She said, "I'll go talk to the manager about keeping your car here overnight. He's a friend."

"Meet you at the car?" I asked. She nodded, and I helped settle the bill with Charlie before assisting him and Willow to my car. Once Nellie rejoined us and took her place in the passenger seat, I pulled out of the parking lot.

Nellie snuck her hand up to mine on the steering wheel and gave it a brief, but intense squeeze. I glanced over when she removed her hand and caught a look of gratitude cross her face. She took a quick steadying breath, as though keeping some emotion at bay, and winked at me.

"Hey," Charlie called out from the back seat. "You should take Nellie home first; she's closer."

I had no doubt Charlie's booze-bruised mind told him he'd recommended something logical, thoughtful even. But as my college wingman, he should have known better. Willow voiced her approval with the idea, saying it was less time I'd have to spend on the road since I was already doing them a favor in taking them home.

I peered at Nellie with an intimate understanding that didn't exist before tonight. Before, I would have assumed her wrinkled nose meant she needed to sneeze, or that her eye roll indicated boredom. But now, I felt a connection with those depression glass sea-green eyes. They told me Nellie also lamented the chance to spend more time together, that circumstances were robbing us of precious moments that could have been spent alone.

Nellie further confirmed by mouthing, *It's okay.*

"Nellie's home it is," I announced, shooting a quick glare in the rearview mirror that made Nellie suppress a giggle in her nose. Charlie caught the stare. A moment later, his mouth and eyes turned into *O*'s. He groaned.

"What?" Willow asked, clearly confused.

Nellie distracted her with a question about Sam. Talking about her toddler dominated the conversation until we reached Nellie's still-dark house. I got out to escort Nellie, using the streetlight reflecting off the wet cement as a guide to the front door. Even if the car ride hadn't gone as expected, we could still end this date on a positive note. Though I could feel Charlie's and Willow's stares from the car windows.

"I need to get my street game back," I muttered with a dose of self-annoyance.

"What was that?"

"I should have parked down the street or behind your neighbor's obliging bit of landscaping. Could have prevented us from having an audience."

Nellie turned around and paused to stare where I'd parked my car. Something caught her eye. Something hilarious, judging by Nellie's smirk and playful nudge into my side. But I didn't turn around and instead focused on her.

When Nellie broke into a laugh, I tried to bring the conversation back to us. I remembered I hadn't told her about Edward and the background investigator.

"I have something that might interest you," I said.

"So do I."

Nellie stepped closer, and I realized she was coming in for a kiss. It happened so fast that what flashed through my mind was Charlie or Willow might be staring from the car.

For a second, my mind hit a brain delay, but as she got closer, Charlie and Willow faded away, the rain faded away, even my surprise faded away. I willed my knees not to turn into Jell-O, but even as I shored up my legs, I lost feeling in my fingers. I raised my hands anyway, reaching for her face.

Just as I felt a brush against my lips, Nellie pulled back. My eyes, which had been tracking her mouth, went to her face to find she wasn't even looking at me.

Headlights briefly crossed her features as a car crept into the driveway and disappeared around the side of the house. A moment later, Nellie stepped back at the sound of the garage door opening. Her body language, now stiff and jerky, had completely transformed.

"So, thanks! This was fun!" she said as she reached out to give me a one-armed hug before pulling away again. When a car door slamming echoed from the garage, she started toward the sound. "Yes, so, um, we'll meet next week for our usual meeting, yes? Oh, wait, there was something you wanted to tell me."

Nellie hadn't stopped walking backward, even when asking me the question. In a moment she would be around the corner of the house.

"No. It can wai—"

"Perfect!" Then Nellie was out of sight, calling, "See you next week!"

I stood there, blinking rapidly into the rain I'd just noticed was still falling. The elation from the evening deflating in my chest as rapidly as a popped balloon. My mind jumped into instant replay, reviewing every second of the past minute in fast-forward. The arrival of the car, or whoever was in it, had caused the change in Nellie's demeanor.

A light inside the house flicked on. Not wanting anyone inside to peek through the window and catch me gaping in the rain, I ran back to the car and entered to find myself in the middle of an argument.

Willow had somehow maneuvered herself from the back of the car to the passenger seat. Probably what Nellie had seen over my shoulder and laughed at. Willow's once-elegant bun now hung low by one of her ears. A few remaining cockeyed bobby pins holding everything together stuck out like knitting needles.

"I want to apologize. You wanted more time with Nellie," she said. Her head rolled as she attempted to focus her eyes, though her voice sounded so sincere I wouldn't have known she was drunk if we'd been talking on the phone.

"We're good," I assured her and Charlie through a glance in the rearview mirror. Then I shoved a hand through my hair and stared at Nellie's front door. To myself, I lied, "We're all good."

Awkwardly securing Willow's seat belt on her, I drove back onto the highway to get them home. As the car splashed through puddles, sending spray onto the windshield, I tried to stay out of Willow and Charlie's animated discussions, only jumping in to correct the record when Charlie tried to retell my "Worst Candy Adventure" story, when Elise and I tried to pick the worst convenience store food for the other to try when stopping for gas on our road trips.

After that, I let the harmless, occasionally hilarious drunken banter between them fade into the background. As entertaining as it was, I couldn't concentrate on it.

What had just happened? Every time we'd met, Nellie had lulled me further and further outside myself. First, as a participant in a crazy agreement. Then literally out of the house to play basketball. Then to a restaurant. Then to a party. Finally, to a proper date. Nellie always led the way.

But this was the opposite. She'd pulled back, retreated—an action that didn't match what I knew of her. By the time I dropped Willow and Charlie off at their apartment and ensured Willow's mother was good to stay, I'd concluded there was no way to know what was happening without talking to Nellie.

I had five days until Thursday and our next meeting. Between now and then, I would find the words to ask her, and then I'd actually ask her. I could call or text her to resolve the situation much sooner. But I wanted all five days to work this out.

I could do it, I promised myself.

Surely five days would be enough time.

Surely.

Chapter 8

I LOOKED UP THE WORD *palpable* on my phone.

Result: "an intense feeling capable of being felt."

What a perfectly descriptive word.

Nellie and I sat in our usual spots in Elise's living room but not in our usual moods. I placed my phone back on the side table next to my chair and doubted Nellie had noticed me pick it up. She remained laser focused on the manuscript in her lap, burning the words through the paper and into her jeans with her eyes. She'd also been reading the same page for five minutes.

The atmosphere had produced a similar lack-of-efficient-work environment for me. At least I'd narrowed down all the submissions to ten finalists. One would complete and perfect Elise's book for her. It was difficult to express how much I was looking forward to that.

In the meantime, I needed to do something to break the unspoken stalemate between Nellie and me. I didn't know how to move this nascent relationship forward without having this conversation.

My muscles wouldn't mind getting answers too. They were tense enough to lose their springs if I didn't act soon. I rubbed my knee absentmindedly, wincing when a flare of pain warned my hand off, the product of extra-long runs every day that week. Initially, I thought the longer runs would give me a chance to clear my head and help me think of what to say to Nellie. On Tuesday, I finally realized I'd used the runs as an excuse not to think at all.

I'd settled on saying, *I don't want to pry, but*—Wait, that sounded stupid. No, no. Why had I selected that as my intro? It'd sounded logical an hour ago, but now it sounded astonishingly stupid in my head. Only people planning on prying would say something like that.

Having courage but no plan, I cleared my throat and said, "It's weird, this being a regular work night. We've been on so many dates in such a short time, it's odd to be meeting for work."

It was too late to take it back now. But it seemed like a good intro. Just a joke with no accusations, no demands, nothing to force Nellie into—

"I need to tell you something." Nellie's voice sat low on her register.

Anxiety lifted me an inch out of my chair before I forced myself back down.

Nellie placed her hands over her face and spoke through her fingers. "This is my fault. I created some unnecessary tension. If you were wondering, yes . . . I meant to kiss you. I wanted to then, and I want to now."

I fumbled for words, but instead of responding, my mouth hung open, and I couldn't find a good way to sit as I shifted back and forth.

Still speaking into her hands, Nellie's words took on a rehearsed quality. "I can't blame you for being confused. I'm sorry for that. I'm . . . working some stuff out. And that's not a good explanation. Like, at all. It was one thing, but then it turned into another. I'm not sure I can explain it right now. I want to move forward with you but am worried I'll mess it up."

Nellie's cagey answer raised a red flag, and I thought back to the private investigator Edward had hired. "Has anyone showed up at the house bothering you?"

"What? No!" Nellie dropped her hands into her lap. "This is something else. Who would show up to bother me?"

I wanted to tell Nellie about Edward, but that would change the subject, and this one still needed some closure. I thought back to Charlie's patience and to all the times Nellie had demonstrated understanding. I wanted to know, absolutely, what Nellie couldn't tell me and how it might impact what we were starting. However, I had no right to demand it.

"There's no rush," I told her. "Tell me whenever you feel is best."

With a low laugh, Nellie tossed her stack of papers onto the coffee table, then stretched and rubbed her face again, the action reshaping it back into her regular smile. "Thank you," she said.

Even though I didn't have the answers I wanted, I could still celebrate that *relief* had replaced *palpable* as the dominant emotion in the room.

"Does this mean you're up for something this weekend?" I asked. "It's about time I asked you to something. Unless you're tired of seeing me twice a week."

I meant it as a tease to ease us from this heavy material back into our usual banter. It worked. Nellie nodded, her smile slowly widening as her eyes roamed over my face.

A thrill of excitement ran circles in my stomach, squirming under my skin with the tenacity of a worm trying to escape the rain. I focused on the new date to distract myself from her stare.

"Where would you like to go?"

Nellie shook her head. "Nope. It's your turn to plan. Where would you recommend?"

"Go-carts?" I meant it as another joke since Nellie never drove.

But Nellie didn't laugh. Or even smile. Her mouth shifted into neutral for too long before acknowledging my suggestion. "How about batting cages instead?"

If something other than date planning had just run through Nellie's head, I couldn't chase it down, not so soon after telling her she didn't have to explain anything to me if she wasn't ready. I quickly considered her idea, ready to move on. I thought my bum knee could hold up to batting cages, and there were several good restaurants near there. We could try out the Ethiopian one.

"I'll set it up," I said.

Nellie reached for the manuscript I'd finished reviewing and placed it with the others inside the box. "We have ten minutes left," she said. She wrapped a loose bit of hair around her ponytail and winked to reset the mood. "What if we start looking at the next story? We'll want to gear it up for submissions, otherwise we won't have a reason to keep meeting every Thursday night."

That was a good point and excellent motivation. "I'll get Elise's laptop." I stood and started to complete a full-body stretch toward the ceiling until my knee creaked in protest. "Just a warning: Elise's second story might need more work than her first. I found it in the trash folder."

Leaving the living room, I crossed through the vestibule and into the little nook Elise had used as an office. Nellie's voice trailed after me as I dug around in the antique desk drawers with iron handles.

"Why were you in Elise's trash folder?"

I returned to the living room carrying Elise's laptop. "Elise didn't know where she'd put something the lawyer needed for her will, so I ended up checking everywhere."

I sat next to Nellie on the couch. She took advantage of the dip in the cushions created by my weight to tilt into me, our legs touching.

"Don't worry," I said, fighting a grin for who knew why. "I'm not being oblivious anymore."

I was now on high alert for anything Nellie did to initiate physical contact with me and was more than glad she'd started again. Only the knowledge that one of Nellie's sisters could show up early stopped me, and probably Nellie, from doing anything more obvious.

I hadn't forgotten she'd said she still wanted to kiss me. I surprised myself by admitting I wanted to kiss her back. Or first. Really anything. Mostly because without meaning to, I'd turned off that part of myself when I'd moved in to help Elise after her diagnosis. All my energy and focus had gone to caring for her.

Now I felt it coming back, the longing to be with someone who excited you, celebrated the best parts of you, and carried you through tough times without the need of repayment. And someone who caught your veins on fire when they sat next to you on a couch, deliberately letting their leg touch yours.

It had been a while since I'd felt like this. Not since dating Janice.

Thinking back to my last relationship, Elise's diagnosis hadn't been the only reason I'd broken up with Janice. It'd accelerated a decision I'd been thinking about for months before. I hadn't been serious with anyone since. But now, sitting next to Nellie and sharing surface area, I remembered why I'd broken up with Janice in the first place.

Janice was undeniably funny and beautiful and could command a room. The problem had been that she was predisposed to stay at home every night. *Every* night. I had that aspect to my personality too and had been held prey to that side of myself over the past few months. If I'd stayed with Janice, I knew I wouldn't have fought that instinct, giving into it to please her. A quiet night at home wasn't bad, but at that time in my life, every night would have suffocated me.

Nellie shook her head slightly, like a needle had poked at a thought. "What would Elise think about you dating me?" she asked.

"She'd think it was hilarious you would ask her first instead of me." Nellie elbowed me in the stomach, then left her arm resting against my side. "Honestly, she'd mock you, just to make sure you could take it. Elise didn't want anyone flaky dating her little brother. And, speaking honestly again, you might be the first girl she would have approved of. She might have even spirited you away for your own girls' adventure one weekend without me."

I wasn't making that up. Nellie's ability to pull me, emotionally and physically, while staying respectful of my boundaries seemed like a contradiction in terms, but it was working. Each meeting was built as a continuation of the last one. Pulled a little further, tested a little more. Tonight, I found myself back in the head space I'd lived in until a few years ago. At least since before the fight between Elise and me—

I pushed away from the thought, not wanting to remember any bit of it.

Nellie wrapped her arm around mine, but not so tight as to keep me from being able to type. A rush of pure gratitude hit me. After the shock of it, a yearning set in. I wasn't sure what had prevented her from kissing me that night, though I guessed it had something to do with Luis. I'd meant what I'd said; I would give Nellie the time she needed and wouldn't push anything until she was ready.

But feeling her warm skin against mine? It was hard. If Nellie had put her hand on my neck, she would have felt my pulse go in for a slam dunk.

An insane urge to run my hand through my hair, root to tips, crept down my arms and into my fingers. Janice, and various other girlfriends, had all confided in me that they found the action irresistibly "cute." I'd found that logic to be cheesy and cliché. Now? I was totally going to find a way to use it.

I opened Elise's laptop. The screen blinked to life, showing a picture of me and Elise about to be swallowed by a towering wave gearing up to crash into us. Taken a few years ago on a holiday weekend vacation in Myrtle Beach, South Carolina, it still looked like a relic from a past life, one I could read about but not relate to anymore. That day Elise had purchased a waterproof disposable camera from a beach vendor, determined to use up the entire roll of film before we left for lunch.

The picture caught me in a bad moment. My mouth half-open, loosing a dreaded but excited yell with my eyes in the act of closing as I sensed the impending doom behind me. Better pictures existed from that day, but Elise had chosen this one to remember it.

I braced for Nellie to mock my expression, or the peeling sunburned skin at my hairline, nose, and shoulders. Instead, Nellie squinted and reached out her fingers to briefly brush the screen over Elise's blond hair, hanging over both shoulders in about-to-be-soaked braids. Nellie halfway covered Elise's smile but not the thumbs up she gave the camera while taking the picture.

Another secret thought seemed to pass behind Nellie's eyes. Keeping to my decision not to pry, I didn't say anything and clicked on Elise's story folder.

Nellie rested her head on my shoulder and asked, "How did you know it was a story when you found it in the trash folder?" Then she answered her own question. "Oh. She named it 'My Second Story.'" She slid her face closer to the screen to look at the file data information. "It's short. Maybe it's another draft?"

"Maybe," I said, preparing to open the file. I couldn't believe I was actually about to read it. When I'd first discovered Elise's stories, I'd only managed to look at the first one before guilt shut down any repeat visits to her Documents folder. But with Nellie sitting so distractingly close to me, I felt a comforting buzz in my fingertips as I hit the Enter key.

Instead of leaning on my shoulder again, Nellie shifted her gaze to me. "Um . . . I can't believe I'm saying this, but are you sure this is something Elise would want other people to read if she, herself, didn't want to anymore?"

I hadn't considered that. The thought shut down the automatic insistence that I had to get Elise published. Looking back, I realized I'd only focused on completing this one last thing I could ever do for Elise. I'd taken her desire to be a writer and married it to her manuscripts and outlines to create the perfect gift. That Elise had deleted this story hadn't been a part of that equation at all. I was just so glad to have found it.

But Nellie was right. This story might have significant flaws. Why else would Elise have thrown it away?

The more I thought about it though, the more I rationalized moving forward. Elise's romance story was flawed. The outline and the written parts weren't perfect. But that's why we were doing this. To find people to fix any mistakes, make it perfect, and bring Elise back to life.

I checked myself. To bring Elise's *stories* back to life. I knew the excited version of Elise's face at seeing her books in a store would only be in my mind. But knowing she would have reacted that way was real. So real that even though it hadn't happened, and would never happen, I could picture it like it was a memory.

I couldn't stop now.

"I don't want to abandon any of her stories," I said. "There has to be something salvageable. Something to inspire another writer to complete and perfect it."

I clicked on the file. As it pulled up on the screen, I suddenly screwed my eyes shut and chuckled nervously.

"Daniel?"

"Why don't you read it? You're the undisputed champion narrator."

Without disentangling our arms, Nellie took the computer off my lap and placed it on her own. I rested my head against the back of the couch, eyes still closed and focused on Nellie's voice. Soft as a hum, perfect for a children's story.

"One day, two bunnies played in the sun. They laughed, ate clover, and chased each other around their tree. They had no mother or father but took care of each other. That night, Daniel Nibble Hop—hey." Nellie elbowed me in the ribs. "This is about you!"

I groaned inwardly at the mention of Daniel Nibble Hop and the reminder I'd never found Elise's two stuffed bunnies. It would bug me forever because I'd looked everywhere and knew Elise would never have thrown them away.

Elise started again. "Sorry, anyway . . . ahh, okay, that night Daniel Nibble Hop wanted to make a fire to stay warm, but E. Bunbun . . . oh, it's about the two of you! Cute. So, E. Bunbun says the fire will spread while we're sleeping. It will scorch us to the ground, and our home will be gone. We will have nowhere to be safe."

My eyes snapped open. The wording, "Scorch us to the ground," brought back a memory. Elise had only ever said it once. The night of our fight. *The fight.*

The memory wasn't a good one. I'd tried burying it next to the memory of Elise's death. The one I hadn't realized I was trying to fully eradicate with this endeavor to get Elise published. Her words sliced open the memory. I wanted to ask Nellie to stop reading but found my limbs and throat paralyzed.

Unaware, Nellie continued. "E. Bunbun said, 'Let's not start a fire. It might be cold and dark for a while, but we'll be together and can keep each other alive until morning. Let's use a blanket instead.'"

Every part of me weighed down into the couch. Except for my pounding heart, I didn't move.

"E. Bunbun put a blanket over Daniel Nibble Hop to keep him safe and warm but woke up later to find he had created a fire, and their tree was burning. Hmm. A bit dark for a children's story . . . but children's horror is actually on the rise." Nellie talked over my attempts to swallow. "As their home burned to the ground—oh yeah, that's dark—E. Bunbun rushed Daniel Nibble Hop to the river, afraid he had been burned too. She hoped the water would save him and heal his burns, but he refused to listen to her and hopped away, leaving her and the destruction he'd created behind."

My breathing came in fast enough that this time Nellie noticed. Like being unable to turn away from a train wreck, Nellie continued reading, though her soft narration voice had vanished.

"E. Bunbun faced the cold alone. Daniel Nibble Hop had even taken the blanket she'd wrapped him in. She had nothing to protect the singed fur she'd endured saving Daniel Nibble Hop from the fire. There was nothing left for her. Her home, gone. All her family, gone. In the fading embers of everything she once loved, E. Bunbun prepared to die alone. She would die alone. She was going to die a—'"

I surged to my feet.

She would die alone.

She had to have written this after her diagnosis, substituting a make-believe fire in her story for our real-world argument.

She would die alone.

Elise's words continued slamming into my mind, rearranging everything. "Daniel?"

All my emotions jammed into my throat. The tiny space couldn't hold them all, and I swallowed painfully. When I spoke, my voice had to fight to get out.

"One night, before her divorce . . . way before her diagnosis, we had a fundamental difference in world views."

It was an odd way to discuss the fight we'd had, but it was how I'd referred to it afterwards. We'd never argued with each other like we had that night. We'd assumed our world views were perfectly aligned, because they always had been. The fight was as unexpected as it was fierce. And as damaging as it was painful.

Still struggling to speak, I said, "I'm sure you can guess it was about politics. Something so life-or-death in the moment. Neither of us even had the power to change anything about what we were arguing about, so, in the end it was, so . . . *pointless.*"

That small speech proved to be a marathon, wringing my lungs dry and desperate for oxygen. "I should have backed down. I didn't. After I stormed out, we didn't talk for almost two years."

At least, not out loud. But I'd argued with her in my head for months. I'd let my petty grievances keep me from reaching out. The fact that I'd heard about her divorce during that time, and still didn't reach out, stunned me.

What kind of horrible person did that?

I could have called, should have called, but didn't. I wasn't there to help her through the worst of her separation from Edward or help her pick up the pieces. If she hadn't called to tell me about her diagnosis and plead for help with tears in her voice, we might never have started talking again.

Elise had reached out first.

The thought still burned me. It should have been me. A million times over, it should have been me.

After I moved in to help her, I couldn't talk about the fight. Ever. I tried my best to make up for it and pretend it never happened. Elise did too, until the end.

Nellie called my name again, asking me what was wrong.

I didn't want to answer that question, but the emotions erupting in my throat demanded an outlet. Once the words started coming out, I couldn't stop them.

"Near the end, Elise tried to talk to me about the fight. She promised she wasn't mad, had forgiven me, but I—I couldn't talk about it. She tried over and over again to get me to talk to her, but I always said, 'We'll talk about it later.'"

My vision fuzzed, and I put a hand over my eyes. "She was dying, I knew she was, she knew she was, but I still said no. Maybe she needed to have that conversation with me. But I—"

Where was the air?

"—now this book—it shows she didn't forgive me: for the fight, for abandoning her, for needing to rely on me." I laughed so harshly I didn't recognize the sound of my own voice. "Maybe for all of it."

I must have tricked myself into thinking that maybe she had forgiven me. But even under that false assumption, I'd never been at peace. A dark shadow had fallen over every laugh we'd shared while I had cared for her. Cruel reminders that we could have been building those memories during the time we didn't talk after the fight, and that I'd never get that time back to spend with her.

And now, my guilt compounded with the knowledge laid bare in Elise's book about how she'd really felt about the fight. About me. And why not? I'd taken her brother away when she'd needed him the most.

I knew what pain I'd gone through at that time. Trying to understand what Elise must have felt meant taking my pain and multiplying that by a divorce, a fateful doctor's visit, and months of living alone with the knowledge that she had no family to support her.

It was impossible for me to fathom. I just couldn't. Like the wave behind me in Elise's picture, guilt pounded and spun me in its cycle without letting me break free for air.

"She didn't forgive me," I whispered.

Maybe I'd always secretly known. Maybe that's why I couldn't forgive myself. How could I, when she hadn't? This story proved how Elise had really felt and revealed thoughts she kept hidden from me.

It really was quite dizzying, the punch in the face about how much pain I'd caused her.

But, something in my mind argued, we really had shared so many good times during her last year, hadn't we? Even with the shadow of her death closing in on us? Wasn't that enough to erase my mistakes?

I stared at Elise's computer.

No. I guess it wasn't.

The rickety safety net I'd constructed with lies and false memories snapped, plunging me into a pit with no bottom.

What I'd told Charlie about needing time to heal wasn't true, though I hadn't realized it when I'd said it. Time couldn't heal the things fundamentally wrong with me. I'd tried burying my guilt with this scheme to get Elise published. Now my real intentions and all the truths I'd been hiding from lay uncovered, refusing to be ignored any longer.

A car horn blared. Nellie's ride.

She said something. I heard the uncertainty in her tone but couldn't understand any words.

I waved my hand and tried to look at her to assure her she could go, but my eyes only traveled to her stomach before dropping back to the floor. I turned toward the kitchen saying, "Meet up next week," or, "I'll call you tomorrow." Or maybe something else entirely.

I made my way around the corner, out of Nellie's sight and the stream of light coming in through the living room. She called after me. I managed an, "Mmmhmm," while I curled my hands into fists and placed them on the counter, leaning on them to keep my balance.

The front door opened and shut. Like the starter pistol of a race, everything burst out of the gates at once. My arms refused to hold the body weight that my legs had already given up on. My knees shook. I gasped lungsful of air but couldn't get all the oxygen I needed.

Dull pain sapped everything away, and my vision fused into blocks of dim color as I collapsed.

I had enough awareness to know that, at my current angle, my head was on track to crack against Elise's marble countertop. With what strength remained in my arms, I pushed away. From one bad angle to another.

My upper body twisted, popping my bad knee. Unlike the dull pain wrapping my mind like a mummy, fresh spikes of searing agony stabbed into my knee like I'd rolled it over a plank full of nails.

On the floor, contorted into a heap, both my hands reached for my knee, but the pain flared with lava heat, warning me away from touching it. Instead, I vice-gripped my calf in a futile effort to stop the piercing sensation. I screamed into my arm, tears already soaking into my sweatshirt.

Through a wall of pain, I heard persistent knocking at the front door. The duller ache around me tried to clamp my mouth shut, but the searing pain in my knee screamed for me to do something.

It took several gasps for me to be able to yell, "In here!"

The door opened, and Nellie called out, "Daniel?"

I tried to tell her where I was, but only croaked out a strangled sob.

I squinted against a sudden blaze of light from the can lights above me as I rocked back and forth, fueled by agony.

"Daniel." Nellie breathed. "What do . . . what can I . . ."

I managed to choke out, "My knee."

Then she was crouching beside me, one hand lightly on my shoulder, as if afraid to press harder. Her voice sounded steady and uncertain at the same time. "Should I call an ambulance? Or can you make it out to the car to go to the hospital?"

Not moving was the one thing both the dull and searing pain agreed on. And, thankfully, the searing pain had opened a few of the pathways in my mind the dull pain had shut down. If moving was out of the question, I needed another option.

"Medicine basket above the fridge," I gasped.

Elise's kitchen had floor-to-ceiling cabinets. In order to reach the one above the fridge, Nellie would need a chair. In her hurry, I heard her slam one into the fridge doors. A part of the chair's wooden frame audibly cracked but held as Nellie leaped onto it. Moments later she jumped off, basket in hand.

Before I could find the strength to even think about giving her more instructions, she was already rifling through the basket contents. I squeezed my eyes shut in a pitiful attempt at pain management. The pain ruled inside, not out. Closing my eyes wouldn't keep it away.

Nellie's hand brushed my shoulder. "This one?" she asked breathlessly.

Peeking one eye open, I squinted at the prescription bottle with my name on it that Nellie was holding up to my face. The last time I'd hurt my knee the doctor had prescribed painkillers, but in small doses. I'd saved the last one should something happen, and I needed it to tide me over until I got to the hospital. Or, in this case, if I wanted to avoid the hospital altogether.

I nodded, and Nellie jumped to her feet. She opened and slammed cupboard door after cupboard door until she found the one with the glasses. After running one under the sink, she skidded back to my side, placing a glass with water dripping over the sides beside me. She screwed the cap off the bottle and handed me the remaining painkiller before holding my head as I struggled to wash the pill down. Though I hadn't moved much, the action drained me.

I tried to scrape up enough embarrassment of crying in front of Nellie to stop. I couldn't. I tried forcing the pains away; somehow, that only strengthened both of them. Within moments, I couldn't control the sobbing or shaking.

"Are you sure I can't get you to the hospital?" Nellie pleaded.

I shook my head and spoke through shivering lips and clenched teeth. "Need fifteen minutes . . ."

It might take up to thirty for the medicine to work its magic, if at all. I was fairly certain it had expired but didn't have the capacity to remember dates at the moment. A hospital could only help with my external pain anyway. I just wanted to stay where I was until everything went away.

I squeezed my eyes shut again as I shook. I heard Nellie get up and leave the kitchen. My dull pain hoped she'd left for good, but the searing pain prayed she hadn't.

The squeak of Nellie's loafers against the tiled floor told me she'd come back. And she hadn't come alone. A soft weight fell across me. I slit one eye open to see Nellie arranging a blanket over me. Then she sat with a couch pillow on her lap and, with care, placed my head on it as she scooted under it.

The sobbing continued. The shaking continued. But, eventually, the battle within me turned in favor of the dull pain. It began its work again of shutting everything down. Whenever I chanced to look around, blocks of color dissolved into gray. Nellie's hands on my shoulder added to the warmth spreading throughout my skin, easing my muscles and quenching the fire radiating from my knee.

I couldn't tell if the gentle rocking I felt originated from me or Nellie, but the humming was definitely coming from her. I didn't recognize the tune and didn't care. I let it carry me through a muted haze as my chest slowed, turning my rasps into rhythmic rumbling.

Gray turned into charcoal and, mercifully, to black.

Chapter 9

NOTHING ABOUT WAKING UP FELT natural. From my weighted eyelids to a fuzzy throat, everything fought the attacking awareness. But whatever woke me acted like a barrier between my mind and sleep.

I blinked to find myself lying on my side, staring eye-level at the threads of Elise's Moroccan rug under the kitchen table. Cutting whiffs of lemon-scented floor cleaner crawled up my nose to aggravate a headache building with every tick of the grandfather clock in the living room.

Groaning, I managed to wrestle my arm around so I could position my wrist in front of my face. Once my blurry vision focused, the time jolted me into squinting consciousness. I'd been out for almost five hours.

The spikes of pain in my knee had dulled to throbbing. Unpleasant, but not a reason for waking up. What was it? There, a spot of intense cold. Glancing down the length of my body, I saw a bag of ice wrapped inside a kitchen towel on top of my knee. The bag must not be closed all the way and ice water was leaking out, soaking through my sweatpants.

I didn't remember getting the bag. I reached for it, and a blanket slipped off my shoulders and onto the tile. The blanket . . . the blanket I remembered. Nellie had brought it in. I brushed the fuzzy woven strands with my fingers as the events of the night played out in reverse through my head, stopping at hearing Nellie read Elise's story about dying alone.

I lurched into a sitting position and would have continued to try standing if my knee hadn't shot a flare of warning into my mind. I ran a hand over my face, still trying to orient myself. I shoved my back against a cabinet and looked down when paper crumbled under my palm. On the floor next to me was a note that read, "If you wake up before I get back, CALL ME," with three underlines under the words "CALL ME" for emphasis. Next to the paper was my phone.

I'd been out for hours with no idea of when Nellie had left. The slow trickle of melting ice from the bag she'd created at some point suggested it hadn't been too long ago.

Nellie had also found my knee brace and put it next to me. Probably in case I woke up and needed it. Her actions, the blanket, the ice pack, the brace, the note, my phone—all of it didn't add up. Nellie now knew what kind of person I really was. Why would she want to help? I certainly couldn't stand me, so how could anyone else?

I threaded my thoughts carefully. Like trying to break away from a rubber band, if I pushed too hard too fast, I'd be flung back into the memory of the fight Elise and I had. I grabbed the bag of ice and put it to my head, hoping the cold would provide a needed distraction.

I gripped it too tightly. The sandwich bag split open, splashing melting ice water over me and skittering still-frozen particles across the floor. Sighing, I flopped my arm against the cabinet door next to me, finally catching it by the edge and opening it. I pulled out the garbage can inside to throw away the sandwich bag but stopped. The can was overflowing at the top with crumpled paper towels.

Searching through my memory of the night's events again, I couldn't remember putting them there. I pawed through them, finding black streaks across them almost like someone had used them to check the oil in their car. I brought one closer to my face to inspect it. I sniffed, nothing. I rubbed the black streak with my thumb. It took a while to place it, but a memory of helping Elise clean her bathroom when her strength was failing brought the answer to my mind.

The smears were mascara and eyeliner.

However long Nellie had stayed with me, at some point, she'd reached onto the counter without waking me to grab the paper-towel roll. Then she sat and cried for quite a long length of time, if the number of paper towels in the garbage were any indication. From the looks of it, she'd cried all her mascara off and kept going, since, unlike her makeup, her tears weren't a finite resource. She cried silently and alone just to keep from waking me up.

On their own, the pain from Elise's story and my knee injury had dug a hole of grief and dropped me at the bottom. Now, knowing I'd caused Nellie extra pain, I felt like boulders were slamming on top of the hole, making sure I could never get out.

Wincing, I brought my non-injured knee to my chest and placed my arms on it to rest my forehead against. I found no relief or explanation. Why would

Nellie do this? She had to have figured out I was only trying to alleviate my own guilt by publishing Elise's books.

Nellie was all about family. She'd probably had to ask her sister to leave her here when she'd come back and found me in the kitchen, and then had to call her again to ask that she come pick her up and take her wherever she'd gone. That sister had rearranged her night twice to accommodate Nellie. Sacrificing for her sister.

Contrast that with what I'd done to the only sister I had. The same sister I'd caused to throw away her cherished childhood stuffed bunnies. They'd survived her going to college, entering adulthood, and getting married. My association with them, what she must have thought when she looked at them, had broken her nostalgic need for them. Because of me, they brought her more pain than joy, so she'd thrown them away, and that's why I couldn't find them.

I'd caused Elise pain, and now I was doing it to Nellie.

My forehead pushed so hard against my arms that my heel had to dig into the rug to prevent me from falling forward.

And Nellie hadn't wanted me to meet her family. Every attempt was rebuffed. There was something about me she'd figured out; I was a bad brother. But then, why go out with me? It didn't make sense. Had I pressured her?

My head popped up. Had I abused our relationship with our power dynamic? I was technically her client. I paid her. Had that been it? Had she cried because of the horrible position I'd put her in? Now that she knew who I really was?

Nothing made sense. But it didn't matter. Even if everything was screwed upside-down and sideways. Even if Nellie really did care, which seemed more and more unlikely given her love of family and sisters, this couldn't work. If my own sister couldn't forgive me, I couldn't expect anyone else to.

I was a husk of a brother, choosing selfish self-guided principles over a simple phone call. A simple text. A simple care. I hadn't managed any of that. Nellie wouldn't want to date someone like that. I wouldn't *want* Nellie to date someone like that.

And Elise was just . . . gone.

Gone like the tradition of watching home videos while preparing and eating our mom's favorite dish, pierogies, on the anniversary of our parents' death.

Gone like all our adventures.

All gone.

Because I'd gotten mad one time and stepped out of Elise's life.

Elise, who knew me better than anyone, thought I'd leave her to die alone. The fact that I ultimately hadn't didn't matter. The knowledge that Elise had lived with that belief for any amount of time clawed grief across my chest, hollowing out any joy and leaving the remnants of the brother I'd turned out to be.

No, Nellie wouldn't want any part of someone like that.

I glanced back at Nellie's note, eyebrows drawing together as I reread, "If you read this before I get back—"

Nellie was coming back.

No. Not now. No.

Risking injury to my knee, I lurched forward to grab my phone off the floor. I couldn't see her. I'd be seeing myself through her eyes. I dialed Nellie's number to tell her not to come before remembering after one ring that I didn't want to talk to her. I should have texted instead.

I pulled the phone away from my ear and was preparing to hang up when Nellie's tiny voice sounded from the receiver. "Daniel?"

She must have been holding her phone at the ready, waiting in case I called. Before I could say anything, she launched into a hurried explanation. "I'm so sorry I left, but I couldn't find any Tylenol and thought you might need some when you woke up because there wasn't any medication left in the basket, so I called Sarah to come pick me up because Jenna has an early-morning appointment. Anyway, we're hurrying in case your medicine wore off, and like I said, there wasn't any Tylenol—"

I tried to cut her off, to tell her the Tylenol was in the upstairs bathroom, and she didn't need to come back, but she spoke right over me.

"—or do you need something else because you may not be able to combine Tylenol with the medication you took . . ." Nellie paused for her first breath in this conversation.

I opened my mouth and instead of assuring her I had additional medicine in the house, I asked, "How did Luis die?"

The silence coming over the phone hung more pronounced in the absence of Nellie's rambling.

"Nellie, did he die in a car wreck?"

It wasn't what I'd expected to say. It also wasn't something I could say I'd ever thought of, at least not in my working brain. But my subconscious had apparently been at work while I was asleep and, planning more punishment for me, had pieced the rather obvious clues together. The fact that Nellie never drove, or drank, or her reaction at the possibility of Charlie and Willow driving home after one too many. She'd never made her decision not to drink obvious, or passed judgement on me, or anyone else, when we had. Something that made my blindness to her actions even more damning.

"Uh," Nellie said in a quiet voice before hesitating. "Yes."

"Were you driving?"

". . . Yes."

"Had someone been drinking?"

"The driver who hit us."

The final boulder fell, burying me completely in the hole my own pain had dug for me. In vivid recollection, I remembered every time I'd teased her about not driving. I'd even done it tonight by recommending go-cart racing. Offering to teach Nellie to drive a few weeks ago was even worse. Or maybe the worst was drinking at Edward's party right in front of her.

"I've been a jerk—"

"Listen," Nellie said in a tone I hadn't heard before. Angry? Upset? No. Commanding. "I never told you that. You couldn't have known. Anything you've ever said in reference to my not driving has been in good humor. Just like you never knew what Elise had written about in the story you found in her trash folder. It wasn't your fault. She never meant for you to read it. Daniel, she deleted it for a reason."

Where Elise had chosen to put the representation of her pain wasn't the point. The point was that I'd caused it.

I shook my head even though Nellie couldn't see it.

"We're almost back," she said. "Hang tight for a few more minutes."

I snatched my brace and hopped into a standing position on my good leg. Trapping my phone between my neck and shoulder, I struggled to wrap and secure the brace around my bad knee. "No. Just don't worry."

"No, Daniel, I promise, we're almost there."

"I'm sorry. It's my fault. I need to go—"

"—hang on! Please don't—"

"No, this is my fault. It's okay! I need to go."

"Daniel, please!"

I hung up. Nellie was coming. How much time? She said minutes. I needed to leave. Where? It didn't matter. Seconds ticked by, aggravating my indecision.

Keys. I needed keys. Bad knee was the left knee. I could still drive; I only needed to use my right.

Hobbling into the foyer, I grabbed my keys and made my way back through the living room. My eyes met with the uncovered sampler Elise had hung on the wall a month before she'd died. *Be kind and compassionate to one another, forgiving each other—*

I picked up the stack of chapters and hurled it across the room before I'd fully formulated the thought to do so. Pages flew off in a storm, but the main heft of the stack smacked into a corner of the frame, knocking it off the nail that secured it to the wall. The sampler crashed onto the floor. The carpet wasn't enough to cushion the impact, and several shards of glass cracked and broke out of the frame.

Elise's laptop still lay on the couch, an accusatory monument of evidence against me. On a sudden impulse to throw it into the Hudson, I grabbed it and burst through the kitchen and out the back door, skip-hopping to minimize the amount of weight on my knee. I crossed the driveway with the determination of a man trying to make it to a lake before dying of dehydration.

As I yanked my car door open to collapse onto the driver's seat, I remembered you shouldn't drive while on pain pills. But the effect had worn off, and I felt wide-awake. Painfully so. My knee wasn't good, but the muted pulses of fire shooting out from it shouldn't impede my driving.

I hoped my squealing tires didn't wake up my neighbors at near midnight on a Friday. If they did, well, they were the last of my worries. I needed to go somewhere. Where?

A hotel? I'd remembered my keys but not my wallet. If I went back to the house for it now, I might run into Nellie. I needed another option.

Charlie? No, he had a teething kid who had trouble sleeping.

I slapped my hand on the steering wheel and clenched it to keep my palm from smarting. I turned down another street, desperately trying to jump-start an idea of where to go. Propping my arm against the window as I drove out of Elise's neighborhood, I clenched my hair into a fist. Where could I go? A memory of Edward offering his place played through my head. Had the offer been serious?

No. NO. The word pressed through my mind to imprint on my impaired decision-making process. I didn't trust Edward.

But . . . a snake of a memory slithered into consideration . . . Edward usually went on international business trips over the weekend. Especially at the beginning of the month. I rejected a call from Nellie and tried to squeeze an answer to my dilemma out of the steering wheel.

I could call Edward. If he didn't answer, he was probably asleep and therefore at home. If he didn't pick up after four rings, I'd hang up. But if he answered, it was more than likely he was in another time zone and not at his apartment.

This could work. I rejected yet another call from Nellie and felt my heart twist.

I moved forward with my plan, with one amendment; I'd made a mistake in calling Nellie instead of texting her. Not wanting to make any more huge errors in judgment, I used my car to text Edward instead of calling.

Are you up?

If he didn't respond soon, I'd have to drive to Bob's Market to find a place to park and sleep. But trying to curl up in the cramped back seat wasn't an action my knee recommended.

A call from Edward blared through my speakers, causing me to strain against my seatbelt in surprise. Of course Edward wouldn't make this easy by texting me back.

I answered and immediately apologized. "Sorry. Were you asleep?"

Edward's voice didn't have any traces of midnight exhaustion to it. "No. I'm at the office. We're having a conference call with our branch in Tokyo." Right. Stupid virtual conferencing.

"And you . . . called me back?" In the middle of a no doubt high-end business call at work?

"We're having a break." Edward played off the excuse like it was no big deal. "I'm actually flying out in a few hours. I was—"

I forgot myself and sighed in relief loud enough to interrupt Edward. "Sorry. Go ahead."

"—planning on leaving the office once we're through with this call. What's going on?"

"Were you, you know, serious . . . um, before?" I continued strangling the steering wheel to squeeze the words out. "About me crashing at your place?"

Even though that was, in fact, the reason I'd called, a part of me hadn't wanted the conversation to come around to this. I hit *Ignore* on the third call attempt from Nellie and swallowed painfully.

"You need somewhere to stay?"

I briefly squeezed my eyes shut, as though that would help, and admitted, "Yes."

Nonplussed and as calm as I was wound up, Edward said, "I'm sending you the address to my new apartment. Don't think you've ever been there. Did you get it?"

My phone pinged. "Yeah. Yeah," I clarified twice for no reason, just wanting this conversation to end.

"I'll also send you the code to get in our parking garage. Park in my spot."

"Won't you need it?" I asked, then remembered he'd just told me he was flying out after his meeting.

"The place is yours for a few days if you need it. No parties though. Right?"

"Ah, no."

"I'll let the doorman know to let you up to my floor. His name is John. Nice guy. If you need anything while I'm gone, he can get it for you." Muffled voices called Edward's name. "I gotta go. Talk soon?"

"Yeah, sur—"

The connection clicked. I stared through the windshield at the varying paths the orange streetlights led to. It took several blocks of mindlessly meandering before I navigated to Edward's new apartment. Traffic increased the more I drove into the city, but it still felt like I arrived at the parking garage sooner than expected. I found the stall with Edward's apartment number and turned off my car.

Without my headlight shining on it, the dark concrete wall in front of my car glowered back at me. Cold. Impassive.

Judging.

I broke down again. On the road with other cars surrounding me, and the thought of seeing a security guard at the garage check-in, corralled my emotions behind a mental gate. However, there was a quiet power in secluded spaces. They promised to guard against the world, letting me reclaim the energy I was using to shield myself. But when I gave into that promise and lowered my defenses, all the feelings I was running from swarmed back in.

Fifteen minutes later, I remembered I still had to talk to John, the doorman in the lobby, to be let up to the floor where Edward's apartment looked down on everything. My head hit the back of the seat rest, and I gave up. I didn't even glance in the rearview mirror to assess what I must look like. Though it had to include crumpled sweatshirt and pants, a splotchy forehead, red eyes and nose, wild hair, and rubbed-raw cheeks.

Grabbing Elise's computer off the front seat, I dragged myself to the elevator. The buttons sat blankly until I remembered to push L for lobby and stepped out to meet John the doorman.

The white hair growing out of John the doorman's ears gave him the grace of a great-grandfather. He didn't bat an eye at me or my appearance as he ushered me into the correct elevator with a nod, and keyed in acceptance for Edward's floor. It could be that I wasn't the worst thing he'd seen come through his polished and shiny lobby that week. Or maybe even that night. Other than a raised eyebrow at my knee brace and favoring of my good leg, he treated me with the polite, distant courtesy he probably used for everyone else in the building.

I lurched into awareness when the elevator arrived on the correct floor. Stepping out, I peered down both ends of the hallway. It wasn't difficult to locate Edward's door, so few were on this floor. But standing outside it, I didn't remember any plan for getting inside.

I scrolled through Edward's texts again when the lock on his door clicked and opened an inch. For a second, I scanned the door frame for a sensor or camera, but decided I didn't care and gave up, letting myself inside.

I leaned against the door to close it and rubbed my face. I would have continued, but the raw pain receptors in my cheeks demanded a cease and desist. A few lights had automatically turned on once I'd entered, though most of the modern wood paneling that covered the walls remained in brown shadows.

If I wasn't careful, this place might become another secluded nightmare.

My phone buzzed. Nellie again. My heart wasn't handling this well, and my thumb hovered over the accept button, but swiped to dismiss the call. I stuffed the phone away and wiped my eyes to look around.

A single piece of oak carved into a side table stood next to the front door. A vibrant purple scarf with lots of curlicue designs lay pooled next to a marble bowl where Edward probably kept his keys when he was home. I stared. It had to belong to Shanna. Or what was her name? Shayla. The girl that jerk, William, had told me about at Edward's party. The one he was seriously dating.

My fear of being in a secluded space switched to being in a place where I wasn't alone.

"Hello?" I called.

The ambient lighting directed by an automatic computer program didn't reveal any supporting evidence that anyone else was in Edward's apartment. Or that someone even lived here. The spartan wood with elements of stone design complimented Edward's style. From the hallway, I peeked inside what must be his room, but no one lay on the bed or was in the open door to his ensuite bathroom.

I was alone. If Nellie had called in that moment, I might have answered.

I passed through Edward's kitchen, where the scent of wood polish permeated the air, and back toward the other room with a bed. The guest room. No doubt sheets with a higher thread count than I'd ever slept on lay under the perfectly angled black duvet. Depositing my phone and Elise's computer on it, I noticed the room had its own entrance to a balcony that wrapped in an L shape around the entirety of Edward's apartment. It might even offer a beautiful view. Instead of investigating though, I homed in on the attached bathroom and splashed my face with cold water from the sink, letting the cold both sting and soothe my skin.

A muffled buzz rang from the bed. I dabbed my face on a towel and hobbled toward the sound. I needed to turn off my phone. Between leaving the house and driving to Edward's, the caller ID must have logged at least twenty missed calls from Nellie, and I couldn't keep doing this.

This caller ID read *Edward*. I swayed uneasily, but obligation forced me to answer. Before I could say hello, Edward asked, "Are you on drugs?"

What? Had John called him from the lobby?

Edward stomped on that theory. "My doorbell cam pinged my phone when you got to the apartment door so I could let you in. You look terrible. Are you on drugs?"

"No!" Wait . . . *oh shoot.* "Well, technically, yes. But they were prescribed." I sank onto the edge of the bed. "I hurt my knee."

"Oh." Edward sounded relieved. "There is something you can take in the cabinet in the guest bathroom." I wouldn't be surprised if Edward had it stocked with other "prescribed" painkillers.

He hung up again before I could say thank you or goodbye. Or *What is going on with you?*

I returned to the bathroom to search through the cabinet behind the mirror, honestly surprised when I discovered a bottle of extra-strength Tylenol instead of black-market prescriptions. Using my hand to scoop water from the faucet, I forced one pill down, figuring I could take a second if the pain kept me from sleeping.

Instead of returning to the bedroom, I placed both hands on the slick, cool black marble sink to steady myself. I had to make some decisions. Logging onto work in the morning was out of the question. I'd need to call my boss. I hadn't taken a single day off this year, and no big meetings were scheduled. Missing work would be fine.

However, work wasn't the real issue I needed to address.

I would need to talk to Nellie.

No, not talk, I corrected myself. Text.

I needed to find some way to explain the contest was off. This experiment of buying forgiveness by getting Elise published had crashed and burned. I needed Nellie to heal and the only way for that to happen was if she was away from me and everything I'd done. An image of a garbage can full of mascara-stained paper towels blasted behind my eyes, making me cringe like I'd stared directly at the sun.

As for the rest of my life, things weren't looking good. The pain in my knee would go away, but my chest sunk under the weight of a four-hundred-pound grief-bear. I couldn't poke it or move it and would have to find a way every day to function under its weight. I would have to be careful. One wrong move and it might crush me.

And Edward? At least I had good news that he would be out for a few days. The unsettling feeling that started creeping through my mind when I'd walked in the front door finally forced me to focus on it. I'd made a mistake coming here. Maybe the worst case of brain delay I'd ever had. Now that a modicum of logic had returned, it started an autoloop of everything odd Edward had done, beginning with the evening he'd surprised Nellie and me by showing up at Elise's home with an unplanned dinner.

I'd make several mistakes tonight, but at least I wouldn't have to worry about this one. In the morning, I'd put together a plan for what to say to Nellie and be out of Edward's apartment by lunch.

I unstrapped my brace and let it drop to the floor as I made my way to the bed. The bathroom light cancelled itself as I shut the door and flopped on the duvet. I thought about getting back up so I could climb in between the sheets, but that would require . . . getting back up.

But as tired as I was, I couldn't seem to get my brain to flip the switch from dulling exhaustion to shutoff. Mascara-stained towels kept running through my thoughts. I tossed around until I started to drift. Then I heard the front door open and close.

My eyes opened with an almost-audible snap.

Maybe Edward had forgotten to pack something for his trip? Passport or company takeover documents? I flung an arm over my eyes, hoping I could make it back to the promise of sleep when Edward left.

A moment later, there was a soft knock on my door. "Daniel," Edward called in a hushed voice. "Are you awake?"

I left my arm where it was and didn't make a noise so Edward would go away. Seconds passed.

A loud thumping caused me to jerk my arm away and stare wide-eyed at the black ceiling. I turned toward the door and saw a lined rectangle of illumination around its edges from the hall light.

"Daniel!" Edward called again, though this time he shouted. "Are you awake!"

No pretending I didn't hear or slept through that.

Somewhere between a groan and a shout, I confirmed, "Yes!"

"Good!" Edward didn't sound at all like someone who'd just woken up an invited guest. "Come out and let's talk."

Everything inside me felt raw, allowing a sudden conviction to hit me bone deep. The motivation for Edward's odd behavior over the past few weeks? It had to be revenge.

Elise had never told me what she and Edward had discussed the night he came to see her at the hospital before she'd died. They'd sent me down to the cafeteria. She must have told him something about me, maybe even read her story to him. As arrogant and condescending as Edward could be, his love for Elise, even after their divorce, was never in doubt.

He'd known all along the truth that had slapped me sideways tonight. I was a bad brother.

Maybe I'd reached the level where I couldn't feel any more guilt. This new revelation about Edward only produced twisted anger. I didn't owe him anything. I shouldn't have to talk to him before trying to make amends with Nellie, someone I had actually hurt.

Just a minute earlier, I would have contorted myself through any excuse not to talk to him.

But now . . .

If Edward wanted to talk, fine. So long as I could talk back.

I stood and limped to the door, before opening it and stepping into the hallway without a second thought to follow Edward into the kitchen.

Chapter 10

I DIDN'T KNOW HOW IT would start, but I was prepared for a fight. Entering the kitchen, I challenged Edward's back as he dug through the refrigerator. "I thought you had a flight in a few hours."

The seams along Edward's tan and tailored sports jacket flexed as he continued to rummage. "You're correct. In. A. Few. Hours," he repeated. "Not this very second. And it doesn't take long to go through security at a private airport. Thought we could chat first."

Making a selection, Edward closed the fridge door and screwed off the top of a glass beer bottle. I didn't recognize the logo. Probably imported. Edward sampled a sip and gagged to keep from spitting it out when he turned and saw me.

Swallowing with a grimace, Edward pointed at my chest, his blue eyes seeming to channel electricity. "Where did you get that?"

I glanced down at the Yale emblazoned sweatshirt I was wearing. I'd been in such a hurry to leave Elise's house I didn't remember I had it on.

I raised my eyes in an unspoken question. Any glance around his apartment would confirm Edward didn't care about "things." I doubted any piece of clothing in his closet dated older than a year. As gratifying as it was to know I was right to hide the fact that I had it, I still didn't know why he would care about this.

Edward continued to study the sweatshirt as he took another suffering sip from the long-stemmed bottle. He must have had the same thought, because he said, "Doesn't make sense, does it?" He chuckled, the smile regaining his composure. "The only professor who ever meant anything to me gave me that the day I graduated."

He didn't elaborate, but the way his face relaxed in that short story of a sentence . . . the sweatshirt had sentimental meaning to him. It was possible. Though he didn't display and surround himself with things the way Elise had, he still had a place in his heart to store them. Maybe that's why they fell for each other in the first place. What two bizarre thoughts.

Stymied, I searched for something to say. I'd come prepared to fight, but I'd been put on the defensive, which was wobbly and annoying. I didn't know how to answer without implicating Elise, who must have taken it from Edward without permission before giving it to me.

Edward smirked. First at the sweatshirt, then at his beer as he endured another sip. "I knew she had it. I just knew it." His tone was a tonic mixture of smugness and . . . victory?

Before drinking anymore, Edward placed the bottle on the giant marble slab of a kitchen island between us. "Don't know why they keep sending me cases of this stuff from Germany. I don't really like it." He turned to rummage through the fridge's blue-lit interior again.

Unsure why Edward no longer cared to talk about the sweatshirt, or ask for it back, I played with the idea of leaving. I wanted answers, but maybe I wouldn't need them if I walked out the door. I could. I could do that. But I wouldn't.

"What's going on?" I demanded.

Edward turned around and shut the fridge before giving me his full attention. "I need to ask *you* that. Look at you."

"You 'need' to ask?"

Edward sighed and pinched the bridge of his nose with the air of a man with too many self-imposed duties. "I don't like owing people, Daniel. It doesn't sit right. What's worse, though, is feeling like I've let someone down, especially Elise."

"How did you let Elise down?"

"You. Because of you."

Here we go. His play to find some way of punishing me. Whether by finding a way to take back the money Elise had left me or hiring an investigator to find dirt on me.

I had to lean against the counter with one hip to take the weight off my knee. Afraid the gesture appeared weak, I compensated by straightening my back and folding my arms. Edward may be taller and have the moral high ground, but I wouldn't back down.

"How did I help you let Elise down?"

Edward leaned against the counter behind him and matched my folded-arms stance. "Elise asked me to take care of you."

He was framing his plan like a cheesy mob threat? I ground my teeth, annoyed. Annoyed that Edward was playing with me, annoyed at his styled hair, annoyed his perfect apartment. At *everything* about him.

"And taking back the money Elise got from you in the divorce is how you were planning to 'take care of me'?"

Edward jerked his head back and stiffened. "You think I need that money back?" He snorted. "I'm guessing her lawyer told you the same thing mine told me. The amount she got out of the divorce was paltry to what she could have asked for. And got." He choked a laugh out through his teeth and stared with incredulity. "You really think I need the money?"

"I . . . don't . . ." Uncertainty chilled my skin, and my voice rose to shore up my weakening accusation. "No, you don't *need* the money. You just don't want me to have it."

In my head, it presented a solid argument. Saying it out loud to the object of my annoyance, only to have him look at me like I was a fool, lessened its impact.

Edward blinked. When his facial expression didn't change, he blinked again, looking like he was trying to simultaneously calm down and understand what he obviously thought was an asinine argument. Edward reached across the marble island to retrieve the discarded beer, the woven cashmere threads of his sleeve hissing as they made contact with the surface. Regardless of his disregard for the taste, he chugged several swallows before sliding the bottle away again.

Edward's mouth twisted as he tilted his head to the side, still looking for calm. The action confused me, and I struggled to keep the emotion off my face, which was hard to do when primed for an argument. Why calm himself? Why not throw every accusation at me he'd been holding inside now that he'd admitted to his plan to "take care of me"?

Edward narrowed his eyes, more discerning than angry, and faced me. "I didn't mean 'take care of you' in that way. I meant it in the usual, human way of wanting to take care of someone." Edward flicked his eyes away and scoffed. "What is going on with you? Did you really know Elise? You seem to jump to conclusions that don't match the woman I knew. I tell you Elise wanted me to take care of you, and your immediate response is, why did we collude to take away the money she voluntarily left you? Of her own free will?"

"I thought I knew her. But she—" Even as I tried to complete my thought, what Edward had said smashed into my argument with breathtaking speed. Elise would never do that to me.

I should never have even come here, not with my thoughts tied up in knots that led nowhere and bouncing around my head, making it difficult to form any retort.

Edward stopped to take a breath before continuing with obvious forced calm. "Do you understand what I'm trying to say?" His eyes forced truth into my stubborn skull. "Elise asked me to take care of you, and I . . . I failed by taking so long to come see you at her house. I didn't know it would take that long before I could bring myself to see her house, her stuff, all there without her—"

Edward paused, sudden grief in his voice. With the night I'd had, Edward's reaction hit with the force of a physical shove. I needed to sit.

My hand sideswiped until it connected with the metal backing of a bar stool. I eased onto it, trying not to slide off the wood top so glossy it might have been polished with the same product Edward used on his hair.

Edward continued, "I had to wait until I was ready, right? Isn't that what stewardesses say on airplanes? Been a bit since I've flown commercial, but make sure your oxygen mask is securely in place before you try to help someone else, right?"

I swallowed, but my throat stayed dry. "Elise wanted to make sure I was okay?"

Edward nodded, even though I'd only repeated back what he'd said. Somehow aware of how my brain delay was attempting a hostile takeover of my cognitive abilities, Edward hesitated before saying, "It would have been so much easier if, when I'd come to see you, you were fine. You're clearly not okay." Edward's natural smirk broke through his forced calm. "You're putting me through a lot of hassle. I don't know how to help you. I keep trying, but you shoot down every attempt. Instead, you're holed up at your house, ordering Thai food that you don't eat. Don't deny it."

I hadn't tried to. Edward wasn't giving me a chance to talk. Better to blame this conversation on that instead of the fact that the words needed to form sentences weren't lining up in the correct order in my brain.

"Elise stopped ordering Thai food after we got married. I let her because I hated the smell so much. Do you know how petty that is? I could be wrong; maybe you do place two orders and really eat all that food. But I'm not wrong, am I? I'll take your silence as a yes. You're struggling to move on, and that makes keeping my promise to Elise harder."

Like buoys, happy memories of ordering Thai food with Elise tried bobbing to the surface of my tangled thoughts. She always ordered the pad thai and made me get something different or new every week so she could try it. Maybe that's why I didn't have a standard favorite dish. The experience with her was my favorite.

Edward sighed. "You know she's gone, but you can't let her go. I'm guessing other than keeping up her house and paying to get her books published, you haven't spent any of her money."

"I bought a suit!" I said.

That was when my mind decided it could speak again? To say I'd bought a suit to try to look good for my date with Nellie? And it wasn't even accurate. I'd bought it with my Christmas bonus. I'd just wanted to counter Edward in some way, to stop this onslaught of annoying truths so I could have time to process them.

"A suit?" Edward repeated. A slow smile came to his lips. He may have been annoyed I'd poked a hole in his theory, albeit a very tiny hole, but he was also pleased. "So, you went out with Nellie again? I had high hopes for her after seeing you together. My life right now would be so much easier if you were okay. Tell me you're still dating. That you haven't screwed anything up."

The thought that I may have really screwed things up with Nellie plunged my internal temperature from chilly to freezing. I stared at my hands and didn't answer while grief and annoyance argued over who got to steer me.

Edward thumped the island with a fist. "Oh no. You messed things up, didn't you?"

Annoyance grabbed the wheel. "I don't have to tell you."

I tumbled off the stool, intending to leave. But my knee vetoed the plan to storm out. And by vetoed, I meant sending lines of fire down my leg. Stumbling, I grabbed the edge of the island with both hands to hold myself up and hissed.

Other than having to suck breath between my teeth for the pain, the next few moments were blissfully quiet.

Edward finally asked, "You all right?" All of his supposed arrogance and suspicion was gone. He sounded genuinely concerned. I had no idea how to react.

"I really did wrench my knee," I said, barely glancing up.

Edward started to slide his unfinished beer my way, then stopped. "You said you took some prescribed painkillers tonight?"

I nodded.

"That's not gonna mix well." Edward kicked open a cabinet door and tossed the beer into the trash with a thud, then returned to the fridge to grab a glass bottle of water. No cheap plastics here. It curved in an arch as it sailed across the kitchen island toward me. I caught it and slid back onto the stool.

In the next few moments of silence, we mentally retreated to our own corners. While I unscrewed the bottle and took a long drink, Edward studied the island's surface, probably planning his next move. Hopefully it involved the realization that pointing out painful truths wasn't likely to put me on the path to "okay." But I didn't think Edward knew how to fix a problem without pointing out everything you did wrong first.

In the silence, I tried to work out what he'd already said. If it was true, it would explain why he'd only attended Elise's funeral for a few minutes before leaving without talking to me—he was just as racked with grief as I was—and why it'd taken him months to be able to come check on me. Instead of telling me what he was up to, he'd brought dinner and left abruptly when he'd discovered Elise's weekly order of pad thai that I couldn't bring myself to cancel. Confounded by the fact that I wasn't okay and that he would have to do some actual work, he'd fled.

So far, everything about that checked out.

Then he'd invited me to a party as an excuse to try to get me a higher-paying job. He'd probably mistook my decision to stay at my current position as proof of more self-punishment instead of loyalty to my employers. And he'd been so afraid of furthering what he saw as my backsliding that he, a man who commanded boardrooms and workforces, schemed to make sure I never learned about Shayla. That the thought of him dating someone, and thereby moving on from my sister, might shatter me.

So . . .

Edward cared? Not just in words, but apparently in actions.

That was a lot of work, or half-hearted attempts, for someone I'd always considered to be an "extravagance to inconvenience you." His actions were taking my perception of my ex-brother-in-law and warping them into an attribute I wasn't used to seeing from him.

Compassion.

But Edward didn't know me. He never had. He was doing this all for Elise. Which meant he was telling the truth. That maybe Elise hadn't secretly hated me. But I'd read her book. She hadn't forgiven me.

Counterpoint, my mind argued, Edward's actions would seem completely whack job if they weren't so relatable. Elise's death had cut him so deeply it'd taken months for him to put himself together to carry out his promise to her. Something else I could readily believe.

Edward turned toward a wall of the kitchen where a massive glass cabinet stretched from counter to ceiling. Amber lights lit up each shelf, making the various bottles of size and color glow. Opening one door, Edward selected one that had to be worth a monthly house payment. He grabbed a glass and sloshed himself an inch worth of liquid into the bottom.

Edward took a sip and cleared his throat like he had a theory he was nervous to test out. "Do you remember the time I came to see Elise in the hospital?" Edward asked. "'Course you do. It was the only time I came to see her after her diagnosis."

There was no reason to lie. "Yeah. You came as soon as she called you from the hospital room."

"Don't make it sound heroic." Edward took another sip and sucked on his bottom lip. "It was actually the second time she'd called me, asking for help. The first was a few days after her diagnosis. She'd been processing the news and knew she'd need help."

Edward fiddled with the glass, his fingers shaking so bad I thought he might drop the crystal. "I couldn't do it. That's when she called you. You were the one who came the first time she called. You did, not me. I could only come the second time she called. Even then, I only managed to stay a few minutes. I wanted to stay longer. But seeing her like that . . ."

Edward's grip tightened, and he drained the glass, as if he wanted to use the excuse of the alcohol hitting the back of his throat to explain the new rasp in his voice. "She knew you would struggle. That you were struggling, and that it would likely get worse once she was gone. She asked if I could help. Could I do that? I told her I could. 'Course," Edward added with a small smile, "it's a good thing she didn't specify a timeframe, since it took all those months to pick myself up to come see you."

More details of that night became clear. Sitting in the hospital's cafeteria while Edward and Elise spoke up in her room. Eating out of the vending machine since the food services had shut down. I'd chosen a packaged cinnamon roll that lasted all of two bites before I threw its cardboard contents in a stained trash can. I'd worried what Elise would be like when I got back to her room. But she'd smiled, so relaxed she'd fallen asleep within minutes of my reading the next chapter of her favorite book aloud.

"Why did you promise her?" I asked.

Edward shrugged before apparently deciding he didn't want to play his reaction off as casual. "Divorce." The word fell like an anvil. "It's amazing, even now to think about it, how much we loved each other. Finding out it wasn't enough to keep us together was . . . brutal. I was . . . I didn't—I was unprepared for how much it would hurt."

Edward put his elbows on the counter to cup his hands together. "She was my best friend even if she wasn't my wife anymore. And even with my best friend by my side through the divorce, it's still the hardest thing I've ever done. Well, now the second hardest."

Ah, Elise's death. Suddenly it hurt to swallow.

Forgetting he'd emptied the glass, Edward picked it back up and tried several times to pour a nonexistent liquid down his throat before registering what he was doing. He put the glass on the counter, barely clinking it against the marble.

He didn't cry. He was board pressure tested and certified. Didn't mean his eyes didn't get beady when he lifted them from his hollow glass to me.

In a voice thick with nothing but emotion, Edward said, "You have no idea what I owe you. You did what I couldn't but should have done. For more than a year, you took care of her. Changed your work, moved in with her, cooked, cleaned, took her to appointments, flea markets, craft fairs, you even left your girlfriend, which, by the way, didn't make Elise feel guilty. She didn't really like her."

My unexpected laughter at Edward's equally unexpected joke bounced off him like a mirror, and he joined in. Our laughs dissolved into chuckles until we started throwing glances at each other to gauge who would stop first.

Finally, Edward held up a hand. "I need to make sure you understand because I don't take this lightly. I owe you. I'll never stop owing you for what you did. For that reason, I'll fulfill Elise's last wish and always take care of you."

The words were a psychological painkiller. My shoulders relaxed, though something still didn't make sense.

"So, um." I readjusted myself in my seat. "If on any given day you want to help take care of me, could you call and give me a heads-up so I can duck? Especially if it means hiring a secondhand private investigator to interrogate my friends."

Edward brought his hands to his face and groaned into them. Exhausted laughter eked out between his fingers.

"Give me a break," he pleaded. "I don't play in that world. I knew someone who knew someone, who knew someone who knew a private investigator. So, yeah, I hired him. Guy was all trash and didn't get much data on you anyway. I just needed basic information to see what you were up to. Maybe that would help me plan how to help, and he couldn't even manage that. Plus, now he won't stop hounding me that some guy named King Marco is stalking him online."

Never one to pass up an opportunity to laugh at Edward admitting he made a mistake, I had to press a hand over my mouth to stop a chuckle long enough to ask, "King Marco?"

"Yeah."

"He's my friend. Smelled your guy from a mile away and has been cyber stalking him ever since."

Edward perked up. "Is he good at cyber security? We're always hiring." Then he massaged his brow and shook his head. "No, wait, let's back off my mistakes and focus on yours."

My chuckle faded out. "Which one?"

"The one that made you think Elise thought badly of you. Seriously, what twisted your brain so much you thought that? She loved you."

There were a lot of reasons. So, so many reasons. I wasn't sure if the one that fought to the front of the line was the right one, but I chose to admit it.

"I've never had one mistake do so much damage. And it happened to the person who mattered most to me."

Edward nodded. "Your fight."

I nodded in return. "Turns out she wrote a book about it but disguised it as a children's story."

I paused. Edward had admitted more flaws to me tonight than I'd ever guessed he would. But Elise's story was still so close, too fresh. I put the water bottle to my lips and found, like Edward and his drink, I'd long since drained it.

Edward raised his eyebrows in teasing understanding.

I sighed. "The story was about those bunny personas she'd given us when we were kids. She even had two stuffed bunnies she'd named after us. No matter where in life she went, she took them with her. I don't know where they are. I looked after she died but can't find them anywhere. She must have thrown them away after the fight."

This sounded stupid. How would stuffed animals convince Edward what I was trying to say? My poor, shoddy evidence to support my twisted reasoning.

I shook my head and mumbled, "I must have hurt her so bad. You know how much Elise loves sentimental things. If she loved something, she'd keep it forever—"

Edward left the kitchen so abruptly that I had to blink to make sure he wasn't still standing across the island from me. After a few seconds, I hopped off the barstool, its hinges squeaking in protest.

"Stay there!" Edward called from down the hall.

I rested my hip against the counter to keep my weight on my good leg and leaned over to peek out of the kitchen toward Edward's voice.

He came back into view gripping two very tattered stuffed bunnies that clashed with his polished sports coat and Rolex. Daniel Nibble Hop and E. Bunbun.

I stared at Edward, whose expression resembled a trickster instead of a thief. "You stole Elise's bunnies?"

"She stole my Yale sweatshirt."

I reached out, and Edward handed the bunnies over before perching halfway onto the barstool I'd vacated. The gray fur matted under my fingers like I'd remembered, as well as their dusty odor, though I might have been imagining that from a memory, since Edward's cologne was currently dominating the airspace. I ran a thumb over E. Bunbun's red ribbon necklace while one thought ran through my head.

Elise hadn't thrown them away.

"I'm confused," I said. "Weren't you saying Elise was your best friend? Even through the divorce? That you'd do anything for her?"

Edward gazed at the bunnies with something akin to fondness. "I could see where the misunderstanding could happen. This doesn't make logical sense, so don't give it any. It would probably seem strange that two people who love each other would take the one item that meant the most to the other person. Or that the other person would know and not demand it back. I suppose we both wanted to keep the other one close in a way that we physically weren't anymore."

I opened my mouth and closed it. What to even say to that?

Edward blinked and looked back at me, unconcerned by my gaze. "What were you saying about Elise writing a bunny story? She told me it was a space story."

That bit of information shocked me out of the mess of trying to understand how Edward ended up with Elise's bunnies. Edward had to be talking about Elise's third story, the one I hadn't cracked open yet. In my mind's eye, I saw its resting location in Elise's file directory.

Edward settled one elbow on the counter and said, "Did you know we spoke almost every week? Usually on Fridays. I thought I could manage that. Just having weekly phone conversations. But soon, they became the highlight of my week. We could talk about anything, and it always stayed inside those phone calls. We never discussed her illness. She would regale me with whatever adventure she'd had with you during the week. They made her so happy and helped her forget about her illness. Then she'd always mention the latest revision she was working on for her space story. She didn't tell you about it?"

I shook my head.

"Funny." Edward's fingers drummed along while he said, "She based one of the characters off you."

I looked at Daniel Nibble Hop. The memory of the last book Elise had put me in broke a new fear sweat across my shoulders.

Edward's phone pinged. He stood and typed a response before turning to me with the air of someone who hated leaving things unresolved.

"I'm just going to say it." But, to contradict himself, Edward blew air into his cheeks for several seconds. "I don't think grief is allowing you to remember Elise correctly. She was like a cat. If she got wounded, she would hide away, not wanting anyone to see her. Sound familiar? She only came out when she was ready. She also was a vicious fighter when cornered. I don't know what you both said during that fight of yours. She never told me. But I would be shocked if you were the only one yelling or saying hurtful things that night. The Elise we both knew wouldn't have sat politely while you shouted at her. She was as much a participant in that fight as you. Am I right?"

He knew he was. And he knew I knew he was.

Edward pressed on, maybe to save me the guilt of having to say it out loud. "She never called you during the time you didn't talk, did she? She only reached out after her diagnosis. She was as much to blame for your rift as you. Would you want her to read an allegory book *you* wrote about her about that fight? Would it be an accurate representation of how you saw and felt about her?"

I would have burned that book before Elise could ever see it. A dangerous emotion, far more dangerous than fear, started infiltrating my thoughts: hope.

I gave the bunnies all my attention. Their expressions were fixed and offered the solidness I craved. They wouldn't change or judge if I lost it right here, right now. I thought I'd gotten rid of everything that made tears, that the tank was empty. Who knew there were backup tanks? Didn't seem fair.

Edward's voice lowered. "I know you remember her at her best. That's good. It's right. She was all those things you loved about her . . . most of the time. However, it wasn't all she was. She was human, like you. You have to remember all of her, everything she was. Else, it's not really her, is it?"

Edward's voice became Nellie's in my head. *You have to love all of someone.* Then I saw her face. A dimpled smile reaching up to eyes that understood and cared. A rush of gratitude for Nellie filled my chest, for her kindness, for her willingness to share, just for . . . her.

I didn't even fathom at the time what a sacrifice that must have been, sharing something that personal to help ease someone else's pain. Pain over a death that I'd been fighting to acknowledge.

With Nellie's words in my mind and Edward standing patiently beside me, I finally spoke.

"I miss her."

Escaped tears hit E. Bunbun's matted fur. Edward didn't respond. At least not with words. But a subtle hitch in his throat told me he'd swallowed hard.

"Daniel," he said my name as though trying to find his footing to cross a lake covered in thin ice. "I'm guessing here, that grief has been eating you alive since Elise called to tell you she was dying. That you've been blaming yourself for the time lost during the years you two didn't talk. Because you want that time back more than anything."

I folded my arms across the speckled countertop and buried my head in them. Squeezing the bunnies that Elise hadn't thrown away in my fists, I struggled to breathe in the hot air trapped in the space between me and the marble.

Edward must have leaned forward since his voice sounded both lower and closer. "Maybe something inside your brain said it would be easier to deal with Elise's death, after the death of your parents, by placing blame on yourself. To focus on that because, even as terrible as that was, it was better than trying to acknowledge that everyone was gone. Now dealing with all your guilt, your stupid, misguided guilt, on top of your grief over Elise's death is too much for you. But if you let that guilt go, you may have enough in you to manage the grief. To move on. To heal. Daniel, it's just a guess, but your guilt is manipulating you. What it won't tell you—something I will—is you're not alone."

His hand closed on my shoulder. He left it there, steady and warm even as my back heaved. "Please," he pleaded above a whisper. "Elise wouldn't want your guilt to twist you like this. She loved you. You know that. Remember it. You're a better man than me, so if I could do it, you can."

Those words allowed me to reign in my breathing and put a stopper in the tanks. I couldn't completely internalize the words; there were too many thoughts and emotions competing in my head. But the weight of their promise was effective all on its own.

It took several seconds, but breath after breath, I inched myself back up until I was standing.

Edward didn't move his hand until he must have concluded I could stand on my own. Then he squeezed my shoulder before clapping it twice and sliding his hand away. He didn't say anything, just gave me time and enough space while remaining close enough if needed.

Taking a few more regulating breaths, I placed the bunnies on the counter and wiped my eyes in one motion.

"You're not the person I thought you were." Meaning the driven workaholic whose sole warmth and color in life was supplied by Elise. But tonight, I was learning what she already knew. Edward carried a deep loyalty streak.

Edward smirked, because even under that loyalty streak, he was still Edward. "And you turned out not to be the annoying prankster punk little brother. Well, not only that." His smirk turned thoughtful. "Perhaps our futures would both benefit from seeing each other and ourselves as Elise saw us."

I tried to clear my throat as inconspicuously as possible to clear out any remaining emotion and nodded.

Edward straightened and thankfully moved the conversation along. "Do you want the bunnies back?"

I managed another throat clearing to say, "No."

I paused to make sure I meant it. Elise clearly wanted him to have them since she'd never sent me on a mission to retrieve them. They meant something to Edward, the man who I thought lacked sentimentality.

"No," I repeated with more conviction. "You keep them. You stole them fair and square. Ah, do you want your sweatshirt back?"

"Cotstoee, no. You've stretched it out." He paused. "What's with the face? I'm fine if you keep it."

I put a fist over my mouth and swallowed a snort laugh shooting for my nose. "It's nothing," I finally said. "Just something else Nellie was right about."

Edward cocked his head and started to speak, but his phone pinged again. Before Edward could say it, I beat him to it. "You gotta go."

"My ride's here," Edward confirmed as he turned to leave. When he reached the hallway, he stopped. "You'll be all right?"

I didn't say anything. Edward and I had left all our cards on the table tonight, but I still didn't want the indignity of hearing my own voice crack and wanted to let him leave without feeling guilty that he'd left me in a state, so I dipped my head and mustered a reassuring grin.

Edward smiled, an upgrade from his smirk, because he actually used both ends of his mouth instead of just one and turned around. I hobbled after him toward the front door as he talked over his shoulder.

"I'll tell John to call our concierge doctor to check on you tomorrow. See what she can do for your knee." Edward gathered his wallet and keys next to Shayla's scarf.

"How's it going with her?" I asked. When Edward lifted an eyebrow in question, I nodded toward the purple fringe. "With Shayla?"

Edward's grin turned goofy, and I had to hide a smile.

"I'm glad," I said.

Edward's hand rested on the doorknob. "It's okay to move on, you know? And keep me in the loop so I don't have to keep using my expert clandestine methods to check on you."

"You could just call me."

Edward considered the notion. "I could, couldn't I? That's not too much work."

I nodded.

"I could do that." With his usual smirk, Edward waved farewell and closed the door behind him.

I shouldn't have been surprised at that point that Nellie had been right about so many things. She'd suspected arrogance didn't fuel Edward. If this night had proven anything, it was how happy I was to have been proven wrong over and over again.

I limped back to the guest room and stood in the doorway, watching the power indicator on Elise's laptop blink at me from the bed. As long as I stayed put, I could pretend I was waiting to process what Edward had told me. And I did have a lot, mentally, to unpack. Then repack in a stronger box and put in the crawlspace of my mind. But I knew I was staying where I was out of fear.

Elise's third book might damn me worse than her second. I didn't think I could survive that. Still, if I wanted to do more than survive in the future, to "move on" from my guilt as Edward suggested, I needed more information. Edward's words alone hadn't erased the memory of Nellie reading Elise's bunny book out loud. Elise's words might. Especially since she'd written the space story after the bunny book.

There was that hope again.

I thought back to what I'd said to Edward when he'd offered to invest Elise's money. *Only risk what you can afford to lose.*

I couldn't afford to lose my sister a second time.

I walked inside, shut the door, and sat on the bed, pulling the laptop into my lap.

Time to start reading.

Chapter 11

WITH A FEW MOUSE CLICKS, I opened the folder where Elise's third book, or as Edward put it, her "space story," waited. There were several copies. The latest version, last revised a month before Elise died, was number sixteen. Judging by the file size, it might be a full manuscript and not just an outline. By comparison, her romance and children's stories had only been one version each.

"It's a good sign, has to be a good sign," I whispered to myself.

My finger hovered over the mouse pad.

Then I fiddled with propping my knee up with one of the six pillows on the bed. Then I propped up my back with two other pillows. Then I stopped myself from getting up to grab another pain pill.

Then I told myself to knock it off.

I clicked on the file and began reading.

It wasn't hard to turn off the analytical side of my mind—the one where I kept my mental spreadsheet of what did and did not belong in a "good" book. I didn't care about those criteria here. I bypassed grammar and formatting in search of the plot and the characters. It didn't take long to find me.

Elise hadn't done much to disguise who she'd based the character on. Even his name, Adneil, was an anagram for Daniel. He served as the first officer on a crippled spaceship as they tried to return to their home world, Pearl, before succumbing to the devastations of space. He kept his "foppish" hair under a cap and constantly attracted the most annoying females on the ship.

Harsh, but a bit real-life accurate.

Elise had done even less to disguise her character, the ship's captain. She'd simply used her middle name, Erin. I even found Edward, though Elise surprised me by going in a different direction than her romance novel. Here, Edward wasn't the love interest, but the financier of the ship's expeditions.

Erin still had a love interest, though. A shy, brawny mechanic named Rowan, who walked around in sleeveless shirts and used quips to make everyone laugh. If he existed in real life, anywhere outside the pages of her book, I didn't know who he was. But the deeper I read into the story, the more I doubted he was real.

> *"Why doesn't he own a uniform with sleeves on it?" Adneil asked.*
> *Erin kept her eyes on Rowan as he sauntered away. "Unfortunate budget cuts."*
> *"Don't you run the budget committee?"*
> *Erin smiled and didn't look away from the view.*

I laughed out loud for several seconds. Another point for Nellie being right. This was exactly the type of cheesy dialogue I'd used to love to redline and mock. But now, it wasn't the words that I was reacting to; it was the emotion. A warm bubble spreading throughout my heart. Understanding all of Nellie's guidance was leading me to understand myself better.

I slowly read all Adneil's scenes. I had to, out of self-preservation, since I knew a repeat of Elise's bunny book would destroy me, as hilarious as that sentence sounded without context. However, the more I read, the more my anxiety turned to anticipation, hooks encouraging me to read faster. Soon I couldn't keep up with my anticipation and followed at a reckless pace to know what would happen next, slowing only to reread the scenes between Erin and Adneil. Those I searched to make sure I didn't miss anything from their conversations. I analyzed them from every angle to see if Elise had written in any hidden accusations.

I couldn't find any. Erin and Adneil formed a formidable team. Against asteroids, alien attacks, and even an incompetent chef with a surprisingly deadly cheese grater.

> *Erin asked, "Now who will cook dinner?"*
> *Adneil smirked. "It will be hard to find someone 'grater' than he was."*

Something changed once I got past chapter seven. While I still reread any pages where Erin and Adneil interacted, I found I'd stopped trying to sniff out a trap. Instead, I read their dialogue several times over because of the lightheaded rush I felt, as though Elise and I were speaking again through her characters, having brand-new conversations. Like she wasn't gone. It created such a dizzying effect that I had to grip the edges of the laptop. I hoped the feeling wouldn't go away.

In chapter nine, Erin and Adneil clashed over how to save the ship, in a terrific confrontation reminiscent of the argument that had split Elise and I apart. But unlike Elise's bunny book, Erin and Adneil moved past it, occasionally snipping at each other, but coming together time and time again to save the ship and its inhabitants from each new threat introduced in chapters ten and eleven.

> *Warning off a raiding party, Adneil threatened the raiders' captain that he would, "Scorch them to the ground."*

The pirates wisely returned to their ship to flee. It was the same thing Elise had yelled at me during our fight and again used in her bunny book.

> *"That's my line," Erin told Adneil when the pirate ship disengaged, approval shining through the space between her words.*
> *"Yeah," Adneil said. Then he winked. "I say it better."*
> *But Erin didn't smile. "I never should have said that to you in the first place."*
> *Adneil threw an arm around her shoulders. "I forgive you. So long as you buy Rowan a full shirt."*
> *Erin finally smiled and rolled her eyes. "Go get a haircut."*

But in chapter twelve, the adventure came to an end.

Erin sacrificed herself to retrieve a mineral their ship needed to complete its return journey to Pearl, their North Star, their home world. It was clear for Erin that Adneil would end the mission without her.

Though it was only eight pages long, chapter twelve took an hour to read. Not only had my reading slowed as I tried to stop the inevitable ending, but the words kept blurring as I read Erin and Adneil's farewell.

Unlike the rest of the book, Erin and Adneil weren't together. Adneil had remained at his station onboard the ship while Erin stood on the surface of an uninhabited world. A faulty radio allowed them to communicate only via voice after Erin had absconded with a shuttle on a lone mission to save all their lives. Adneil begged her to return to the ship, saying they would find another way, but Erin wouldn't risk his life.

> *"Adneil, you have to forgive me. I don't want to leave you, but this is the only way."*

The line was a cliché. I knew it was. But it squeezed my chest like I'd never heard, seen, or read anything like it hundreds of times before. I'd never expected a known cliché to hit me so hard.

Erin filled her shuttle with the needed material and returned it on autopilot to the ship, where its inorganic makeup allowed it to be decontaminated and put to use saving those on board. Erin stayed behind, permanently infected with a substance that would turn deadly should she leave the planet.

Adneil tried to disobey Erin's orders, to take the shuttle back to her and stay with her, but she stopped him, insisting only he could lead everyone home. He alone had to finish the journey they'd started together.

> "But I promise that somehow we'll see each other again. I'm not sure when or how, but we'll both make it back to Pearl. Believe in that and be strong. And remember that though we're apart, you're not alone."

I slid down the headboard, my arms at my sides while Elise's laptop maintained its precarious perch on my stomach. I stared at the ceiling, 100 percent overwhelmed. Since Elise's death, I'd felt like I'd reached my emotional limits so many times. As though I'd been swallowed by a wave of unforgiving guilt over and over, wondering when the cycle would pound and tear out everything I had left in me.

And while I couldn't deny what I was feeling probably fell under the definition of "emotional limits," the roiling through my chest was different.

Instead of crushing me, these emotions hugged me tightly. Instead of trying to tear everything out, they put everything back where it should go inside me and held me to make sure it all stayed in place. Instead of guilt, I felt love. Aching, yes, but still love.

Apart from the occasional swipe at my eyes at the inevitable itch tears produced, I didn't move until the lightening layers of morning coming in through the windows started to dissolve the gray light on the ceiling. The moment I registered the early-morning hour, the red low-battery indicator began to blink on Elise's computer.

I pushed myself back into a sitting position, increasing my reading speed to finish the book. Even though Adneil stayed on the ship, Rowan, Erin's love interest, took the shuttle down to stay with her. Maybe between the two of them, they could find a cure to reunite with the crew at Pearl.

So I'd been right about Rowan. He wasn't real; Elise had just written someone to be with after sacrificing herself to save Adneil and the ship. Rowan was the personification of what Elise hoped to find in the next world, who she hoped she would be with after she died. Someone hot and funny. I rubbed my face as laughter bubbled out of me.

In the end, Erin looked over the planet's unknown landscape, recognizing its alien terrain and dangers but not frightened by them. She chuckled to herself at Adneil's stubbornness but knew he would eventually find the forgiveness he needed. I knew from Nellie's writing videos that Elise had written Adneil to be a flawed hero, only she didn't call him that.

> *Before the ship flew out of communication range, Erin told Adneil, "I'll see you again in Pearl."*
> *Adneil tried to respond but choked on the words. Erin understood them anyway, and the last thing Adneil heard before static filled the channel was Erin chuckling, just as she always had, just as she always would.*

The computer's battery ran out on cue, right as I finished the final sentence.

> *Though their journey together ended, their separate adventures would continue.*

Elise's screen flicked to black with a little descending electronic whine. My eyes drifted to the far wall, where the promised sun painted the wood paneling a golden tone.

This story broke so many of the guideline rules. Filter words, tense changes, head hopping, run-on sentences, comma splicing, plot holes, cheesy dialogue, and even what Nellie defined as "pink purple prose."

I didn't care. Nellie had been right. Flaws hadn't ruined the story. I loved it even with its flaws because it had endured them, triumphed over them. I doubted the final victory would have even felt earned without those flaws.

Like Elise, and like me, the story didn't have to be perfect to be loved.

Huh. Nellie'd said that too.

The sun's light continued to climb the walls as I sunk back into the pillows. I couldn't forgive myself on the spot. Yet I had to admit that, for the first time, it was a possibility.

The warmth of Nellie's guidance, both spoken through Edward and in Elise's story, which had been patiently waiting for me to listen, spread across me. My eyelids sputtered, and I fell asleep before the pneumatic hum of the automatic shades finished lowering over the windows.

***

I knocked on Charlie's door, eye to eye with the peephole, wearing what I hoped he'd interpret as a psychotic grin on my face.

Footsteps sounded on the other side before a pause, then the door opened so quickly the air vacuum tossed my hair across my eyes. Charlie stood in the doorway with Sam on his hip. Sam wore only a diaper, showing skin that reflected Willow's russet-brown tone while his forehead was all Charlie.

For a moment, I envied Charlie's buzz cut that never revealed the last time he'd showered or slept. I'd caught him in his Sunday-morning attire—basketball shorts with a black, long-sleeve T-shirt, all grounded by his wife's fuzzy purple slippers.

"Where have you been? You send us one text over two days ago saying, 'I'm fine,' then go dark?" Charlie's tone caused Sam to alternate his stare between us with wide eyes. He didn't start wailing but received some obvious comfort by doubling the sucking rate on his binkie.

I shrugged. "I didn't want you or Nellie to file a missing-person report or anything."

"Where have you been?" Charlie demanded again.

"Hanging out with John. Have you ever thought about getting a doorman? They're wonderfully addictive." I glanced down at my new knee brace.

Charlie's head tilt read "not amused" when combined with his glare. Sam started sucking even harder.

I dropped the nonchalant attitude and admitted, "I've been at Edward's."

Charlie's jaw dropped. "Creepy Edward?"

"I've got a story for you," I said as Charlie stepped back to let me inside. "And a possible job offer for Marco."

Charlie shut the door and followed me into the living room as I navigated the minefield of bright smiley toys to take a seat on the L-shaped sofa. Willow had brought the ivory piece of furniture into the marriage. Now several blankets covered it to either protect the coloring from new stains or hide existing ones.

Charlie knelt on the floor next to a plastic pad with a wipes container on it. A cautionary sniff confirmed he'd just changed Sam's diaper. Charlie grabbed one of those pieces of clothing toddlers wore that melded a shirt with underwear and started sliding Sam into it.

"Okay, now tell me what happened," Charlie said.

I had no idea how he thought he could correctly bend Sam into the awkward piece of clothing without breaking him while also carrying on a conversation with me.

Before I could answer, a timer dinged in the kitchen. With an exasperated sigh, Charlie stood and handed me his half-clothed child. He ran into the kitchen yelling, "I'll be right back."

I held Sam under the armpits and away from me. We stared at each other with a mutual understanding. If the other didn't move, neither of us would. But as hurried noises escalated inside the kitchen, Sam's eyes and mouth got wider and wider until the binkie slobbered out and flopped onto the carpet.

"Charlie," I called, now hoping my grin looked reassuring and not psychotic at all. "I think a wail is coming . . ."

Charlie dashed back into the living room to rescue Sam before I caused him any childhood trauma. Not that Sam didn't give Charlie a reproving look that said, *This isn't how we usually do this*, while Charlie finished dressing him. Then father and son nestled in a rocking chair opposite the couch with Sam contentedly downing a warmed bottle after a final warning glare in my direction.

"Never leave me again," I said out of the corner of my mouth. At Charlie's raised eyebrows, I admitted, "Apparently I narrate children now. It's all part of Nellie's language."

Charlie flashed me a determined smile. "Speaking of Nellie, tell me what happened."

I inhaled a long, deep breath (it would have been deeper if not for the recent diaper change) and launched into a recap of what had happened, starting with Nellie's reading of Elise's bunny story. Unfortunately, this entailed having to admit to the guilt I'd been living with, but at least it helped better explain my conversation with Edward. I ended with describing what I'd found in Elise's sci-fi story.

It was easier explaining all this to Charlie than I'd feared. Maybe it was one of the benefits of working toward self-forgiveness and a place where I felt worthy of love. *Anxious* for love. Now that I wasn't feeding my guilt with unquestioning fealty, it seemed as eager to be rid of me as I was to replace it with something infinitely more hopeful.

Charlie's eyebrow expressions ranged from shocked to incredulous. For any other topic of discussion, I would have teased him about it. Instead, I spread my hands and said, "So. Elise didn't hate me. She'd forgiven me."

Charlie's eyebrows hit a new peak. "Well, yeah," he said, punctuating his words with obviousness.

I backed farther into the couch cushions. "I know. I've spent the last two days getting my head straight. But I'm still . . ." I took a breath that shuddered with a forced laugh. "Ya know . . ."

"Yeah." Charlie dropped his eyebrows and gave a small grin. "I know." He regarded me through discerning eyes. "You look better, though."

I didn't have to glance down to understand what he meant. I'd stopped by Elise's house and showered before coming over. Now, sitting in a fresh pair of jeans and a hoodie, I felt clean in a way I hadn't in years. Scrubbed. New. Almost all over. Almost. There was still a rat's nest of a problem in my mind.

"You asked about Nellie, and that's kinda why I'm here. I know she—" I straightened and twisted at the waist to peek toward the hallway. "Is Willow sleeping? Is she gonna come out?"

Charlie shook his head. "No, man. She's at the office trying to get a few things done before we head to brunch. We got . . ." He expertly checked his watch without disrupting the angle he was holding Sam's bottle at. "At least thirty minutes."

I blew out a short breath. I liked Willow, but it would be easier to talk to Charlie about this one-on-one. I'd left out some key information in my recap, like how Nellie had cried her makeup off onto a roll of paper towels. Or the actual number of times she'd tried contacting me before I'd sent the text to her and Charlie letting them know I was okay. After that, I'd turned my phone off for two days while I processed Edward's and my conversation and Elise's third book.

When I'd powered it back on, there were no missed calls from Nellie. A fact that disturbed me more and more with each passing minute. I'd started obsessively checking the screen for messages or voicemails and cursing every alert ping that turned out to be a text ad or weather update.

Charlie used his heels to rock the chair as Sam's eyes began to close longer with each blink. "So, Edward wasn't after the money? Or revenge? He's just guilty of hiring a bad private investigator. And acting crazy strange. Huh."

I gave Charlie a pointed look.

"Right," he said, getting back on track. "So, you and Nellie. Does this mean you still want to keep seeing her?"

I pointed at my chest and nodded, trying to explain the inflating balloon of need growing inside me. "I really do."

Charlie gave a small smile and clenched his fist in a triumphant way that I hated to correct.

"But I might have massively messed things up."

"Wait." Charlie perked up and placed the empty baby bottle on the table beside him. "You need romantic advice?"

His widening grin challenged my decision-making matrix.

"Yes," I said slowly.

"And you came here?"

". . . Yes."

Charlie used the arm not holding Sam's sleeping form to pump the air. "Yes!"

Knowing I had Charlie in my corner ready to go was exactly what I'd been hoping for. But at his overexuberance, I had to ask, "Why are you so excited?"

"You and Nellie are good people. Also," Charlie pointed at Sam, "for my services, I charge a night of babysitting so Willow and I can have a night out."

I couldn't help myself. "As long as you promise to get a designated driver."

Charlie covered his eyes with his hand and rested his head against the chair's overstuffed back cushion, seemingly designed for parents to have a crisis of consciousness just like this. "Oh man."

When he dragged his fingers away, all the joviality had drained from his face. "We're really embarrassed about that. The board had just approved two of my books for publication and Willow had won her last case, and it'd been so long since we'd both had a night out. We wanted to celebrate." His eyes drifted to Sam, nestled in his arm and drooling down it. "We were stupid. We'll both own up to it. Designated drivers from here on out."

I nodded, relieved by Charlie's reaction. "Soooo, about Nellie."

Charlie smiled again. "Have you talked to her? I mean, since you left Edward's?"

"Nope."

Charlie narrowed his eyes. "Do you want to talk to her?"

"Yes."

"Do you know what you want to say?"

I shook my head.

Instead of being discouraged, Charlie seemed happy to have a starting point. "We can work with that. You want to let her know you don't want to get Elise published anymore?"

I nodded.

"Okay. So you still want to see her but don't know if she wants to see you."

"Yeah." My good knee began bouncing. "I freaked out on her, but she stuck around and helped me. So maybe, even to someone who loves family as much as she does, it wasn't a deal breaker for her. Or she was just being nice. It's the kind of person she is. But then I up and disappear for a few days and don't return her calls. That doesn't speak well of me either."

"Can't you tell her what you told me?"

I looked straight at Charlie. "What if it's not enough?"

Charlie got up and placed Sam carefully inside a popup crib next to the couch and started to pace. "It may not be enough," he finally said. "But you'll regret it if you don't. If she means something to you, you'll always wonder. Besides," Charlie lightly kicked at my running shoe on his next pacing pass, "it's the kind of guy you are. You'd never leave a girl hanging."

I put my head down, a bow to the inevitable. I held out my phone. "Would a text be enough?"

"No way. And don't do it over the phone either. Invite her to meet with you to talk."

I groaned loudly, causing Charlie to frantically wave his hands and point toward the form of his sleeping child.

Sorry, I mouthed.

After waiting for a moment to make sure Sam hadn't stirred, Charlie said, "You need to do this in person. For you and because you owe it to her."

For better and for tougher, his concurrence solidified my own thoughts. Not only would I have to talk to her, but I had to be prepared for her to shut me down if that's what she chose. I finally straightened, coming up for air. My neck flexed as I held my breath and started typing.

"You're doing it now?" Charlie asked.

I had to while I had my wingman nearby offering support and kicking me to prove points.

Charlie and I froze in place as we both listened to the ring tone buzz. And buzz. And buzz.

"Hey! This is Nellie Vasquez from Writer's World Publishing. I'm away from my phone—"

I hung up. "Aghhhhh!" Intense relief and disappointment twisted around my spine like a chocolate-and-anchovy-swirl ice cream cone. That Nellie used her married name on her voice mail threw cold water on my plan. I just hoped it was because she hadn't updated it in a while.

Perching on the end of the rocking chair, Charlie held out his hands, ready to make a deal. "Okay, let's not assume she's avoiding you."

The disappointment in me laughed, but I remembered, "Nellie does forget to charge her phone. A lot. It died twice on our dates."

I took up Charlie's pacing duties, finding a path right next to the couch where I wouldn't have to kick toys out of the way. "Do I go to her house?"

Charlie's eyes bulged. "No. No, no. Not in front of her family. This is between you and her. Don't bring in extra participants to influence the conversation."

I ran through my few remaining options. I could keep trying to call. Um, no. Too much stalker and too much passive action. I could wait until Monday and go into her office. Again, no. As Charlie pointed out, her coworkers would add extra participants, which could influence what we said. And I didn't want to place pressure on or embarrass Nellie in her place of work.

I stopped pacing. "Sarah."

Charlie frowned.

"Sarah. The sister who always side-glares at me when she drops Nellie off. Nellie used my phone in my car to call Sarah one of the times her phone died. I might still have the number."

I scrolled through my outgoing calls made on the date of Edward's roof party and held out the screen for Charlie to see where I found a number without a name attached to it.

"This is it."

So I had the number. Now I just had to talk to someone who probably despised me. How badly did I want to do this?

"Are you gonna—whoa, dude!"

I'd pressed dial.

Charlie's shout elicited an annoyed murmur from Sam's crib as he threatened to wake up. I raised my shoulders in an exaggerated motion: *I don't know what I'm doing.*

Flinging his arms out, Charlie pointed to my head and made an explosion gesture: *This is crazy!*

Charlie pressed fists into his eyes, and I folded my lips together.

Sarah's phone buzzed twice, and a dry voice picked up. "Hello?" Her voice sounded exactly how a knife would when scraping over burnt toast.

Thankfully, the need to keep Sam asleep, because a wailing child was just what this conversation needed, helped keep my voice nice and low, perfectly calm.

"Hey Sarah, this is Daniel. I work with Sarah. I—I mean Nellie. I work with Nellie."

Silence.

I winced and bobbed at my waist while Charlie gestured helplessly. This wasn't the introduction I wanted for finally "meeting" a member of Nellie's family. Brain delay was hitting hard, and I had to move quickly with what words I had ready before that stream dried up.

"Hi. So I'm just trying to reach Nellie, but her phone is just going straight to voicemail, and I just don't want to bother her at work or at home and just wanted to see if maybe she could call me back or just—"

"Hold on."

Charlie and I, and thankfully, Sam, didn't move. The sound of shuffling papers came over the phone.

"I don't know why Nellie's not answering her phone. You'd have to ask her about that."

I gritted my teeth at the clear contradiction. How could I ask Nellie if she wasn't picking up her phone? Sarah must really not like me. Worse, I couldn't blame her.

Sarah's voice, sounding even less engaged than before, said, "And she'll be out of the office for most of next week. She's flying from JFK up to Buffalo for a writing conference."

Charlie bent over to grab a charging laptop in front of the entertainment center and opened it, probably to start checking for flight information. Was he expecting me to go to the airport?

He waved to catch my attention and mouthed the words, *When is she leaving?*

Caught in a mid-shrug toward Charlie, I had to tilt my head back to the phone when Sarah sighed. "Anything else?"

"Yeah, eh . . ."

I stalled while Charlie rolled his fingers, indicating I needed to keep the conversation moving while he mouthed again, *What time?*

"So, I don't want to interrupt her at the airport. How long would you recommend I keep trying to call her before she leaves?"

That was weak. Charlie's grimace confirmed it. I held my breath.

Sarah sighed again, annoyed, and I heard more papers being shuffled. "Her flight leaves in two hours."

Charlie snapped his fingers, mouthed *BINGO*, and focused on his computer.

"Thank you," I said. The phone clicked dead in return.

"Don't worry about her," Charlie said. He jammed his finger at something on his screen and spun it to face me. "There's only one flight leaving JFK for Buffalo in two hours." The airline and flight number were next to the search result.

I sat slowly. "You're suggesting I ambush her at the airport."

Charlie glared and set the computer aside. "Ambush sounds stalker-y, but yeah, that's the basic idea."

A headache blossomed, and I massaged my forehead. "Not sure I can do that."

"This shows her you're making an effort. Find her, ask if she'll give you five minutes over coffee."

"The airport will be full of people."

Charlie scoffed. "No one is gonna notice you. Everyone is focused on their own stuff and getting to their own place."

It was hard to argue when I wanted to see Nellie. And I wanted her to want to see me. If she didn't, well, a rejection in front of hundreds of people who didn't care was probably what I deserved.

I winced. Obviously, I still needed to work on not immediately feeding the guilt beast.

"Okay," I said. I was doing this.

I started searching on my phone for the cheapest ticket available at JFK to get me through the gate and into the terminals.

"You ready?" Charlie asked as I bought a red-eye flight to Washington, DC.

I tucked my phone in my back pocket and smiled. "Nope."

"Good." Charlie slumped back in his chair, letting his arms dangle over the sides. "If you were thinking you were on top of things, I'd be worried."

"Thanks for the support." We looked at each other and broke out in nervous snickers. I rubbed my head again. "Don't worry; whatever the outcome, I'll still come babysit Sam so you and Willow can have a night out."

"Oh no. I don't trust you alone with my kid, man. Just make sure you bring Nellie with you, and we've got a deal."

I glanced away and chuckled, only to have to glance back when Charlie's tone became serious. "But I am worried. If this doesn't turn out the way we're hoping, if she calls it quits—" Charlie gave me a significant look reminiscent of helicopter parenting.

I knew what he was trying to say. I nodded. "I'll let you know. I won't go dark again."

"And?"

"And I'll come to b-ball every week. After, you know, my knee heals."

"And?"

"And I'll buy Marco pizza for the rest of his life."

Getting what he wanted to hear, Charlie stood with a wry smile. He led me to the door and asked me again, "Know what you're gonna say?"

I stepped outside and squinted into the shaft of spring sun escaping through the clouds, unnerved by its promise of summer when it could just as easily snow this afternoon. Flashing Charlie a smile full of all the positive hope I didn't have, I said, "Nope."

With nothing else to say, I turned to head to the airport and a conversation I was dying not to have.

Chapter 12

I PULLED INTO SHORT-TERM PARKING at JFK and flicked off the windshield wipers. It was hard to say if the rain was a sign of new beginnings or a harbinger of doom.

I endured the crawl and shove of the security screening by unhelpfully checking the time every thirty seconds. Only after passing through the body scanner and sitting to put my shoes back on did Sarah text me with the news that Nellie's flight had been moved to nine p.m. that night.

Sigh.

I hung my head and nearly got bumped off the bench by several high school band members lugging their instruments. I didn't want to have to go through security again. I'd rather stay and waste time here than in my car.

Leaving the airport without seeing Nellie wasn't an option.

Still. I checked the time again. Ten hours was a long time.

I texted Charlie to give him a heads-up with yet another promise to contact him no matter how late. Normally . . . wow, what a wonderful word *normally* was. I couldn't wait to get back to any semblance of normal.

So, normally, I would use a good chunk of the waiting time to exercise. I considered looping through all the terminals but discarded the idea and stayed in the one where Nellie's flight would be. Technically, my knee was on the mend. Best not to antagonize it.

Besides, I had work to do. I had an amazing and honest apology to construct and commit to memory. Brain delay would hit hard when it came time to deliver it, and I didn't want any complications. I also had to prepare for Nellie to reject any offer of continuing to see me. I quickly deduced there was no real way to prepare for that. If it happened, it happened. I should spend my time refining my apology instead.

For some reason, I thought it'd take all day to compose. However, when I checked my watch, it only read noon. Nine more hours.

I played around with the idea of leaving, knowing I could come back before Nellie's flight left. I stopped at the food court to grab Mexican food for lunch—unfortunately Venezuelan fare wasn't an option—while I decided. Midway through my meal, I practiced my apology to my water bottle to make sure I had it well and truly memorized. I started a second time but stopped when the woman sitting at the next table side-eyed me and moved to another seat.

The time now read 12:45.

I could still leave and come back. Concerns about traffic and if there would be any issues with security with re-entering on the same ticket, something I'd never done before, worried me.

But if I were being honest, underneath all the layers of excuses, I didn't want to leave. Nellie was coming here. Was going to be here. Until I'd see her, I was drawn to this mill of human travelers with the force of a magnet.

I paced the food court until I realized I didn't want security to flag a suspicious guy in a hoodie talking to himself near the juice bar. I found a place to camp out at the nearest gate, only getting up to refill my water bottle. Gulping it down as the time inched closer to nine p.m. became a nervous tick.

I moved between different gates periodically, constantly fighting the nostril assault of cleaning chemicals versus the mass of human body odor that all airports reeked of. Relief only came when I passed pizza stands or coffee shops selling cinnamon rolls.

To help pass the time, I watched people come in from their flights and narrated them in my head. It wasn't until around seven that inspiration hit to add romance to the mix.

It wasn't entirely my idea. A guy with flip-flops and a five o'clock shadow arrived on a Ft. Lauderdale flight, carrying a pink teddy bear large enough to have needed a separate seat purchase. Instead of following the crowd toward baggage claim, he scampered in the opposite direction. Intrigued, I followed him seven gates over, where he waited thirty-five minutes for a flight from Des Moines to arrive. Once a woman with an over-the-shoulder braid that reached her waist entered the concourse, flip-flops rushed forward, capturing both her and the bear in a hug.

Excited giggles escaped from the woman. Or maybe from an automated voice box activated on the bear. With all the twirling, it was hard to tell.

I watched the couple leave, narrating their exit in my head with the cheesiest dialogue I knew. That's when the idea of a romantic gesture hit me.

The excitement of the idea overrode my instincts, and for the next thirty minutes, I cobbled together a fake proposal in my head. I borrowed ideas from the romance movies I'd seen with Elise and from the countless submissions Nellie and I had gone over since our first meeting in January.

I'd wait until she was nearing the ticketing agent, then burst from the crowd holding my boarding pass overhead and yelling I'd purchased a ticket to stop her from getting on the plane and leaving New York City to take that glamorous fashion job in . . . Buffalo, New York.

Okay, the location didn't match with the profession. No one would move from the city to Buffalo for a fashion career. I'd need to tweak that part.

I took my rehearsed apology and morphed it into my new script. The line "I never should have donated your Christmas gift to the zoo's charity auction" was taken from what Nellie said at the night of Edward's party. Would she remember that? Or would she remember "My heart is so full of love it will explode like a water balloon filled with chocolate milk"?

The clock was nearing 8:15 p.m., only fifteen minutes away from when Nellie's plane would be boarding for its nine o'clock departure.

For someone who'd been killing time all day, I suddenly had some to save. I rushed to the other end of the terminal where the information board reported the gate for the flight to Buffalo.

Scanning the crowd, I searched for Nellie's face, afraid I might see her before I could enact Plan Romantic Stupidity. Because it *was* stupid. I knew that. It was why, with every step I took, my judgment fought against the thrilling excitement of how Nellie might react to such a "go big or go home" gesture. Everything about it was "us," if I could use that term.

Normally, I wouldn't attempt something like this . . . then again, was that true? Before our fight, Elise and I used to pull stunts like this all the time. Even a few on Edward, who, to his credit, tolerated them. That must be why there was an air of familiarity in my spine shoring up Plan Romantic Stupidity. I didn't just want to show Nellie I was willing to do something stupid and fun for her, I wanted to be that person again for me too.

Guilt's weakening strangle grip on me was also loosening several dormant personality traits. But as I neared the waiting area for Nellie's gate, still scanning the crowd for her face, reality forced me to admit I wasn't that person. Maybe not anymore, or maybe just not yet, but the version of Daniel I'd been living with for the past several years was too entrenched.

"Attention passengers, this is a full flight to Buffalo. If there is anyone willing to check your carry-on baggage with us free of charge . . ."

The message rambled on as I tried pumping myself up, to force myself to act when I saw Nellie. I could still pull this off.

Though the possibility dimmed as the gate agent called for the first boarding group. By this time, everyone in the waiting area had stood, either to take their place in line or mill as close to it as possible for when their group was called. The planes attached to the gates around us must have recently taken off, because this section of the terminal was vacant except for those on this flight.

I scanned more faces, then desperately moved a few steps to the left to look at everyone again. I took another step but tripped. Catching myself, I turned in a circle. Still nothing. Empty faces, unfamiliar eyes. Hope drained out of me with every quickened breath. All led to the same conclusion.

Nellie wasn't here.

Plan Romantic Stupidity was a no-go.

I backed off from the crowd, rubbing my neck and wondering how I could have allowed myself to think this was a good idea. Coming to the airport, let alone concocting the plan to throw myself at Nellie's feet for a fake proposal. Sarah might have lied to me. Or Nellie's plans could have legitimately changed again. Either way, she wasn't here, and I didn't have it in me to call Sarah again.

As the gate agent called for the second boarding group, I backed farther away, my eyes no longer scanning faces but shoes. My shoulder bumped someone. I whipped my head to look, but it was a bearded gamer so intent on the game on his phone he hadn't seen me.

"Wait! Don't go!"

I stopped, the voice down the hall trapping me between denial and reality.

"Daniel!"

I turned around slowly enough to watch most of the crowd do the same. It was Nellie. She held a single boarding pass in the air like the hero of her own romantic comedy. She ran toward me dressed in the same sun-yellow sweater I'd met her in with curls bouncing over her shoulders.

She grabbed my hands, her cold fingers cooling mine. "Please stay." Shock locked my jaw as she continued. "I never should have auctioned off your birthday present at the zoo's charity. Or called you a boiled lobster when you got upset."

Since my mouth wouldn't open, my surprise found an outlet by bulging through my eye sockets.

Nellie pressed her forehead to our clasped hands and went down on one knee. A jolt of adrenaline shocked my system as my mind finally kicked into working gear.

A woman behind me emitted a shriek ending in a swooning sigh. Several people grabbed their phones and pointed them toward us. I glanced over to see a boy dressed in blue dinosaur pjs totter away from his father and gesture at me with a grin on his face.

I looked back at Nellie with her mouth half-open to "propose" to me. My old self, the one Nellie had been coaxing out of my guilt haze over the past few months, reemerged.

I raised my eyebrows and let my mouth drop to indicate surprise. "But you swore you'd closed off your heart, to never love again." The awful line almost caused me to grind my teeth into powder.

Nellie's facade almost cracked. This close, I saw how she had to clench her teeth to keep laughter from escaping her mouth.

She inhaled sharply through her nose and swallowed a hiccup. Speaking a touch louder than necessary for two people actually exchanging these sentiments, Nellie countered, "For you, I would. My heart is so full of love it will explode like a water balloon filled with chocolate milk." She blinked away ready tears, and one of my eyebrows tweaked up in respect. "Stay with me," she whispered. "Forever."

The guy who'd bumped into me earlier and who, as far as I could tell, had never once looked up from his phone, said, "Bro, you'd better say yes."

I turned and shrugged at the crowd as if asking for advice. The passengers nearest me made shooing motions with their hands to tell me to, "Do it!"

One woman, craning her neck to look back at us as the line pushed her through the door to the plane's gangway, shouted, "I want to see what happens!"

"I'm supposed to ask her," I said sheepishly to the crowd.

Several voices yelled, "Yes! Say yes!"

Game-guy was close enough I heard him mutter, "Chauvinist," all while his buxom lady avatar played visibly across his screen.

Killjoy.

I nodded a yes to an outbreak of applause. I hauled Nellie to her feet and into a hug she sold so enthusiastically that even game-guy snapped a quick picture before moving forward as group three was called.

Even as my arms wrapped around her, I struggled to wrap my mind around the situation. Nellie was here, doing exactly what I'd planned to do. That we'd had the same idea wasn't lost on me. Nor was the fact that her cheek was pressing into mine.

Content to stay in that moment, even if surrounded by strangers impeding on our romantic moment, I almost pulled back when Nellie wrapped her arm around mine and started leading us away from the crowd. Her eyes flicked to my knee brace, and for the second time, her facade almost cracked. But she waved to everyone and led the way as quickly as she could without making us run.

A few yards away from the departing cheers, I asked in a low voice, "Will you get in trouble for missing your flight to the writing conference?"

Nellie squeezed my hand tighter. "That wasn't my flight. I just bought the cheapest ticket I could. I think it leaves for DC at midnight."

"Mine too."

Nellie grinned and kept her eyes ahead of us.

"So, what Sarah told me . . ."

"Oh, I was in the room with her when you called. I wrote down for her to tell you about the airport." She paused her stride to look at me. "I couldn't wait to do this."

I breathed out some pent-up anxiety and found a feeling like sinking a game-winning shot taking its place. But I had to ask, "You wanted to make me wait ten extra hours?"

Nellie turned to continue leading us out of the terminal, though her eyes strayed back to my face several times as she said, "I wanted to see if you'd still come."

It'd been a test. Nellie's fake proposal was the passing grade.

I managed to catch her eye and offered an understanding grin. I stopped so she'd have to face me. "Has your phone been off this entire time too?"

"Yes. Well, partly yes. It was at the beginning."

I nodded, knowing I had no place to fault her for pulling back from communicating to deal with something confusing and potentially hurtful.

Instead of walking out of the terminal and into the main concourse where groups of people were milling around shops or rushing to destinations, I pointed to a small restaurant across the main walkway. The kind that charged more for a quieter and more secluded place to sit and eat. The sign advertising the day's specials in pink chalk listed closing time at nine.

Nellie nodded in agreement. What laughter remained in her expression from our fake proposal left entirely, leaving the mood decidedly more serious.

I led us in to find low-lighted tables and a red-vested waiter whose expression clearly said he was more concerned with getting off work early than the possibility of earning one more tip for the evening.

Grimacing, he grabbed two menus and led us to a table next to the restaurant's lone window. The only other occupants were a family who must have been from another time zone, if not another country, considering how wide-awake their two small kids looked.

As we passed their table, I asked Nellie, "Do you think anyone on the plane will figure out we were lying when there aren't any empty seats?"

"Probably the same people who got suspicious when we didn't kiss after we got engaged."

The eavesdropping mother at the table gave us a startled double-take and nudged her husband. I offered a quick wave before the waiter sat us. We refused the menus and ordered fountain drinks. The waiter didn't complain, probably hoping we'd drink quickly and leave.

Once he left with the unopened menus, Nellie began studying the bar without seeing it. I looked out the window at the rain-slicked tarmac. Carts of luggage were being guided by halogen headlights and red-lighted markers to the plane we weren't on. I still couldn't decide if the rain was a good or bad sign for my future with Nellie.

We'd just publicly shared a private joke. That felt good. The fact that Nellie had thought to catch me in the same dramatic fashion I'd been envisioning was encouraging. Though now we seemed reluctant to break the silence and fill it with the discussion we both knew we needed to have.

I didn't know if Nellie's uncharacteristic silence was due to nervousness or if it was another test. Regardless, I needed to go first. Luckily, the secluded atmosphere softened the cacophony of outside voices to a wordless hum as Nellie's perfume lightly cocooned the space around the table.

I flexed my fingers and clasped them in front of me. "I need to apologize."

That drew Nellie's attention. She didn't automatically laugh or play it off, just looked at me with a quiet patience. She knew I was being serious and was responding with the same courtesy.

"Whatever else we talk about tonight, whatever else we decide, I have to make sure this gets said. I, ahhh . . ." I attempted a laugh and suddenly wished Nellie was a water bottle. I forced myself to meet her eye. "I'm sorry for how I treated you. How that hurt you. I'm sorry I ran. You helped me so much that night, and so much before it; I should have communicated better."

That was it. It took an hour to come up with, fifteen seconds to say, and yet my heart was thumping as though I'd run a marathon.

Nellie nodded, gathering thoughts and information. "Thank you." Then she asked, "Do you still want to move forward with the contest? To get Elise published?"

The waiter arrived and put our drinks down with more force than necessary. Nellie leaned forward to catch my answer as soon as his back was turned.

I shook my head, adding, "I'll honor the contract for the work done and for the unexpected cancellation." I didn't see any signs of annoyance. I still said, "You have to know this isn't a reflection of your work."

Nellie huffed and crossed her arms. "I know. I'm not concerned about that." Judging by her skeptical expression, she'd rolled through what I'd said and didn't find the answer she wanted. "What changed? Was it the bunny story? You wanted Elise published more than anything. Right? Because that's what she wanted most when she wrote those stories."

"Turns out it wasn't what she wanted most." I snuck a quick sip of my drink, relieved when the carbonation cooled my throat instead of making it itch. I was also glad that the speed the waiter used to deliver our drinks meant he hadn't had time to spit in them.

Nellie tilted her head to the side, confused, but gave me space to explain.

"Yes, Elise had always talked about wanting to be published, so it took a while to realize that she wrote those stories and outlines just for her, to help her deal with everything during her last year. She got what she wanted or needed out of them at the time she wrote, or deleted, each. There's nothing to gain by publishing them now. They weren't what she wanted most."

"Then, what was?"

The way Nellie peered into my face and down into the thoughts my heart hadn't expressed yet meant she already knew, but she wanted to see if I did. It was a fair critique, because up until two days ago, I didn't.

Then I spoke the truth that had taken over a year and a conversation with Edward to understand. "Ephesians 4:32."

"What?"

"Elise wanted me to forgive myself. That—not her name in print—is the last gift I can give her."

Nellie's face looked much like my inside had felt when I'd finally come to that realization. That it affected her meant more than . . . more than any clichéd wording could explain. All I knew was that it made me feel like a comforting bowl of soup with a shot of bourbon in it. Warm and fiery.

If I didn't move on quickly, I'd become a weepy puddle in this restaurant with a rude waiter and a nosey family standing by to judge me. It'd taken me two days to plug the hole in my reservoir of tears, and I didn't want to let that dam burst again. Not when I still had important work to do.

Clearing my throat, I moved on. "Not to mention, I think publishing Elise's books would hurt Edward. Elise's romance novel had them getting back together. That could make him feel guilty. Plus, the sci-fi book didn't have him as a love interest at all, which could also hurt. So, no. He's been through enough. Elise wouldn't have wanted him to feel either way."

Nellie waved her hand, indicating she wanted to go back to something I'd just said.

"What? Oh yeah, I went to Edward's."

Nellie, who had taken a sip through her straw, coughed so hard into it that she created a bubble that erupted toward the top of her glass.

Sputtering, she said, "Edward's?"

I slid a napkin across the table and glanced at the waiter. When he saw me looking at him, he pointedly checked his watch.

With half an eye roll, I returned my attention to Nellie. "Turns out, Elise had asked him to watch out for me. Every odd thing he did was him trying to do that. His intentions were genuine. He wants to help. He's just," there was no polite way to say it, "really, really bad at it."

Nellie covered her mouth to hide her shock and breathed out a surprised, "Wow."

"Yeah. Edward being bad at anything is hilarious." My smile faded. "There's more. I read Elise's third book."

Nellie's eyes narrowed. Having been there for the reading of Elise's second book, she was understandably on edge about the third. "That's the sci-fi book you mentioned?"

"It's okay," I said. I opened my mouth to say more, but a breathy laugh came out, interrupting my words. Trying to find them again, I could only offer a smile.

Nellie seemed to understand. "It was better."

"Yeah." I upgraded my smile into a dashing smirk. "Turns out I'm a flawed hero."

"I can believe that." Nellie's expression was a kinder version of Charlie's and Edward's when they'd implied some blindness on my part, not unjustly, for not seeing Elise's love.

Nellie rubbed her hands together. "I have some questions for you. How's your knee?"

The question came out so rapid-fire, I straightened in my chair. "Better."

"Good. Why did you run from Elise's house that night?"

I said the answer before I could mull it over, so it had to be an incidental truth. "I was afraid of what you thought of me."

For the first time in the conversation, Nellie looked shocked. Maybe a little hurt.

The pain on her face pressed into my chest, making it hard to breathe. "Because you're all about your families. You collect them. I've never met anyone with as many sisters as you, and I'm Irish. I had one sister, and you had a front seat to see what I did to her. How . . ." I inched closer across the table and dropped my voice a shade above a whisper. "How do you not despise me?"

Nellie squinted as though she wanted to make sure she'd heard me correctly. She took a moment, then said, "You're hilarious."

The dryness in her voice reminded me of Sarah. I didn't know if that meant Sarah was a biological or foster sister, since the trait could either be a learned mannerism or genetic. I also didn't know if Nellie was being serious or not.

Nellie leaned so far across the table that she invaded my half of it. "You are the most family-oriented person I've ever met. And I'm me."

She sat back slowly, watching me with what could be described as a glare if not for the earnestness in her eyes. "Your dedication to Elise went far beyond whatever guilt you were feeling. Every time we've been together, whether for work or for a date, there are reminders of everything you did for her. Out of love. And you—" Hearing her voice about to break, Nellie stopped to swipe at her eyes before finishing. "You dyed your sister's hair, didn't you? With the Golden Crown color?"

I looked down and grabbed my drink all just to have something to do with my hands. I took a gulp so big several ice cubes snuck past. After conquering guilt, accepting praise would, apparently, be my next hurdle. Maybe because the praise reminded me of things, of memories, that hurt because of Elise's absence.

Wincing, I forced the ice down my throat and swallowed. "Up until she didn't need it anymore."

Nellie's gaze grew distant. "It drove me crazy, wondering how you knew about brands and had the hair-dyeing equipment in your kitchen. When I started seeing pictures of Elise, I figured it out. Most brothers wouldn't do that for their sisters." Before I objected, Nellie brought up a hand. "I have a lot, believe me. And you're wrong, you know. My hair color is actually Gilded Harvest."

Her eyes smiled, and again, yes, they can do that, as she twirled a curl between her fingers.

I didn't want to assume anything. Even though I'd been rightly corrected by Edward and Charlie over the space of one weekend for not seeing the obvious, I still asked, "You've seen my worst. Why doesn't that bother you?"

"Because I've also seen your best. You don't get angry quickly, else you would have flattened William at Edward's party. You're caring and thoughtful and hilarious when you let yourself be. You put family first. Yes, you and Elise had a blowout fight, and that's unfortunate, but that's family. What's important is that when Elise asked, you came. Dropped everything and came. That's how I know you made Elise happy. And that's how she knew, too, every day."

A penetrating warmth thawed out the back of my throat. The sensation lasted four seconds.

"Then why don't you want your family to meet me?" I asked.

The back of Nellie's chair creaked as she pushed against it and laughed in that sort of uncomfortable way that indicated a personal struggle. I wasn't the only one going through something, I reminded myself.

Using the straw, I swirled the remaining ice in my drink and looked back out the window to give Nellie time. I'd told her before that I wouldn't pressure her into telling me. I still didn't want to, but with everything else shared, and with everything at stake, and with as hard as my heart was pounding, I hoped she was ready.

Her shaky intake of breath and even slower exhale didn't inspire confidence, but at least she was gearing up to speak.

"It's a two-fold problem." Nellie looked as though she was staring down the slide of a roller coaster. "I was falling for you fast. I had to pump the brakes hard to make sure I didn't push you into anything that would also push you away. Or that you weren't ready for. There was so much trial and error to see if you were even interested in me or felt steady enough to be in a relationship."

I laughed, surprising us both.

"What?" Nellie demanded, sounding worried.

The thought that Nellie had been holding back, carefully cultivating our relationship even as she'd been pushing me, turned my neck into a heat generator. Or maybe it was her admission of falling for me. It might be that.

It was definitely that.

Now I had the same problem she'd had. Nellie's admission was the starter on an engine. I just didn't know how much to step on the gas.

"You fell for me?" I asked.

"Yes, quickly." She played it off like it was just another part of her story, but I caught the quick shrug and the way she grabbed at her sweater to pull it away from her skin, which might also be acting like a generator. "Do you remember when I told you I was dealing with stuff because you were the first guy I'd dated since Luis died?"

I nodded. Then again when she said, "And you know how grief hits when you're not expecting it? Course you do. Weird stuff kept popping up. When I went to kiss you after the restaurant, something hit me. I chickened out. Nothing to do with you. And nothing to do with my falling for you. It was one of those weird moments, and I just wasn't expecting it. And then Margarita pulled into the driveway. She's Luis's sister, and my mind maxed out."

Cold rematerialized in my throat and stretched down through my esophagus. "Does Margarita not want you to date again?"

Nellie snorted. "She's been the one hollering the loudest for me to let her meet you."

"Oh man." I raised my arms the way an exhausted marathon runner would at the end of a race. Our waiter started to rush over, probably thinking I was asking for the check. I waved him off and glanced back at Nellie before I caught any dirty looks. "I thought they didn't like me."

Nellie raised an eyebrow. "Like you thought Elise didn't like you?"

"Hey, it was an easy leap to make. They always stayed in the car, they weren't at the house when I picked you up for our third date, and Sarah always glares at me."

Nellie tilted her head, then shrugged. "Okay, yes. But Sarah glares at everyone. And you get it too, right? I didn't have my family meet you at first so you wouldn't feel pressure. Then some rude part of my brain played me like a grief puppet when I wasn't expecting it. I was afraid to tell you I didn't kiss you because my sister-in-law drove up to the house early; you might have misunderstood and thought I wasn't ready. That I didn't want to date you."

Nellie's long sigh reminded me of air escaping a tire. She continued, "I want to date you and don't want these odd moments of unplanned grief to get in the way. And I really want to kiss you. To make sure I don't get hung up or surprised again, I've even been practicing—"

My eyes widened, and Nellie clapped both hands over her mouth. She splayed her elbows on the table so her chin almost grazed the surface while her eyes shot to the ceiling, looking anywhere but at me.

Luckily our waiter had his back turned. However, the couple with the kids was watching with unabashed interest. They were easy to ignore when I had these questions on my tongue.

"When you say 'practiced,' do you mean kissing?" Then, "How . . . would that even work?"

Nellie shook her head, keeping her eyes locked on the rustic metal light fixture covering the Edison bulb above our table.

"Practice, as in you . . . imagined it?"

Nellie squeezed her eyes shut and nodded. She stayed locked in that position until I couldn't hold back my laughter. My attempt to keep it contained only made it more explosive.

With the speed of a tectonic plate, Nellie slowly lowered her hands as she straightened in her seat. By the end, her elbows were back at ninety-degree angles, and the red imprint across her face from her hands was the only expression her features wore to suggest she was anything but calm.

"Moving on," she said.

Another round of laughter exploded through the hand I'd clamped over my lips to keep it in. Nellie glared. I'd never loved her sea-green eyes more than when backlit with this intensity.

I gave her some cliché prose, meaning every single word. "Your eyes are so bright and shiny."

It melted her glare into a half smile. Then the glare came roaring back. Nellie balled her hands into small fists like they were plugging an emotion trying to shoot out of her.

"You are so aggravatingly sweet and annoying! And that's just your personality. Everything else—" She gestured at me while keeping her hands curled into adorable little fists. "You're so physically cute! With your basketball physique, casual ignorance of that, and that hair you never know what to do with . . ."

Her eyes strayed to my hairline, and her fingers broke free from her fists and twitched as if already imagining running themselves through my curly mess.

I reached for her hands, emboldened to say what I did next when she didn't pull away. "It's my turn to tell you about you."

Edward, Charlie, and now Nellie had all been telling me about me. While hearing you're not a horrible person is always great, and something I needed to ingest, it wasn't what I wanted to talk about anymore.

I had all the words in the romance genre to choose from to describe Nellie. My feelings for her were right there, flooding down my arms to where my skin met hers. Which was why I was so confused to find that words were failing me.

I squirmed, annoyed at myself. I didn't just have romance prose to fall back on; I had actual memories to draw from. Nellie, coaxing me onto my feet a dozen times, persuading me to leave my house and join her on the basketball court, stuffing herself with me behind a van while strategizing what to do about Edward together, leading me onto a dance floor, holding me up at Edward's party, and then kneeling in front of me for a fake proposal.

Nothing. Nope. No elegant string of words or phrases to tell the woman in front of me what she meant to me or what she had done for me. Where were the best words?

I remembered Charlie challenging me to describe Nellie during our date to the Blue Parrot. Words had failed me there too. But I hadn't *completely* failed, had I? Nellie had loved what I'd said even though the words weren't perfect.

I sighed and trusted in whatever I was about to say.

"You're everything that's my favorite."

Nellie blinked. Then again. After the second time, her eyes were brighter and shinier than before. Her thumb ran over our clasped hands.

I inched forward. "I have three questions for you."

Nellie pressed her lips together as she held her breath.

"One. Do you know I'm going through some stuff? It's looking up, but I still have stuff."

Nellie nodded.

"Two. Do you know that *I* know that *you're* going through some stuff? It's looking up, but you still have stuff."

Nellie nodded again.

I breathed her in, unable to stop the goosebumps running up my spine. "Three. Do you want to go through some stuff together? We can take it slow if that's what we need. But I want to take it somewhere. With you."

This time Nellie didn't nod. She lowered her chin a fraction and leaned forward, the stare so intense it ignited a flare in my chest.

"I lied," I said. "I have one more question." My lips twitched. "What was it like when you imagined kissing me?"

The way Nellie's eyes drifted toward my mouth told me she and I were thinking the same thing.

The only problem came when she moved a heartbeat faster than I did.

Nellie stood, pushing the table toward me at an angle so that when I stood and rushed forward, my stomach rammed into the corner. I doubled over in a grunt while Nellie's barely touched drink tilted, bubbles fizzing over its side.

Nellie's hands grabbed my shoulders as the waiter yelled something about getting a room. Wincing, I half stood and reached into my back pocket to grab my wallet. Since I only carried twenties, the waiter got an undeserved overtip.

At the other table, I caught a glimpse of the husband's red face before he turned away laughing. The wife just gave Nellie and me two thumbs up.

With one arm wrapped around my aching waist and the other around Nellie's shoulders, we made our way out of the restaurant. Back in the main walkway, Nellie and I held hands and hurried along as though afraid of being caught skipping school, throwing glances all around us and being unable to hide goofy grins. When we reached the trams leading to the main ticketing area, we hopped on the last car with a few airport employees who exited at the next stop.

Temporarily alone, and aware it wouldn't last long, I pulled Nellie toward me. Her elbow bumped into my stomach where I'd rammed the table. She flinched when I made an "Oof" sound, and I found myself groan-laughing into her curls. Placing her hands on my hips, she guided her body a few inches to the left as I cupped her chin and turned her face to meet mine.

Before our lips met, Nellie whispered, "This is my favorite part."

Then, between two terminals, we finally had our first kiss.

***

A chorus of shrieks broke out as the escalator brought us to the main concourse level.

"She forgot to tell him they were about to be mobbed," Nellie muttered.

Before she could say anything else, we reached the landing, and I discovered the source of the noise. A group of women, all holding signs with Nellie's name like she was a celebrity arriving from a trip, was waiting for us.

Now I understood why Nellie had shot down my last-minute suggestion to head to each terminal to reenact our "proposal."

Raising her voice, Nellie grinned and said, "You wanted to meet my family. They're here to cheer me up if this didn't work out. Or to meet you if it did."

The group surged forward and surrounded us. I lost track of names but saw several faces I recognized, having seen them through car windows across Elise's front lawn. The most memorable was Sarah's. Her white-blonde hair was squeezed tightly into a strict ponytail. She regarded me through circle-framed glasses. The whirlwind of intros slowed as she coolly assessed me.

But then she looked at Nellie while laughing with either her foster mom or mother-in-law and looked back at me. Sarah didn't smile but nodded and slapped me on the arm.

I took it as a ringing endorsement.

One of Nellie's mothers, Juanita, pulled me aside and invited me for dinner the next night. No pressure, but the entire family would be there, including Nellie's brothers. Margarita planned to make all these dishes, and did I have a favorite? And again, don't worry or stress out. It was just a family dinner. With everyone. No pressure.

Since Nellie kept getting yanked into quick whispered conferences with her sisters, it took a while to get through all the introductions. Everyone wanted to speak at once. Was it overwhelming? Yes. In that, if quizzed, I wouldn't remember anyone's name. But did I mind this Tilt-A-Whirl of smiles, shrieks, and pats on my cheek? Not a bit.

The noise and family excitement of smiling faces helped bring something back into me. A part that had been buried under guilt that would have instructed me to hide from a situation like this. But the guilt was gone, and so was the compulsion to run. This was a continuation of the healing that had begun with Edward's and my conversation, buoyed by a sister's love that had never ended.

Eventually it was decided Nellie would ride with me back to Elise's house. Nellie's sisters would take Juanita's van, since they could all fit in it, and follow us. I told them I could drive Nellie home, but they insisted. It was tradition to pick her up from Elise's house, after all.

After we arrived, Nellie and I walked hand in hand to Elise's front porch. She kissed me again, something that elicited several squeals that the van's metal exterior couldn't completely muffle. With a promise to meet tomorrow before dinner with her family, Nellie left with her sisters, no doubt being interrogated and bombarded with more squeals.

When the taillights faded, I went into the garage and grabbed my basketball. I dribbled against the concrete down to the park, a spray of rainwater exploding with every bounce, making the streetlights sparkle in a hundred droplets. Once I made it to the basketball court and positioned myself on the three-point line, I released the ball off my fingertips. It sailed through the air until it hit off the backboard and swished through the net.

I held my shooting pose, uncaring of the rain soaking my clothes or dripping off my hair to run down my back. Then, raising my hands into fists,

I basked in the promise of everything this spring would hold for me, smiling at nothing and everything.

As I walked home, I called Charlie. Though he didn't squeal, our conversation left me feeling like all the sisters in Nellie's van. After we hung up, I vacuumed the broken glass off the living-room carpet and rehung Elise's embroidery sampler. I knew now she'd bought it for me. I brushed a finger over the stitching, *forgiving each other,* and whispered. "See you in Pearl, Elise."

Chapter 13

FALL'S ORANGE DISPLAY BEYOND THE window teased everyone working inside. Yet, between the excitement of finishing the second coat of paint in the waiting room, or finally selecting the shade for the conference room, no one complained as they rushed around to prep the new office space.

Three of Nellie's coworkers were on their tenth round of "Row, Row, Row Your Boat" in the small kitchenette area as they scrubbed out the cupboards and installed new hardware. I'd started calling everyone by the name of their shoe brand, since I'd been painting the baseboards and rarely looked above knee height to see who was talking. And Nellie continued narrating her wall-patching work in her best telenovela accent. Apparently, the relationship between the spackle and the sandpaper was heating up.

It's possible we were all high on acrylic paint fumes.

But the money being saved by the literary agency Nellie worked for was worth the donated Saturday. Not that everything was running smoothly. There was an argument currently underway on whether we should close the windows propped open to help the paint dry. A gust of wind had blown a large red maple leaf into the room where it'd stuck to the freshly coated wall.

This led to another argument about whether the leaf should be tossed or remain encased in the paint since it gave the office "character." I took a strong opposition stance on the first issue and stayed out of the second.

Anita, still sporting short, shellacked black hair, directed the crew. She'd been more than supportive of Nellie coming back to work as a literary agent, so I hadn't hesitated to volunteer to help her today.

Unfortunately, I was on her faux hit list for using the trim paint to write quotes on the walls of the unfinished rooms. The quotes were by Dorothy Parker, Nellie's favorite poet, so I suspected Nellie was the real culprit. She'd probably snatched my brush and paint can when I'd left to pick up the pizzas for lunch.

I finished touching up the base trim in the hallway and caught Nellie's eye when she poked her head around the entryway. Raising my paintbrush, I mouthed, *I know what you did.*

Nellie offered a deliciously wicked wink and strode over to my spot on the floor. I put the brush down so Nellie could pull me up with both hands. She kept one as she started to lead us to the folding tables, but she followed me instead when I gently tugged her around the corner to where her new office would be.

"What are we . . ." Nellie's confused smile fell away when we reached her door. With Anita's permission, I'd attached a golden plaque that read, *Agent Nellie Sudder/Chocolate Milk Connoisseur.*

Nellie tried to hold it in, but a smile broke out faster than water through a busted dam. She tightened her fingers around mine and bumped me with her shoulder. Her face got red with the tears she was more successful in holding back. Saying nothing, we remained that way until we finally strolled back to where only a few pizza slices remained in their grease- and tomato-stained cartons.

After loading our paper plates, we made our way outside the small two-story brick building and sat on the sun-warmed front steps to eat. Before I grabbed a slice, though, I reached my hand out. "Dessert first."

"Dessert first," Nellie agreed as she tugged a wrapped brownie out of her bag and split it with me.

The day was brilliant. The kind that met you halfway to the perfect temperature. I stopped myself from thinking it would have made Elise happy. Instead, I reminded myself that Elise *was* happy. We both were. I missed her but no longer resented what wasn't and could celebrate what was.

And I felt grateful for what Elise had given me: my life with her, memories to cherish, and a future with Nellie. Because of Elise's stories, I could now write my own. Cheesy dialogue and all. I couldn't wait to tell Elise all about them one day.

Nellie snuggled against me and sighed through the last bite of her dark-chocolate walnut brownie. "Do we want to go with Jenna to the game next weekend?"

"No, sorry."

Nellie tilted her chin down and frowned until I clarified.

"It's Edward's and my monthly outing."

"Ahhh." A small smile on Nellie's face tripled in size. "Whose turn is it to pick the activity?"

In a malicious tone I couldn't hide, I said, "Mine."

Every month since that night at Edward's apartment, we'd gotten together to do something. What started as an honest effort to find things we had in common quickly devolved into a competition to find an activity that would make the other person the most uncomfortable. The ante was getting ridiculously high.

"What's on your agenda?" Nellie asked.

"Mini golf."

Nellie frowned at her pizza. "You don't like mini golf."

"Edward likes it even less."

"Might that be a little cruel for someone with a caddy on speed dial?"

I picked my plate off the steps beside me. "Apparently, the picture Edward snapped of me puking over the side of his deep-sea charter fishing boat went viral around the boardroom."

Nellie nodded, ready for battle. "Where do you need me?"

"Just off the third hole. Make sure you get the giant clown head in the background behind Edward when you take the picture."

Nellie giggled and took a bite of pizza, pepper slices falling off the edges into her lap. She wiped her mouth on the only part of her sleeve not covered in paint stains and pointed toward Edward's car coming down the street. "Speaking of clowns . . ."

Edward pulled up and graced the asphalt with the presence of his designer leather loafers. He grabbed a large box from his back seat and carried it toward us. I stood and took it from him when he reached the top of the steps.

I grinned at the weight of the box. "You got them."

"Yep. Well, I had Marco get them. He started work last week." Edward winked and grasped Nellie's outstretched hands before pecking her cheek in greeting.

I set the box down to open and paw through the stack of the basketball jerseys inside for the boys' team Charlie and I were coaching.

"Thanks again for sponsoring," I told Edward.

He waved it off as Nellie and I abandoned our lunch to take him inside and show off our progress. In between the appropriate oohing and ahhing over Nellie's new office, Edward leaned closer to me and asked if he and Shayla could come over to Elise's house for dinner.

"I think we're at the stage where Shayla is ready to learn more about Elise if it's okay with you?"

The question was a welcome one. Nellie and I had gone out several times with Edward and Shayla, and I agreed with Nellie's assessment that Shayla was "perfectly lovely." That she wasn't feeling threatened by the memory of Elise and wanted to make the effort for Edward made me happy for him.

"Absolutely," I said.

"Any chance it could count as our activity for the month?"

"Absolutely not."

Edward conceded with a sigh and an appealing glance at the ceiling. "Where are you taking me?"

I grinned and didn't answer. Nellie sidled up next to me, and Edward pointed at our matching shirts, electric blue with the words *Writer's World Publishing Agency* across the front with a typewriter logo.

With a teasing eyebrow raised, Edward said, "You know she's marking her territory by having you wear that shirt."

Nellie gasped and clutched at nonexistent pearls. "That is *such* a cliché." Then she wrapped her hand in the front of my shirt and made a fist to pull me closer. "But true."

I heard Edward's laugh as he turned away. Where to, I wasn't sure, as I was better engaged for the next few seconds.

Nellie released me as Anita called out the last work goals for the afternoon. I walked Edward back out to his car and deflected his final attempt to trick the location for our activity out of me.

Edward gestured toward the office. "Things are looking good."

I chuckled in agreement.

With a parting grin and flash of sunglasses, Edward waved and climbed into his car, which purred down the street, leaving a swirl of leaves in its wake.

Returning to the steps, I intertwined my arm with Nellie as we finished off our pizza. After our last bites, we sat in silence, enjoying the moment to bask in the glow of the autumn sun through the trees while we rested against each other. A small crash and raised voices inside returned us to the present. Nellie stood, brushed off her pants, and held out a hand. I took it and let her lead me inside to our next adventure, whatever genre it turned out to be.

About the Author

WHEN NOT AT WORK, K.A. Ross is finding new stories, discussing old stories, or writing her own. If she's not thinking about stories, she's either trying not to be too invested in sports or climbing up a mountain so she can run down it. She lives in Utah but considers any open space with a view home.

Learn more about K.A. Ross and her upcoming works at her website, authorkayross.com, and follow her on social media.

Facebook: Kay Ross (K.A.)

Instagram: @authorkayross